Graeme Aitken was born in Central Otago, New Zealand. He now lives in Sydney, Australia, where he works as a bookshop manager. His short fiction has been published in several local anthologies. This is his first novel.

'An entertainment, a gentle, poignant story of a fat boy who fantasises romance and glamour without yet having a name for what he is . . . Aitken writes with a distinctive voice, one that is wonderfully evocative.'
DENNIS ALTMAN, *THE AGE*

'A wonderful cast of characters, lovingly drawn and lightened with the right dash of maliciousness . . . Aitken manages to make something extraordinary out of the ordinary . . . (and) shows so much skill and gives so much pleasure.'
CAMPAIGN

'*50 Ways of Saying Fabulous* is an honest, funny and sometimes painful read. Confidently and convincingly written, it is a welcome addition to the gay coming of age genre; the collection of works in which we see ourselves reflected and refracted, and find fifty ways of saying "me".'
MELBOURNE STAR OBSERVER

'Its humour will guarantee you stares as you snicker on the train. Aitken understands the hopelessly daggy and uncool nature of the 12-year-old and he reproduces it as if it were yesterday. Popularity and acceptance take a lot of time and pain to procure. I think he'll be guaranteed it with this book.'
NEIL DRINNAN, *OUTRAGE*

'. . . an important work . . . What Aitken has demonstrated fabulously is his skill in the art of telling a good story . . . his honesty and fearlessness in confronting those squirmy adolescent secrets is to be admired.'
CANBERRA TIMES

'. . . one of the very best novels released this year. Witty, warm and original.'
CLEO

'. . . a secret and magic story which is grotesque and infinitely funny . . . a zany book, highly entertaining, and with enough twists and turns to keep you glued to the end . . . *50 Ways* is fabulous, whichever way you say it.'
BARFLY

'Touching and sad, *50 Ways of Saying Fabulous* also has some very funny moments.'
THE TIMES

'A sort of gay Adrian Mole . . . There are laughs aplenty but also moments of agony . . . Told with bare-faced honesty, it is a warm, cruel, funny tale.'
THE SUNDAY AGE

50 Ways of Saying Fabulous

Graeme Aitken

Green Candy Press

This is a work of fiction. The novel's characters, incidents and dialogue are the product of the author's imagination and are entirely fictional.

50 Ways of Saying Fabulous
by Graeme Aitken
ISBN 978-0-7394-7081-7

Published by Green Candy Press

Cover photographs by Craig Wright
Printed in the U.S.A.

To my parents, who are nothing like the characters in this novel

With thanks to

Andrew Moors, Kate Evans, Keith Buss, Craig Stevens, Dean Baxter, Rosanna Arciuli, Laurin McKinnon, Gary Dunne, Jane Palfreyman, Julia Stiles, Rois McCann and Andrew Freeman

1

When I was twelve years old, my most precious possession was the tail of a heifer that had died giving birth. My father cut it off and handed it to me when I asked for it, presuming I wanted it as a trophy, pleased that I was finally taking an interest in his cows. Rather, I had recognised a potential in that tail my father would never have dreamt of. I trimmed the dags off, washed, dried, brushed it tirelessly with my own hairbrush and tied the end of it with some red ribbon. After days of top secret preparation, with Babe banned from my bedroom, it was ready. Before going to bed, I announced that there would be a surprise at breakfast the next morning.

Morning came. I could barely dress myself for the excitement. My fingers were trembling. I gave up on the idea of a shirt and pulled on a skivvy instead. I put on my woolly hat (though hats weren't allowed indoors) and tucked one end of the tail beneath it. When I made my entrance into the kitchen, the cow's tail draped over one shoulder, Babe clapped her hands together in delight. My parents looked up from their porridge. I informed them that they were to call me Judy from now on. Babe applauded even louder. My parents looked bewildered. Babe explained that I was Judy Robinson out of 'Lost in Space'. With that long white ponytail, I was convinced I looked exactly like my favourite television star.

'Porridge is on the stove, Judy,' was my mother's only comment. She regarded it as yet another of my fantasies. My father tried his best to ignore it. There were no reprimands. Neither of them told me not to wear the cow tail. But they didn't tell me I looked ravishing and just like Judy either. Which I did.

Their lack of enthusiasm prompted me to find an outfit to enhance the resemblance. My mother's lavender bed jacket was the obvious choice. Its clinging fit and shimmering satin made it the most futuristic garment in the house. When I modelled myself for Lou, she insisted I take her black swimming cap. It was far superior to my hat in terms of space age fashion. Studying myself in the mirror, I was impressed by my transformation. I insisted that Lou and Babe play 'Lost in Space' with me in the turnip paddock *immediately*. The dogs acted as various forms of repulsive alien life to run from screaming.

Being Judy, I got to scream the most.

To get to the turnip paddock we had to trek across the Field of Blood, which Babe and I wearily pretended to be terrified by. This meant Lou could lead the way, bragging and making up stories, saying the sheep found the grass sweeter in this paddock, as it had been nourished by the blood of Maori warriors. Certainly the sheep did have their heads down, chomping away furiously, but that seemed to be their perpetual state wherever they were. I wasn't entirely convinced that this was the site of the battle my grandfather was always telling us about, but it was near enough. We liked to brag at school that there'd been a massacre on our land.

The turnip paddock held greater appeal. It was incredibly sci-fi. There were all these half-eaten turnips sticking up out of the mud and the effect was distinctly lunar crater-like. We played the most wonderful games of 'Lost in Space' there. Lou was always Don, and Babe was ordered to be Dr Smith which would make her cry, but as she was the youngest she had no choice. I, of course, was Judy.

Judy screamed at the aliens who got terribly excited and jumped up on her, barking. Don rushed to save her and Dr Smith snivelled in terror. Unfortunately, the lavender bed jacket always ended up getting extremely mud splattered from the dogs' paws, and my mother got sick of sponging it off before she could wear it. She banned its participation in any further games. It was never as realistic without it.

My parents had humoured me in my new impersonation and I felt encouraged to wear my new hairpiece to school. I wanted to show it off. I was so thrilled by my new appearance that it never occurred to me that others wouldn't share in my enthusiasm.

'What's that you've got hanging down your back?' demanded Arch Sampson as soon as I got onto the school bus.

'It's my hair,' I replied demurely.

I was about to instruct Arch to call me Judy, when he yanked the cow's tail out from under my hat and waved it in my face. 'Are you trying to be a girl?' Arch said, in a loud voice.

Several people turned round to stare at me. Behind me, I could hear the Hammer brothers snickering together. I suddenly realised that was exactly what I was doing, though it hadn't occurred to me quite so bluntly until then. Now that Arch had put a name to my behaviour, I understood that it probably wasn't the fun that I thought it had been. It was something to be ashamed of.

No one wanted to be a girl. Even girls. Like Lou, for instance, who was always hanging round up at our place, helping out on our farm, because her mother, Aunt Evelyn, wouldn't permit her to do 'dirty work like that'. Lou wore old clothes of mine when she did my chores. She could get as dirty as was necessary without her mother being any the wiser. All anybody ever talked about in school was being allowed to ride their father's motorbike, or shoot a rabbit, or shear a sheep. Even the girls aspired to these rural rites of passage, though they shied away from slaughtering. With the exception of Lou. She was the fiercest and most ambitious out of the entire school. She always carried a sharpened pocket-knife.

So it was strange that I could never summon up any enthusiasm for these pursuits, a zeal which came so easily to my peers. To my mind, they were merely chores which I would have preferred to avoid altogether. I never admitted my disinterest, but joined in with the others claiming extravagant achievements for myself. None of it was true. I couldn't kick-start the motorbike, let alone ride it. I couldn't bear the agony of suspense waiting for a gun to fire. Even the gunshots on television made me cringe. As for shearing, just holding the handpiece made my whole body, which was kind of flabby, vibrate in a most alarming manner. The runtiest of lambs could kick itself free of my feeble hold before I even got the shearing machine running.

I was inept. But Lou covered up for me. She did the chores my father left by herself and never claimed any credit. I would tag along with her and admire her skill at whatever it was I was supposed to be doing. Then I'd lose interest and start playing out some game of my own; acting out an episode of 'Lost in Space', or pretending to be one of the go-go dancers off 'Happen Inn', or maybe even looking for clues to an adventure 'Famous Five' style. Lou did my chores and I entertained her while she worked. My cow tail lent a superior authenticity to my performances.

When Arch challenged me, my first thought was to try to make him understand how much fun it was to dress up and pretend to be someone else. Maybe, promise him the tail off the next cow that died and he could be Penny ... but it would have to be a black cow and my father didn't have black cows. The scorn with which Arch looked at me made me think better of that idea. I decided to try and down play it.

'It's only a tail, Arch, I was bringing to school to show everyone,' I said.

'We've all seen a dumb old cow's tail plenty of times before,' sneered Arch. 'Why'd ya have it hanging out of yer hat like a ponytail, like a girl?'

I blushed. Everyone was listening and looking at me. 'That was just a joke,' I muttered.

'You're a joke alright,' said Arch, beginning to laugh in a fake, malicious way. 'Seems more like you were acting the poof.'

I didn't know what that meant, and by the bewildered looks of everyone on the bus, no one else did either. 'What's that supposed to mean?' Lou demanded, moving down a seat to sit opposite Arch.

Arch didn't like Lou. She could beat him in arm-wrestling and he lived in constant terror of her challenging him in front of an audience. 'It's somethin' me dad warned me about,' said Arch quickly.

'What is it?' said Lou.

Arch seemed lost for an answer.

'Don't you know?' Lou continued. 'You shouldn't use words you don't know the meaning of. It's pretentious.'

Everyone gasped. Lou had the most sophisticated vocabulary of anyone at school, on account of Aunt Evelyn, who had been a school teacher before she married Uncle Arthur.

Aunt Evelyn was always trying to improve Lou's mind and anyone else's she could get to. Sometimes, she'd fill in at the school when the teacher was sick or away on a course, and accomplish more in a single day than the teacher did in a week. Everyone was relieved that the teacher was in pretty good health generally.

'So what does that mean then?' said Arch.

'It describes silly boys like you, using words you don't know the meaning of.'

'I know what it means,' Arch flared, going a little red. 'It's men who act funny, you know.'

Lou stared at Arch. 'No, I don't know. You explain it.'

'Well, they're men but they wear wigs and dress up in frocks and . . . *they've got fifty ways of saying fabulous*.'

Arch crossed his arms and stared at Lou defiantly. Lou stared right on back at him. The whole school bus was watching the two of them. Suddenly, Lou snatched the cow's tail out of his hand. 'Arch,' she said, in her most sarcastic voice. 'This isn't a wig. It's the tail of a purebred Charolais heifer that Billy-Boy was bringing along to show the school, 'cause it's valuable. That heifer that died was worth a lot of money. More than any of your father's boring old Hereford cows.'

Arch snatched it back. 'So how much is it worth then?'

I saw my opportunity and grabbed it. Before Arch had time to register what I'd done, I had the tail safely stuffed inside my school bag. I didn't want him getting ideas that it was valuable enough to interest him. There was no way I wanted to lose that tail and spoil my new game forever. It was going to have to become top secret.

I clasped my bag to my chest and stared down at my feet, avoiding the eyes of Arch and the others on the bus. The panic of the confrontation was ebbing away and a new sense of wonder slowly took its place. *Men who wear wigs and dress up in frocks and have fifty ways of saying fabulous.* Dressing up was my favourite thing to do.

It was always me who was the keenest to get out the dressing-up basket. I'd have to tempt or even bribe Lou into joining me. The dressing-up basket contained all these wonderful garments cast off by the women of our family. They were mostly my grandmother's clothes that Grampy had bundled up after she died but couldn't bear to destroy. There were fringed silken shawls and chiffon scarves and stiff floral dresses made out of material that looked like curtains and coats with real fur collars and elaborate hats Nan used to wear to church. But the most illicit item in the basket was a pair of Aunt Evelyn's long lacy bloomers. Unbeknownst to her, Lou and I had rescued them from the rubbish to be burned.

Playing dress up became so much more *real* once I had my cow's tail. Previously I'd had to use the tent as a wig. It was the right colour (gold) and exceptionally long, but otherwise it wasn't wildly convincing hair. Lou used to say I looked like the Virgin Mary with the tent clasped round my face. It wasn't the image I was striving for at all.

I wanted to be like the heroines I read about in books; the ones who suffered dreadful handicaps or hardships but who always triumphed in the end with true love assured and a miraculous recovery from their invalidism. I snitched ideas from those books and devised my own plays and insisted Lou and Babe take part in them. I always cast myself in the central tragic role. I had a penchant for crippled heroines rather than blind or mute as there was an old pair of crutches in the wash-house. They were an excellent prop and I could never resist incorporating them. Every year, on Christmas Eve, Lou, Babe and I gave a concert which Aunt Evelyn always tried to take over.

Aunt Evelyn was the local star. She had ambitions to be

an opera singer which she'd 'sensibly' put aside in favour of teacher's college. She took major roles in shows throughout school and college. But after she married Uncle Arthur, her aspirations faltered. The Glenora Musical Society put on Rodgers and Hammerstein musicals once a year. 'Are there any others?' the society's secretary had asked Aunt Evelyn in surprise.

Aunt Evelyn always took the leading roles in those shows but she also complained to anyone who would listen that it was no challenge to her. She wanted something that would inspire her. That was why she got so excited one year, when she saw an advertisement in the newspaper inviting actors to audition for *Hair*. Aunt Evelyn couldn't drive, so my mother drove her to Dunedin for the audition. They had to keep it a secret from Uncle Arthur who wouldn't have approved of them travelling one hundred miles for such a flimsy reason. Trips to Dunedin were for important matters like visiting the accountant or taking advantage of a special offer on sheep drench.

Aunt Evelyn was tremendously excited about *Hair*. She had been thrilled when she heard it was coming to New Zealand. She said it was avant-garde. Most other people said it was disgusting, celebrating as it did drug taking and free love, with full frontal nudity to boot. Aunt Evelyn had no qualms about tossing off her clothes on stage. 'It's a challenge,' she said dreamily. 'At long last, a challenge.'

Three days after her audition, Aunt Evelyn got the phone call to say that she didn't get a part. The director had been looking for a more youthful cast. Aunt Evelyn was terribly disappointed. 'Not that Arthur would have allowed me to do it anyway,' she said. 'But you know, I wanted the part so badly, that I just might have insisted.'

She suggested to the Glenora Musical Society that they

might like to do their own version of *Hair*, but they voted unanimously in favour of *The King and I* instead. That year, instead of dancing naked on stage at Her Majesty's Theatre in Dunedin, Aunt Evelyn waltzed demurely round the stage of the Glenora hall with John Mason. He had been cast in the role of the king, as he had the least hair out of any of the musical society's members. No one was prepared to be shaved bald for the role. Not when it was the middle of winter and sub-zero most mornings.

I adored watching Aunt Evelyn in that show, transformed into this shimmering creature in her elaborate costumes. I used to test her on her lines as Lou wouldn't or I'd act out scenes with her for practice. We rehearsed 'Shall We Dance?' countless times and Aunt Evelyn used to gurgle with pleasure when we'd finished, and called me John Mason's understudy. She never guessed that I was understudying her role. I longed for her to fall off the stage during rehearsals and be consigned to crutches. I knew her role almost as well as she did.

'You prefer culture to cows, Billy-Boy,' Aunt Evelyn often said. 'Like me.'

In fact she said this so many times that it wore thin as a compliment. I began to wonder if in fact she wasn't mourning her own daughter's lack of interest. Nevertheless there was an affinity between Aunt Evelyn and me, and it was her I thought of when I found myself confronted by this enigma. For that was what *acting the poof* became. I couldn't find out what it meant. All day at school I puzzled over what Arch had said, trying to find some clue in it. How could you have fifty different ways of saying fabulous? I consulted all the dictionaries and encyclopaedias at school. Poof wasn't listed. I was loath to ask the teacher. There had been disdain in Arch's voice when he'd described it. He had practically spat out the words. His tone made me hesitate. Was it something *not* to be encouraged? But then he'd heard about it from his father, who had no time for anyone having any fun.

Old Man Sampson was the meanest farmer around. Everyone said so. Especially when it came to money. He'd recently hired someone with a really weird name to help out on his farm. This person had no previous farm experience at all, so he didn't have to pay him much. Old Man Sampson allowed Arch to do just about everything round the farm. He even kept Arch home from school if he had a big day ahead like lamb marking or mustering. So it stood to reason that he wouldn't be encouraging Arch to fool around, play-acting or whatever *acting the poof* actually meant.

I didn't entirely trust Arch's definition. He didn't have much of a memory for anything he was told. But I couldn't question him. That would betray my fascination. Aunt Evelyn was my only hope. She had a wealth of experience in the world of theatre, and to my mind *acting the poof* seemed bound up in that realm. It sounded theatrical, flamboyant, the sort of exotic masquerade that I adored. My imagination became more fevered. Perhaps there was a course for it at drama school or university. I resolved to ask Aunt Evelyn at the first opportunity.

That moment on the bus was an epiphany for me. When I went to bed that night I felt that I had finally resolved my contradictory ambitions for myself. *Acting the poof* sounded like the sort of occupation that I'd be good at. Not like farming, at which I was an unmitigated failure. Finally, I had the answer to the question adults were always asking me. 'What are you going to be when you grow up, Billy-Boy?'

If my father was around when I was asked, I always felt obliged to say that I was going to be a farmer or an All

Black. 'Not that I'll be very good at it,' I'd add later, in a whisper.

But if he wasn't in earshot, I'd invent a more exciting career for myself. I'd say I wanted to be a pop star or an actor on television or that I wanted to write plays or travel through outer space.

'Oh, you want to be an astronaut,' some friend of my mother's would exclaim.

'No, I just want to be like Judy,' I'd reply and the woman would look baffled.

But now I knew. Now I finally knew exactly what I would say. When I grew up, I was going to *act the poof*.

That night, in bed, I lay my ponytail across my chest and tried to recite fifty ways of saying fabulous.

2

Throughout my childhood I was puzzled by the incongruity of my parents ever getting married in the first place. They seemed so at odds with one another. Not that they quarrelled. It was their aspirations that set them apart and proved a constant source of antagonism between them. My father believed in hard work and more hard work, and watching the rugby on television for relaxation. My mother had ideas. Rather original ideas by the Serpentine plain's standards. No one, least of all my father, could understand them.

I used to ask both of them independently about how they met and eventually married, but neither of them would reveal very much. 'I've been asking myself that same question for years,' was my father's standard reply.

My mother merely muttered that 'it happened a long time ago', as if that explained everything.

Quizzing Grampy and Aunt Evelyn was more enlightening. Perhaps Grampy felt neglected. His television set held more appeal for his grandchildren than anything he had to say. He attacked the subject with zeal. 'Jack and your mother met over a meat pie and now she refuses to eat them any more. It's a bad sign, a bad sign,' he lamented, before launching into his version of the story.

Aunt Evelyn was wonderfully indiscreet. But I asked her

in a weak moment, on the drive home from the opening night of *The King and I*. There had been a party afterwards with bottles and bottles of Cold Duck. When the time came to go home, Aunt Evelyn wouldn't allow Uncle Arthur to drive. 'You're drunk. You'll kill us all,' she said dramatically. There was no alternative but for Lou to take the wheel. Aunt Evelyn sat in the back seat with me and told me things she probably shouldn't have. 'Reebie used to confide in me back then,' she said. 'Before she got all those weird ideas.'

Both Grampy and Aunt Evelyn insisted, and even my father admitted as much himself, that before he met my mother he was getting anxious about finding a wife. Jack was twenty-five years old. Practically everyone else his age had already married years before and snatched all the likely girls from the district in the process. To make matters worse, his younger brother, Arthur, had married the school teacher from Crayburn, Evelyn Wills, just a few days after Jack's twenty-fifth birthday. Grampy set Arthur up on the adjoining farm, which he'd had the foresight to buy several years earlier. This meant Arthur and Evelyn had their own farm to run with their own house all to themselves. Arthur had escaped. Even if it was only two miles down the road, it was still a decent distance from Grampy and his relentless advice.

Jack realised that to find someone, he was going to have to venture beyond the Serpentine county. This was all very well, except his father regarded an excursion to the nearest range of shops at Glenora as a frivolity. To Grampy a holiday was going down to the river block to check on the sheep and taking along a picnic lunch. Jack loved the farm life, but he loathed always being told what to do. Grampy upheld that there was only one way of doing things; *his way*. When Arthur had lived at home, it had been possible on occasion for the two brothers to persuade Grampy of the value of their own ideas. But on his own, intimidated by his father's disdainful stare, Jack's initiative faltered, his voice betrayed him with hesitations and stuttering. Even to his own ears, his suggestions sounded weak and doomed for dismissal.

Grampy regarded Jack as a boy. Even though he knew he was twenty-five, he treated him as if he were years younger. To do otherwise would mean confronting the fact of his own age and the retirement his wife was constantly anticipating as if it was Christmas. Grampy had only recently granted his eldest son the privilege of a beer after a hard day out on the farm, and that only after a terribly humiliating scene. Grampy had needed two of the neighbour's sons, Bob and Jimmy Spratt, to help him with their big muster. When they'd all finished, just as the sun was going down, he invited the Spratts in for a drink. He poured them both a beer (Lion, when everyone drank either DB or Speights), then offered Jack a lemonade. Jack left the room rather than accept the drink, hoping Bob and Jimmy hadn't noticed. They had of course, and let him know it, next time he saw them at rugby practice. Inevitably the whole team heard about it and for the rest of the season everyone was ragging him and offering him a lemonade instead of a beer after a game. Jack was older than both Bob and Jimmy by a couple of years, a fact he pointed out to his father. Grampy looked incredulous. 'Is that so? Somehow they seem older.'

It was his mother who explained to Jack that both Bob and Jimmy were married, and Bob already with two kiddies. From Grampy's point of view you were still a lad until you got yourself wed and started setting up your own family. 'You've got to find yourself someone, Junior,' said Nan. 'Then he'll start treating you like a man and giving you responsibilities.'

Nan had her own reasons for pushing Jack into marriage. Once Jack was married and starting a family, she could argue that the house was too small for all of them and Grampy and her could retire down the plain to Crayburn, preferably next door to her best friend Janet Scott. Nan was an avid golfer and bowler and had been extremely frustrated the past winter to have missed several important matches due to the roads being clogged with snow. She also wanted a brand new house like Janet's, except with central heating throughout and not just in the sitting room.

Nan drew up a list of the local possibilities for Jack, headed 'Girls you might marry', and left it on his pillow one evening. Jack glanced through the list before screwing it up. It only confirmed what he already knew. There was no one around the district that he was in the least bit interested in marrying. They were all too young or played golf. Jack was definitely not going to marry a golfer. They were always off playing a round and leaving their husbands to put the dinner on, Nan being the prime offender. He was going to have to take a holiday and look around for a wife. Nan was rather suspicious of outsiders and slightly affronted that her list had been discarded. She had taken some time over it and ranked the possibilities in order of congeniality. However, she could understand, and promised to persuade Grampy to give Jack a holiday.

'What does he want to go gallivanting off for? And where does he think he's going to go anyway?'

'Jack, he's twenty-five years old. He's a man with needs of his own.'

Grampy didn't want to consider what these needs might be. He quickly gave his assent rather than dwell on them or have his wife explain them to him. And so Jack took himself off to Dunedin to stay with his old high school friend Herb Day, who'd gone on to work in the Cadbury Hudson chocolate factory and got himself engaged to one of his co-workers.

The visit was not a success. Herb wanted to spend his evenings at home in his parents' sitting room, chatting on the phone to his fiancée, Barbara, about what had happened to them both since they'd last seen each other at work, a few hours previously. Sometimes talking on the phone wasn't enough and Herb would visit Barbara at her mother's house where the two of them would revise their guest list and menu plans for the wedding. This was torture to Jack, cruelly reinforcing his own hopeless bachelorhood. There was nothing he could do. The one time Jack finally suggested the two of them might go out to the pub for a drink, Herb replied that Barbara didn't like pubs, even lounge bars, and wouldn't want to come. 'But that's okay. We can go, just the two of us,' said Jack.

'Barbara likes us to play cards on Friday nights.'

So they played five hundred. At Barbara's house. Jack was partnered by Barbara's mother. The next day Jack told Herb that something had come up on the farm and he had to get home to help. 'That's a shame,' said Herb. 'It's Barbara's church dance tonight. Barbara's mother loves to dance. She was looking forward to a foxtrot with you.'

Jack mumbled something he hoped was interpreted as disappointment and left as soon as he decently could. He drove down past the oval and decided to stop and watch the girls playing hockey. One girl on the team took his fancy and he cheered every time she hit the ball, to try to get her attention. She didn't seem to notice, but her boyfriend did. He came over and told Jack to put a sock in it or he'd knock his teeth in. Jack retreated to his car. He consoled himself with the thought that if she played hockey, she would probably have turned to golf later in life.

Jack set off on the long drive home, brooding on the

hopelessness of his situation. To cheer himself up, he decided to stop off at McGregor's tearoom in Palmerston, for one of their famous meat pies. Food was always a good consoler. It was there, at McGregor's, that he saw Reebie for the first time. She was sitting at the table nearest the window, staring out into the street with such a sorrowful expression on her face that Jack felt convinced she must have been jilted by some fellow.

McGregor's was busy. Jack took advantage of this to approach Reebie and ask if he could share her table. She nodded, but barely glanced at him. Her eyes were on the street. Slowly Jack ate his pie and in between bites stared at Reebie. When he had finished, he went and bought himself another and ate that one in exactly the same manner. When that pie was gone too, there was nothing to do but stare at Reebie without any distraction whatsoever.

'Are you waiting for someone?' Jack finally asked.

Reebie turned her attention to Jack. She gazed at him with such a grave expression on her face, that Jack felt quite fearful. Something was profoundly wrong. 'Tell me,' he said gently, 'what's the trouble? Maybe I can help.'

'I doubt it,' she replied.

But she confided in him anyway. 'It feels better to tell someone,' she said, managing a smile.

Reebie was a nurse at the Cherry Farm Psychiatric Hospital. She and one of the other nurses had taken several patients out for a walk after Sunday lunch, when Maxwell Powell (antisocial behaviour and petty theft) had suddenly burst into a wild sprint across the park and disappeared out the hospital gates. Reebie set off after him, but she was too late. She reached the road just in time to witness Maxwell climbing into a truck he had somehow persuaded to stop.

She waved frantically at the truck, trying to make the driver understand that he was taking a certified psychiatric patient aboard, but he was oblivious to her. The truck set off down the road again. Reebie's training had never broached such a situation. She couldn't imagine what she should do, when surprisingly another truck, headed in the same direction, pulled up alongside her. The driver leaned across the seat, opened the door and told her to jump in. Reebie had inadvertently flagged a truck down. She had never hitch-hiked in her life and had been warned of its dangers time and time again. Yet, without hesitation, she clambered up into the cab. 'Follow that truck,' she commanded, vaguely aware that she sounded like a Hollywood movie heroine. 'There is an escaped patient aboard.'

'What's he in for?' asked the driver, pressing down on the accelerator.

Reebie refrained from answering. The patient was a notorious pantie stealer, whom the doctors were currently considering for chemical castration. Reebie noted that it was a bright summery day, with a bit of a breeze. Perfect washing weather. Everyone would have their smalls out on the line today.

They lost sight of the truck somewhere between Waikouaiti and Palmerston. A farmer waited for the first truck to pass and then decided to chase his sheep out onto the road. The truck Reebie was in was forced to practically stop, and timorously edge its way through the mob. Reebie was beginning to feel extremely agitated. Not only was her charge speeding away from her with every wasted second, but the driver had begun to eye her in an appraising fashion. 'It must be interesting being a nurse,' he ventured. 'You'd have such a wide knowledge of the human body and all its functions.'

Reebie didn't like to think what he might be implying. 'My training concentrated on the mind and its aberrations,' she said tersely.

'Oh yeah,' said the driver. 'Like perversions and that sort of stuff.'

Thankfully they cleared the last of the sheep and conversation became impossible as the driver revved the truck noisily through its gears. Reebie gazed hopefully at the road ahead. Gradually she became aware that the driver was regarding her in rather the same way and wasn't keeping his eyes fixed on the road as he ought to.

'I think I'll get out at Palmerston and search around for him there,' she said quickly.

The driver sighed. 'I enjoy a bit of company on the road.'

When he stopped to let her out, he mentioned hopefully that he regularly drove past the nurses' home. 'Do you?' smiled Reebie. 'I'll look out for you then, and wave.'

Reebie set off towards the houses and the washing lines with their strings of vulnerable undies. She trailed up and down every street, but it was all in vain. Maxwell was nowhere to be seen. She didn't dare ask anyone if they'd seen him for fear of provoking alarm. Finally, she gave up and wandered back to the shops to revive herself with a cup of tea at McGregor's. She took the seat by the window in case Maxwell should saunter past with someone's washing, and that was where Jack came upon her, dolefully contemplating her failure and anticipating the reprimand she would receive upon her return to the hospital.

'But you did all you could,' said Jack. 'Even putting yourself at risk with that truck driver.'

Reebie sighed. She would probably be transferred to one of the villas where the patients were largely immobile and all they could do was shit themselves.

'Here, I'll drive you back to the hospital and you can explain. I'm sure they'll understand that you've done your best.'

Jack ushered Reebie out of McGregor's and into his car.

He gave a little skip as he hurried around to the driver's side. What exciting circumstances to meet under. Jack had already decided that Reebie was the one for him. He would take her away from this work, which seemed terribly dangerous and quite unsuitable for such a nice girl. She seemed far too tender-hearted and good to be in such a position, fretting about some pervert, who in Jack's opinion should have his throat cut. That was how it was on the farm. The sick and the deformed of the flock were slaughtered.

They drove in silence back to the hospital. Reebie absorbed in the dreadful ramifications that would surely befall her as a result of losing her charge, while Jack was wondering what sort of cook she might be, and if she'd be the type to pitch in and help around the farm. He was convinced that she wasn't the golfing type. When they reached the nurses' home, Jack nervously asked Reebie if he could phone her the next day. 'I'd like to know how it all works out, and also to make sure that you're alright,' he said solemnly.

Reebie was startled. For the first time, she took a long hard look at Jack. She hadn't really paid much attention to him. He sat there at the wheel of his car, dressed in his good jacket and tie which he always wore on special occasions, like travelling to and fro from Dunedin. His hair was flecked with blond, his eyes a startling blue in a face burnished red by the sun. But it was his smile that appealed most of all to Reebie, his wistful curl of a smile.

'I'm in Room 12,' said Reebie. 'You'll need to know that if you call.'

'Oh, I'll be calling alright,' said Jack, encouraged. 'There's no two ways about that.'

Reebie got out of the car and Jack cursed himself that he'd missed the opportunity to kiss her. That would have been something to tell the boys at footie, though he supposed he could claim the achievement anyway and no one would be any the wiser. Reebie walked self-consciously up the path to the nurses' home, certain that Jack's eyes were following her. She turned to wave and also to check, and sure enough, he was still hanging out the window, grinning at her. She waved and he waved and she waved again. Then he thought to start the car and drive off.

Reebie phoned the charge nurse from the nurses' home. She couldn't face him. But to her enormous relief, Maxwell was safely back in the villa. He had been apprehended in the lingerie department of Farmers in Oamaru, undressing a display mannequin. Reebie was praised for her dedication and resourcefulness in trying to find Maxwell.

Jack rang the next day to see if everything was alright and to ask if he could take her out for tea to McGregor's on her next day off. Reebie happily accepted. Their excursions to McGregor's became something of a ritual on Reebie's days off. It was over a McGregor's meat pie that Jack asked Reebie to marry him. Reebie agreed. She was always delighted by something new. 'Just don't buy me a ring yet,' she insisted. 'Wait a few months until we're absolutely sure.'

Jack agreed happily. He preferred not having to spend money until it was essential, and supposed that Reebie thought the same way. It didn't occur to him that she was only saying maybe. He realised the significance of a ring when he started taking Reebie out and introducing her as his fiancée. People would look to her finger for the ring and not finding one, would smirk and whisper. Reebie didn't even notice. She was too preoccupied dreaming about her new life on the land. She had visions of herself tending a flourishing orchard, wandering through the hills composing lines of poetry, baking her own bread and perhaps tossing the odd bale of hay to some grateful sheep. Her first visit to the farm, a month after Jack's proposal, seemed to confirm these notions.

Jack had insisted that they all take a day off work and concentrate on trying to impress Reebie. Not many outsiders married into Mawera. Patrick McDonald's fiancée had broken off their engagement after her first visit, when she discovered where he expected her to live for the rest of her life. Not that it was that bad. Admittedly, there was no shop, no pub, no post office or bank. However, those facilities were available only sixteen miles away in Crayburn and another sixteen miles beyond that there was Glenora, the seat of the county council and quite a thriving little town. There had been a pub in Mawera once. It had been the heart and soul of the community, incorporating the store, post office, telephone bureau and library as well. But it burnt down in 1953. The community lost all its businesses and services in one fierce blaze. They were never restored.

Mawera was tucked up in a valley, high above the Serpentine plain, in the south-west corner of the county. That was where the Red River started. Up in the hills behind Mawera, fed by creeks and streams. The river twisted across the Mawera valley and then dropped down through a gorge to meander across the great expanse of the Serpentine plain. The twisting course of the river provided the county with its name.

One thing Mawera could boast over Glenora was a tourist attraction: an old stone-walled gaol built in the 1860s which luckily was left untouched by the 1953 hotel fire. Those with an interest in the history of the early settlers came to inspect it and gasp over the chains that the prisoners had been cuffed to, still dangling from the stone wall. These tourists didn't mind in the least that the tar-sealed road petered out halfway to Mawera. They liked to step back in time. The gaol had been used by the police escorting the gold transport through from the central Otago goldfields to Dunedin.

The weather was the other thing Mawera was famous for. They always got more snow than down the plain. Sometimes feet of it. When that happened only tractors could negotiate the roads and no one could get in or out of the valley. There had been occasions when the twice-a-week mail and grocery delivery truck couldn't get through for over seven days. The county grader always seemed to have other priorities before getting to the only road in and out of Mawera. School would be closed sometimes for days, and the children would help their fathers instead, digging sheep out of the snowdrifts and feeding out hay. The electricity could be off for days too. Nan kept the old coal range in order for just such an eventuality. It was weather of extremes: hot in summer, cold in winter. Very cold.

Luckily, Reebie paid her visit at the height of summer. Jack slowed the car down once they reached the beginning of the family property, so that Reebie could admire 'the feed' and 'the stock'. She ohed and ahed and didn't admit her ignorance of the terms.

Nan had hot scones with her homemade raspberry jam waiting for them up at the house. She rushed to the phone as soon as she saw the car turn up the drive, to advise Janet Scott of their arrival and her own excitement. The car slowly made its way up the willow-lined drive, the dogs running to greet it, yapping and biting at the tyres. Nan trotted down the path from the kitchen door to welcome them. Grampy emerged out of his workshop, and stood there by the door, watching. The car pulled to a stop and Reebie opened her door and hopped out. Almost at once, she was surrounded by the dogs, barking and sniffing and jumping up.

'Get down, get down,' snarled Jack, but it was too late.

They had already put their dirty paws all over her dress. Nan could see her dream of central heating in Crayburn going out the window. Patrick McDonald's fiancée had screamed when she saw his dogs, had jumped back into Patrick's car and refused to get out until they were all tied up. But Reebie was smiling, actually laughing and stroking the dogs and even encouraging them to jump up higher. 'They're so friendly,' she said.

'That's typical of the country,' said Nan, coming forward. 'Everyone's friendly in the country, even the dogs. I'm Junior's mother, just call me Nan. And this is his father, Jack.'

Jack winced at being called Junior, but Reebie seemed delighted at the name. She moved forward to meet Grampy, who was ambling towards her. 'Welcome,' he said, and then quickly pecked her on the cheek.

'Thank you,' she said, looking round, taking everything in.

The sun was beginning to fade and the colours in the landscape were at their most vibrant. Sunlight spilt out from behind frothy clouds, flushing them dusky pink, catching on the water in the streams and swamps and glinting silver. The hills rose up from the valley floor, crumpled into lavender brown folds, like some carelessly tossed eiderdown. The snow still gleamed on the mountains beyond, smooth and glossy, like glazed royal icing on one of Nan's Christmas cakes. Reebie felt exalted, inspired. She rather wished she had a pen and paper with her to jot down a few lines of her first poem.

This landscape confirmed Reebie's vision of her new life. When she began to prattle on about her plans for composing verse and baking bread, no one said anything to contradict her. Both the Jacks stared at their shoes pretending to be preoccupied, leaving Nan to say, 'that would be nice.'

No one wanted to ruin anything.

Driving back to the hospital the next day in the car, Reebie snuggled up to Jack and told him she was ready. 'It's time we started making some plans.'

Jack didn't stop when they reached Cherry Farm despite Reebie's laughing protests. They drove on to Dunedin, to Weatherall Jewellers, where Jack got out his cheque book and told Reebie to choose her ring. They were married five months later at the Presbyterian church in Crayburn. Reebie was enchanted to arrive and find the church half-buried in snow. It struck her as a symbol of the pure and fresh new existence she would lead. Her father was less impressed. He got the car stuck in a ditch concealed by a snowdrift, and had to carry Reebie the last five hundred yards to the church. By the time she got to the altar she was shivering so much she couldn't make her vows. The locals were intrigued and delighted. Jack had to borrow Nan's fur coat and wrap Reebie up in it before she could finally utter the magical 'I do'.

The snow put paid to their honeymoon plans for Queenstown. By the time they were ready to leave the reception, the radio was announcing that the road there was closed. There was nothing for it but to spend the night at the farmhouse. So it was there, in Jack's bedroom, with the two single beds pushed together, that Reebie discovered that Jack was as keen to begin breeding himself as he was for his finest Charolais bull. And he went about it in a similar brutal, overwhelming fashion. Several times.

They never did get away on their honeymoon. The demands of the farm held them captive. Reebie soon realised that she was expected to toss more than the occasional bale of hay to the sheep. She was expected to feed out over two hundred bales a day, seven days a week, whatever the weather, while her husband drove the truck. Her other plans went similarly awry. The climate was so severe, it was inconceivable to plant fruit trees. 'The only things that grow up here are thistles and tussocks,' Jack informed her.

As for wandering through the hills composing poetry, she was told to take the shotgun with her and dispose of a few rabbits as she went. Poetry was impossible when she was expected to leave a slaughter in her wake. And when she asked for yeast at the Crayburn Superstore, she was told they didn't stock it and why would she want it anyway? Bread was now delivered twice a week, a new innovation. It was ludicrous to make work when there was more than enough to do already. Reebie's desire to bake bread became the favourite derisive story of the district for weeks.

Two months into her marriage, Reebie had not written a single line of poetry, but had fed out over twelve thousand bales of hay. She felt unsettled and bitter. Things had not unfolded as she had imagined. She tried to speak to Jack, but he brushed her complaints away. A nagging suspicion that somehow she had been deceived began to fester in her mind, at exactly the same time as the new life deep within her began to make its presence known to her.

When the doctor in Glenora confirmed what she had suspected, she ran out of his surgery, out of the waiting room where Nan sat waiting gleefully for the news, out onto the road. And still she ran. Blindly. Until the street and the town ended abruptly in front of her. There was nothing before her but the wide, frozen expanse of the Serpentine plain, stretching out as far as she could see. It was there that Nan found her, down on her knees, weeping, at the edge of the town, accusing her and all of them of trapping her into a life she had never wanted for herself.

3

One year, my father made the calves pink. That's my first vague shimmering of memory. My mother always smiles when I remind her of that day, though she protests that I must've been too young to remember. 'You would only have been two and a half the year we made the pink calves.'

But I do remember. It was so piercingly cold that morning, how could I forget? The cold nipped at me and I howled my protest. But my father had insisted that I had to be brought to see his *first* Charolais calf.

It was like a winter's day, though it must have been spring. There was snow everywhere, with a frozen crystal crust that I could walk upon without sinking into. It was like concrete when I inevitably fell over. I remember my mother gathering me up in her arms, soothing me, whispering in my ear, distracting me from the pain. 'Look at the pink calf,' she said. 'A pink calf. Look at the pink calf.'

And I remember turning to look and being struck by the wonder of it. The calf, still wet and bedraggled, but against that pure white backdrop of snow, radiating an extraordinary colour, the shade of a delicate sunset.

My parents were both so excited by the calf. My father jabbered away to it in some nonsense language as if it was a baby, encouraging it to walk, as it stood there shaking on its four legs. My mother was flushed with elation too. My mother who these days barely pays attention to my father and his various schemes and dreams for the farm. There was a look close to rapture on her face. She was entranced by the sight, absolutely still, concentrating. Then her lips began to move, though no sound came out. I was pressed up against her cheek and I would've heard. She wasn't speaking to me or my father. Those were secret words.

Later, maybe even a year later, when I was sick with the measles, she told me a story about the pink calf that she'd made up herself. It was a very clever story and all the words rhymed. Maybe she thought I'd be too feverish to remember because she seemed startled the next night when I asked her to tell it to me again. She was shy. 'You wear a story out if you tell it too many times,' was her excuse and she hurried away.

I doubt she would ever have repeated her story if I hadn't tried to recite it back to her one night. 'No, no,' she protested, 'you've got it all wrong.' And with a solemn expression on her face she told the story again. I clapped when she'd finished and she hushed me. 'It's our secret,' she said, and I knew what she meant.

The story wasn't for my father's ears. He wouldn't have approved. To him it would have been a waste of valuable time.

Bedtimes became clandestine. My mother had lots of her own stories up her sleeve but she only ever told them occasionally. 'I have to be in the mood,' she said.

This state of mind was frustratingly rare. I soon realised there was no point in begging for her stories. It only seemed to embarrass her, and she would hurry out of my bedroom without even saying good night.

So it was unlucky, given that she relented so seldom, that one night my father managed to overhear us. Perhaps he sensed he was being excluded from something. When my mother finished her story, one I'd never heard before, I looked up and noticed him standing there, grinning in the doorway. He didn't say a word. He just smiled in a way that wasn't really a smile. My mother didn't see him. He was gone by the time she stood up to turn off my light. But he must have said something scathing to her in the privacy of their bedroom because there were no more stories after that. My mother was never 'in the mood' again. I didn't dare to ask for one. Something in her face warned me not to persist.

But I knew she went on making up those stories and even wrote them down. There were times when I came upon her unexpectedly, seated at my father's desk, and from the expression on her face I knew she hadn't been merely attending to his accounts. There was that same intensity in her eyes that I remembered from that morning all those years ago when the first pink calf was born.

When Babe was old enough to understand the story of the pink calves, the two of us used to beg my father to make the calves pink again. But he'd always shake his head. He was aiming for white calves, the absolute white of a purebred Charolais. The year of the pink calves was the first year he crossed his new Charolais bull over his red Shorthorn cows. They were the beginning of the long process of building a purebred Charolais stud.

Grampy didn't like the Charolais. 'White beasts,' he called them. They didn't like him much either and one of them almost did him in. It was my father's first Charolais bull, Bruno, the one he had brought over all the way from France, that bailed Grampy up against the railings of the cowshed. I was probably only four, but I remember my father and Mr Spratt carrying Grampy up the drive to the house and lying him on the kitchen table. His clothes were torn, and I could see the skin beneath was swollen and broken. Nan was crying as she and my mother sponged off the blood. She begged my father to go out and shoot the brute at once.

My father refused. Not his beloved Bruno, the French bull he'd paid thousands of dollars for. But it wasn't even the money. My father had a vision. Probably, he'd deny it if I mentioned it now, but I remember him dragging me onto his knee and telling me that by the time I was halfway to being a man, there'd be a whole mob of white cows, just like Bruno, gleaming in the paddocks along the roadside. 'They'll be so white,' he whispered to me, 'they'll dazzle the eyes half out of your head.'

But I didn't want white cows. It had been the white beast who had hurt Grampy so that he walked with a limp from then on. I wanted pink calves again, like the one that magical morning, like the one in my mother's secret story. To my mind pink calves were a good compromise between the white cows my father so ardently desired and the red cows that Grampy still stubbornly complained were superior. But they both ignored my suggestion.

Grampy moved out of our house because of the white cows. He didn't want to have anything to do with them and started spending more time at the Crayburn house. He'd bought it to retire to, before I was even born, but he didn't like it. 'I've lived almost sixty years in this here farmhouse,' he said to me. 'It isn't easy to just up and leave. I can't sleep in that new place.'

He refused to help my father with the 'white beasts.' There were a lot of jobs that required two men and that mercifully were beyond me. Grampy figured that my father would eventually get tired of struggling on by himself and go back to Shorthorns. But he did no such thing. Instead he hired a boy to help and told Grampy he'd have to move out of his bedroom to make room for the new worker. For once

Grampy was lost for words. He just drove off in his car. Babe and I helped Nan pack everything in their bedroom, accumulated over fifty years of marriage. We were both in tears. 'He'll grow to like the new place,' Nan consoled us. 'It's got central heating everywhere, and a dishwasher.'

Nan loved working the central heating. When we visited them in the new house, she always turned it up as high as it would go so we could appreciate its full impact. Grampy complained it was like living in a glasshouse with windows that couldn't be opened because of the double glazing. 'It's withering me up,' he muttered to me one day. 'Making me old before my time.'

There were locks on the door of the new house that Grampy shunned. He didn't even want to know how they worked. 'We never needed locks before.' Nan would deliberately lock him in and go off for an afternoon's golf. 'Keep him out of mischief,' I heard her tell my mother. 'He's getting to be an old man and he doesn't like it one bit. He needs to rest but he won't hear of it.'

My grandmother should probably have taken her own advice. She crumpled into Grampy's arms one night as they were stacking their dinner dishes in the new dishwasher. Grampy grunted his approval. He thought she'd fainted from the oppressive heat of the house and that finally he'd be permitted to turn it down. It was only when her limbs began to twitch that he realised she was having a stroke. He carried her to the car and drove her to the hospital in Glenora. He didn't want to waste any time. But when he got to the hospital, the doctor wasn't there. Eventually he was found at a birthday party in the neighbouring county.

Nan never recovered. She was denied the house with all the modern features she'd waited so long for. The stroke plundered her body. She didn't know anyone. She could do nothing for herself. It was as if her very soul had fled with the shock of the seizure but the body had been too slow and heavy to follow. She lingered on for several weeks in a private room in the hospital, her eyes betraying her bewilderment at the family weeping round her bed who were strangers to her now.

Grampy seemed to grow attached to the new house after Nan died. He even kept the heating turned up because it was the way she had liked it. He wouldn't hear of moving back to the farmhouse. He bought a colour television. He was the first to get one in the entire Serpentine county but he didn't seem to realise how wondrous it was. He'd even criticise it, while Lou and Babe and I watched it in awe, speechless.

'Some of those television people looked better in black and white. The colours they wear together are hard on the eyes.'

It was the seventies after all.

Grampy had bought the television to entertain himself when he was alone. When we visited he turned it off, much to our dismay. He wanted to talk. He'd give us each a bottle of lemonade, which he considered a tremendous treat, and sit us down at the kitchen counter and begin one of the tales we'd heard countless times before.

His favourite story was the Field of Blood. Grampy had heard about it when he was a boy, from some of the old shepherds who worked the big stations until they divided them into small runs for settlement. Before he started, he always brought out the greenstone relics and chisels that he and his brothers had fossicked for as boys. He'd lay out the evidence and encourage us to pick up the strange stones as he told his tale.

Two Maori tribes had met on the same trail, a trading route through to the Clutha valley, near the mouth of the Eweburn stream where it flows into Red River. The tribes fought each other to the death until the two waters ran red and that was how the river gained its name.

When the three of us heard the story for the first time, we raced down to the paddock to search for Maori artefacts. We spent an entire day down there, restaging the battle and then scrabbling around, digging holes in the pasture, vainly hoping to come upon some relic of the battle. We found nothing. Lou started pestering my father to plough the paddock, convinced that it would turn up all sorts of treasures and maybe even an ancient skeleton, but my father wouldn't hear of it. 'That paddock will never be ploughed,' he said. 'I don't want to go digging up any spirits and bringing bad luck upon myself.'

He'd heard Grampy's stories too and held the field in a certain reverence.

Grampy warned us to keep away from the paddock. 'Don't go down there. It was a terrible thing that happened there. Steer clear of it. Never swim there. You'll get a cramp and the water will pull you under.'

Naturally, being told not to go there made the paddock irresistible. We sneaked down at every opportunity, thrilled by the prospect of vengeful spirits and ancient curses. We never swam there. We weren't allowed to swim without an adult supervising us. But we did sit on the river bank, dangling our bare feet in the water, tempting the currents. Then one day, we saw a big eel rise up only a couple of feet from where we sat. Hastily, we withdrew our feet. We didn't tell anyone what had happened as we'd been technically disobedient in the first place. But it reinforced the gravity of Grampy's warnings and the authenticity of his stories.

Despite the amount of time we spent down there and all our hopeful searching, we never did find any Maori weapons of war. All we ever found was a strange bone. Lou was being a Maori warrior and she trod on it while negotiating a swamp. We brought it home to Grampy, who identified it as a moa bone. 'It was the swamps the moas fled to,' Grampy said when he heard where we found the bone. 'There was a huge fire, hundreds of years ago, centuries ago, a fire that almost consumed the entire South Island and the moas ran to the swamps to try and save themselves. But the fires were so fierce that the water couldn't stop the flames. The moas were burnt to death, the swamp waters boiling around them, and that's how the moas became extinct.'

It sounded a bit far-fetched, but we nodded our heads and gasped in the appropriate places. That was the local folklore we grew up on and at first it was fascinating. We clamoured to hear my grandfather's stories. But then we got television and began to crave more exciting worlds. We wanted to be the Robinson family lost in outer space. We wanted to be a family of singers like the Partridge family and have a mother who drove an old bus. We wanted to carry guns and shoot rustlers like in 'The Big Valley'. None of us wanted to be moas running from the flames any more. It just wasn't exotic enough.

It was usually Lou, the boldest of the three of us, who'd ask to watch his television once Grampy had finished his story and before he had time to launch into another. He always looked a little startled but he never refused us. Aside from the television Grampy also bought five hundred acres of land outside Crayburn. At seventy-two, Grampy announced that he was going to breed Shorthorns again. He was determined to compete against his son in the interbreed cattle section of the Glenora Show. And win.

Neither of them ever managed to.

Victor Caldwell of Crayburn had a New Zealand champion Hereford bull that he monotonously entered every year and which the judges always felt obliged to honour. Both Grampy and my father longed for Victor's bull to go lame.

Meanwhile, my father, spurred on by these repeated losses to Victor and by Grampy's revitalised career as a farmer, bought a second bull from France, Dante. This was a terrible mistake. Dante proved to be trouble. He wouldn't stay in with the cows.

Dante was a monster. He was so huge, that when he arrived in the back of the transport truck, he wouldn't fit down the loading ramp at the cowshed. The truck driver and my father had to prod him out of the truck and make him jump to the ground. 'Hope you like 'im,' said the driver. 'You're gonna have to buy a wider ramp if you ever wanna get rid of 'im.'

My father wasn't listening. He was so in awe of Dante. He was much bigger than Bruno. 'Imagine the calves he'll produce,' he gasped.

But the problem was that Dante didn't seem to like the Shorthorn cows he was expected to impregnate with his purebred Charolais semen. He showed no inclination to fulfil the task he was acquired for, preferring to exert his superior weight in fights with the other bulls instead. Trying to shift Dante away from the bulls and in with the cows was a real ordeal. It always ended up taking almost an entire day and usually several fences ended up getting wrecked in the process. These would then take hours the next day to repair. It required all seven dogs snapping at his hooves, my father belting him across his rump with an aluminium crook, and Lou and I shouting as loudly as we could and waving our arms about, to make Dante amble forward at all. And even with all that commotion, he wasn't inclined to go particularly fast.

His favourite trick, once we'd managed to get him halfway to the mob of cows, was to turn around and take off back the way we'd just come. Back to the bull paddock, ignoring the dogs and charging straight through any fences that happened to be in his way. My father would swear and swear, as if it was some sort of incantation that might magically bring Dante back again. Sometimes his swearing carried all the way to the house, and when we got home for lunch, my mother would reprimand my father for using such language in front of Lou and me.

No one called him Dante any more. He'd been called That Bloody Bull so many times by my father that the name had stuck. We all called him that, though we didn't let my mother catch us. We always said it as if it was an aristocratic title, like we were saying Her Majesty the Queen. My father said it in a different tone altogether.

He began to despair of ever getting Dante to stay in with the cows. He blamed everything he could think of for Dante's inertia. The trip on the ship from France. Mawera for being a strange new environment. He even wondered aloud one day if perhaps it was a curse for grazing the cows in the Field of Blood. He wouldn't admit that he'd paid thousands of dollars for a dud bull, which is what Grampy insisted he had done. 'Fussy French bugger,' Grampy said to me one day. 'I'd cut my losses if I was your father and send him to the works. He'd lose money but he'd get the last laugh on That Bloody Bull. You can't be a farmer and let yourself be beaten by a brainless bull.'

But Dante was far from brainless. I admired how he seemed able to outwit my father. I wished I was as accomplished at getting my own way, and avoiding all the jobs my father was always finding for me. I remember one time, we spent all day trying to get Dante in with the cows. Finally, it was done and we wearily made our way home, shutting all the gates along the way. We'd taken him by a circuitous route in an attempt to confuse him, so that even if he did jump out from the mob of cows he could never find his way back to the other bulls. The bull paddock was next to the house. We were stopped at the final gate, about to drive up to the house, an hour overdue for dinner already, when my father glanced over to admire his bulls and noticed Dante standing there amongst them.

He'd beaten us back.

It was Grampy who suggested taking a steer along with Dante for company. He said it as a joke, but my father was desperate enough to try anything. 'What's a steer?' I asked my father, as we trudged along behind an unusually cooperative Dante and the young steer.

'It's a bull who isn't a bull anymore,' replied my father.

I still didn't understand. But Grampy's joke worked. Dante trotted along quite happily with his new companion and for the first time was happy to stay in with the cows and even do his business on top of them. My father hated the fact that Grampy had been right, but he was so relieved that all the money he'd paid hadn't been wasted, he had to give Grampy the credit due him. He rang him up and thanked him. Grampy acted like it was the most obvious thing in the world to do, but he confessed to Lou and me that he was astounded. 'French cows are queer things,' he warned us. 'Steer clear of them. When you have the farm yourselves, get shot of those "Sharlaze" quick smart.'

I agreed with him, swearing to have nothing to do with Charolais when I grew up. I didn't elaborate on the fact that I planned to have nothing to do with cows or sheep or *anything* remotely connected with farm life. Such ambitions were best kept secret.

4

Everyone called me Billy-Boy. It wasn't short for William. It was just one of those nicknames that develops and sticks. I'd been christened after my mother's father, though neither of my parents actually liked the name. My mother convinced my father that they ought to make the gesture. My grandfather wasn't well at the time of my birth and had been in and out of hospital. My parents didn't tell him what they were planning. They wanted it to be a lovely surprise. As it turned out, he was whisked back into hospital and couldn't attend the christening. If he had been there he would have protested.

After the christening, they brought me to visit Grandfather Pearce in the hospital, and announced that I was his namesake. He moaned when he heard the news. He moaned with such anguish that my father ran to summon a nurse. 'How could you do such a thing?' he lamented. 'How could you inflict this poor baby with such a curse?'

'We thought you'd be pleased,' my mother said tersely.

'The sentiment is admirable,' said my grandfather, 'but the name is a shocker.'

My grandfather's name was Athol. It had been a source of mockery to him for most of his life. Throughout school, and even beyond, he was known as Arsehole. The other schoolboys pronounced it with a lisp. Aaaathhholl. That was his reluctant legacy to me. He died soon after that visit, and in her darker moments my mother fretted that she had finished him off with the unwelcome compliment.

My name became a misnomer. No one wanted to use it for fear of reminding my mother of her father's fatal reaction. Everyone was at a loss as to what to call me. My second name wasn't much of an alternative. Palmerston. This was the town where my parents had met and although it had great romantic significance for them, it didn't readily abbreviate into a useable name for me.

It could have been worse. They were also thinking of McGregor in which case I would have been named after a meat pie.

My mother had thought my name sounded distinguished. It wounded her greatly that it could so readily be reduced to 'arsehole'. She became sensitive about my name. People were always approaching her in the street, admiring me, cooing at me in my pram and naturally enquiring as to my name. At first my mother would defiantly tell them. But their polite responses were belied by their startled eyes and tittering laughter when she moved away with the pram. My mother became embarrassed to pronounce the name. She began to mumble it which definitely didn't help the situation. People didn't like to ask her to repeat it, in case it confirmed what they thought they had heard. The whispering, the insinuations, the criticism, all became too much for my mother. She began to invent new names for me. She'd say the first name that came into her head if anyone happened to ask her. She even began to call me by those names herself. One week I was Sam. The next I was John. The week after that Peter. Plain names. My mother had learnt her lesson.

Finally, my father took up the same initiative and started calling me Billy. It was the name he'd favoured from the beginning. My mother had objected, saying it reminded her of camping out and damper bread. Everyone else followed my father's lead and the name stuck. My mother resisted until I was old enough to work her reluctance to my own advantage. When she called me to do a little job for her round the house, I'd refuse to answer, on the grounds that it wasn't my name. I'd stay where I was, usually huddled in front of the television. When my mother came to find me, I'd shrug and pretend I hadn't realised she was talking to me.

The first time she ever called me Billy was the day she had one of her disasters. Even though I was watching television at the time, I still heard the shriek of the truck's brakes over the volume of the television. Then my mother's frantic wail. 'Billy, Billy, come quick, I've run over the puppy.'

We drove the pup to the vet in Glenora. My mother kept peering into the back seat where I sat cradling the little puppy in my arms. She had whimpered furiously for the first quarter of an hour, then fallen into an ominous silence. All the way, my mother called me Billy. She was far too anxious to think of anything else to call me. 'Is she still breathing, Billy?' she'd ask, or she'd fret aloud, 'What if I've killed her, Billy-Boy?'

As it turned out the pup wasn't badly hurt and was just suffering from shock. She'd only had her tail run over. My father was furious when he heard that we'd taken the pup all that way to the vet. 'What a waste of time and money,' he raged. 'You should've wrung the silly thing's neck if you thought it was badly hurt.'

My mother and I shuddered. Both of us loathed the brutality that farm life sometimes demanded. Meanwhile Lou was boasting that she'd have done the deed if only she'd been there at the time. She was going through a bloodthirsty phase, fascinated by how easily life could be extinguished. Mostly her experiments were confined to trapping rabbits and possums for my father. I refused to take part, despite the allure of three dollars a skin, so the task had fallen to Lou or rather, she had volunteered for it.

My father didn't make the fuss we all expected when the bill came in from the vet. That happened a month later, and my mother was still calling me Billy-Boy like everyone else. Perhaps my father figured that a bill from the vet and the cost of the petrol going to Glenora was worth it for me to finally have a name that everyone was agreed upon. That's how I came to be known as Billy-Boy. Most people didn't even know my real name. I preferred to keep it that way.

No one called my sister by her proper name either. She was always Babe, being the baby of the family, four years younger than me. Her babyhood had been somewhat extended by the fact that she'd taken forever to grow hair. She'd had lots of it when she was first born, but it had all fallen out a couple of months later and didn't grow back again until she was almost three years old. When it finally did, it was very fine and wispy. My mother was scared to comb it. Her hair was never cut and she tended to hide amongst it. Some days she seemed to be nothing but a haze of blonde. She threw terrible tantrums if my mother suggested a trim. She'd seen the photographs of herself bald. Lou had told her she looked like an alien.

Babe was very shy around strangers. She always hid behind one of my parents whenever she was introduced to someone new and couldn't even bring herself to say hello most of the time. She'd peek out at them, usually from between the gap in my father's legs. Around family she was completely different, and jabbered away non-stop, as if making up for the time lost while the intimidating strangers were around.

Lou was a profound influence upon Babe. She was always trying to ape whatever Lou did, though in her heart of hearts she didn't much care for the things Lou was passionate about. But she idolised Lou. She wore jeans and old shirts of mine to be like Lou. She tried to squeeze her mass of curls into a ponytail like Lou. She even painted freckles over her nose with some varnish she found in the workshop to look more like her hero.

Lou didn't even notice. She regarded Babe as a nuisance, always slowing her down, keeping her from what she wanted to be doing. It was at my insistence that Lou would relent and allow Babe to tag after the two of us. She'd trail behind us plaintively calling for us to slow down and wait for her, rather like one of the uncertain newborn lambs bleating at its mother, who'd prefer to concentrate on eating grass.

As much as Babe worshipped Lou, there was one thing she couldn't resist and which damned her as ridiculous in Lou's eyes. She loved to wear dresses. Most of Babe's dresses were hand-me-downs from Lou and it was a dilemma for her that Lou scorned them so vehemently. She always agreed with Lou's dismissive remarks but her face betrayed her pleasure whenever a new dress was given to her. Lou boasted that she'd never even worn most of them, so successful was she at avoiding her mother's best efforts to get her into a frock. Babe tried to imitate Lou's scowl if Lou happened to be around when she was wearing one of them. Somehow she just ended up looking smug.

Lou was an only child, but she never lacked for company. She was six months younger than me, so naturally we spent a lot of time together. Uncle Arthur's farm adjoined ours but it was still a couple of miles between our two houses. Once we were old enough to have bikes, this distance became insignificant and we were always over at one another's places. Lou played upon the fact that she didn't have any brothers and sisters to make Aunt Evelyn feel that it was important that she spend time with Babe and me. Poor Aunt

Evelyn always hastily agreed. She couldn't bear to be reminded of Lou's lack of siblings. For there had been another baby after Lou, a boy who was stillborn, that no one ever talked about.

Aunt Evelyn never made too much fuss about Lou spending so much time at our place, though it meant she missed out on her piano practice, a loss Lou rejoiced in. She almost always came home with Babe and me after school and did my chores for me. At weekends, she came home with us on Friday and didn't go home again until Sunday lunchtime. Aunt Evelyn always cooked a grand dinner on a Sunday, and Lou made sure that she didn't miss out on that.

Lou and I often discussed our circumstances and what a mix-up they seemed to be. We both envied each other's situation. She longed to be her father's helper on the farm and be entrusted with regular chores the way I was. I would've preferred to stay at home with Aunt Evelyn, testing her on her lines for her latest show, joining her in a duet on the piano, even helping her in the kitchen. Lou and I were like twins in our intimacy. The oddest, mismatched pair of twins possible.

Lou was a confirmed tomboy. Aunt Evelyn knew it and didn't like it. She wanted her daughter to look and behave the way she imagined girls should, the way she was brought up herself all those years ago in Christchurch. There was constant friction between them, usually over Lou's appearance. Lou had the longest hair of anyone at school, halfway down her back. She hated it. Aunt Evelyn adored it and wouldn't hear of her having it cut. 'To even cut an inch off that hair would be like cutting into my flesh,' Aunt Evelyn always said.

So Lou stuffed her long red ponytail down the back of her skivvy and tried to pretend it wasn't there. She reckoned she looked better that way and I agreed with her. It was simplest to agree with Lou. Secretly, I sympathised with Aunt Evelyn. I was crazy about long hair. Lou's hair was almost like Laurie's in 'The Partridge Family'. Except it was red. Lou always wore her hair in a ponytail so that it looked short from face-on. Whenever Aunt Evelyn insisted she wear it loose, Lou looked terrible. Her perpetual scowl didn't help. But somehow she just seemed overwhelmed with all that hair hanging round her face.

She had a thin, angular face, a dusting of freckles across her nose, and brown eyes that were always narrowing into a suspicious grimace. She wasn't one to smile much. She was usually too preoccupied giving her opinion or thinking of ways to avoid Aunt Evelyn and her latest plan, to have time to smile. People constantly mistook her for a boy and called her 'sonny', which delighted her. She encouraged them in their mistake. If they happened to notice her ponytail, she'd grin at me and try and pass it off to them as a cow's tail. A Shorthorn's tail.

Aunt Evelyn did not appreciate having her daughter mistaken for a boy. Her other strategy to feminise Lou was to force her into frocks as often as possible. Aunt Evelyn made all Lou's frocks herself and insisted Lou wear them to school, though they were often too elaborate and formal for everyday wear. Aunt Evelyn and Lou used to have the most terrible fights over those frocks, so terrible that one frock actually got ripped from bodice to hemline in the heat of their argument. After that, Lou pretended to relent. She would set off to school in those fussy outfits with Aunt Evelyn proudly admiring her own handiwork from the veranda. Once Lou was out of sight of the house, hidden by the trees that lined the driveway, she changed into a skivvy and pair of pants and was transformed by the time the school bus arrived. No one ever knew except me and Babe, and we were sworn to secrecy.

Aunt Evelyn boasted to the other mothers how neat and well behaved Lou was, and how she always came home from school with her dress just as perfect as when she had left that morning. She'd have been mortified if she ever learnt the truth; that Lou was wearing the same sloppy outfit for an entire week to school, which became more and more grass stained and dirt streaked as the week progressed.

Lou was always the organiser of games of schoolyard soccer and rugby at playtimes. She was as skilled as any of the boys and usually scored the most goals. Inevitably, she would be captain of one team and got to pick who she wanted on her side. She always picked me first, though I was one of the most inept players out of all the other kids at both games. She probably thought she was making me feel good. We both knew it was charity. I'd have been happier not to play at all. I preferred more sedate games like 'four square' or 'echo-stop'. But at Mawera School there wasn't much choice in that sort of thing. The school roll was always so tiny, fluctuating around twenty pupils, that to have a decent game of soccer or rugby, the entire school had to play. That was the way it was and everyone went along with whatever someone, usually Lou, had decided.

Lou was the unacknowledged leader of the school, even though she was barely twelve years old, and there were several boys older than her who might have had more of a claim out of seniority or gender. But Lou led the way with the sheer force of her personality and no one liked to contradict her. She possessed a sharp tongue and if that failed, a quick pair of fists. She could pin just about anyone to the ground in a couple of seconds and demand they surrender. Bigger, older boys weren't game to risk having their masculine pre-eminence shattered by Lou's lithe strength.

In addition to dominating the playground, Lou also ruled in the classroom. The teacher in Aunt Evelyn couldn't resist educating Lou as soon as possible. She could read by the time she was four and had romped through the spelling levels and basic arithmetic before she even started school officially at age five. Aunt Evelyn demanded that Lou skip the primers and begin straight in at standard one, but the teacher resented his authority being usurped and refused. He informed Aunt Evelyn that pushing Lou too early could have 'psychological ramifications' later on. So Lou stayed put in primer one where the teacher insisted she relearn to write in the new cursive style, a cross between the old-fashioned longhand (Aunt Evelyn's favoured style) and printing. This caused terrible problems for Lou, as Aunt Evelyn would insist she do her homework in longhand, while the teacher would refuse to mark it unless it was in cursive. Lou had to do two copies of her homework for an entire year, until Aunt Evelyn finally conceded that they were 'living in a modern world and change was inevitable'. Around the same time, she had Arthur buy one of the new colour televisions.

Nevertheless, Aunt Evelyn endeavoured to keep Lou's education advancing at home, which was another reason why Lou always wanted to come to our place, to avoid Aunt Evelyn and *Shakespeare for Children.* When it was inescapable, Lou insisted that I join her. I never admitted around Lou to enjoying those 'lectures' as Aunt Evelyn termed them, but I did. I loved them. Aunt Evelyn always made her interpretations of Shakespeare entertaining. She would borrow costumes from the Glenora Musical Society, dress up in the role of Lady Macbeth or Ophelia, recite their most famous speeches and then analyse their relevance.

The school teacher never dressed up. He wore his navy shorts and knee-high socks with a regularity that somehow suggested his authority was vested in them.

Despite her love of the avant-garde, Aunt Evelyn was rigid

in her view of how Shakespeare should be performed. She wouldn't hear of allowing Lou to read the swashbuckling parts that she wanted to. And even though she told us herself that in Elizabethan times boys played the female roles, she wouldn't hear of me doing the same in the 1970s. 'It's too disorienting,' she insisted.

In private, Lou and I played the parts we wanted to. We had our own secret place where we could do exactly as we pleased. We called it Dragonland. In fact, it was just a massive rock which from a distance looked like the head of a dragon. Or Lou said it did and Babe and I agreed. Dragonland was perched on a ridge, high above our farmhouse. It took a good hour and a half to toil up the hill to it, so we didn't visit that often. Yet almost every day we'd glance up at it and wearily vow, as if it was located up the other end of New Zealand, that *soon* we'd make the expedition to Dragonland. This reluctance was heartfelt on my part. The walk always gave me a terrible stitch.

Up close the rock didn't look anything like a dragon, though we pretended that it was ten times more terrifying. Babe was too scared to venture too close. Lou had convinced her that the rock could actually turn into a dragon and she cried every time we set off there. 'You might never come back,' she wailed.

When Lou did manage to talk me into making the trek to Dragonland, we'd enliven the journey by inventing some extraordinary circumstances for ourselves. I would usually be half-crippled or blind, rendered helpless by some cruel handicap, which meant I was reliant upon Lou's strength and charity. I would stagger up the hill, quite convincingly, as I was usually puffed by the time we reached the first fence. Then I'd collapse in a heap, blaming the legs I lost to crocodiles or the eyes wasted by scarlet fever for my lack of stamina. I adored these games. I would issue demands for sustenance or rest, which Lou as the chivalric hero was obliged to fulfil.

In these games, Lou usually went by the name of John and nothing pleased her more than hearing herself addressed as such. It was the name of her brother, the blue baby. That was how I'd overheard my mother describe him. 'Evelyn's blue baby. He was born with a hole right through his little heart. She only caught a glimpse of his wretched little body before they took it away, but the memory still chills her through.'

I was fascinated by the notion of a baby being born blue. So fascinated that I persuaded Babe to paint her favourite doll with the pale blue paint that had been leftover from when the kitchen was redecorated. Babe was keen on the idea initially. However, once I had painstakingly completed my handiwork and held the doll up for her to admire, she burst into tears. Inevitably, my parents found out and my father took me outside behind the wash-house and disciplined me with the dog collar. I had to give Babe all my pocket money for three months to pay for a new doll. My mother burnt the desecrated doll. She realised what it was supposed to be.

I never let on to Lou that I knew why she called herself John. From instinct, I was sure that she would've denied any association. As for my own name, I was always Judy.

The thing about Dragonland was that it took so long to get there, that we were usually bored with our game by the time we actually arrived. We had fun on the way, encountering fleeing lower life forms (startled rabbits), powerful intergalactic force-fields (sagging fences) and mysterious signs of alien life (sheep droppings). But there wasn't anything to equal these wonders once we got to Dragonland. It was just a rock and we were too tired to pretend it was anything else.

The only thing at all fearsome about the dragon close-up

was its mouth. This was a cave near the base of the rock. It was very dark inside that cave, so dark you couldn't actually see where it ended. Even Lou, who was generally so fearless, had never had the courage to venture right back to touch the rear wall. We used to terrify ourselves making up stories about the dragon's mouth. Lou claimed that there was no back wall to the cave, that it went deep down into the earth with something unspeakable, inconceivable at its very end.

One day we were huddled in there and Lou began to identify the dragon's teeth and then its tonsils. Staring into that unfathomable blackness, her voice hissing in my ear, I began to believe that I could see them too. Suddenly, she rolled backward screaming, swearing that she was being eaten alive by the dragon and begging me to save her. In that dark silent cave it seemed all too plausible. I leapt forward into the sanctuary of daylight, screaming, thoroughly terrified. I think Lou even frightened herself in the process of teasing me. She'd rolled back further than she'd ever dared go before and when she emerged from the cave, having realised I wasn't going to venture back to rescue her, she looked pale and devoid of her boisterous swagger.

By tacit agreement we avoided the dragon's mouth after that day. Instead we'd clamber up onto the head of the dragon, and sit there, getting our breath back after the long walk. We always looked to see if the Field of Blood was greener than the rest of the paddocks around it. Sometimes we were certain it was. Lou liked to survey the farm and brag about the changes she'd make if it was hers. Her comments shattered our make-believe world. It was impossible to continue when she so crudely injected reality into our situation. Inevitably she'd spy my father doing something in one of the paddocks and become impatient to join him. She'd leap up, convinced he couldn't manage without her and insist we go down and help. It was the last thing

I'd want to do, *volunteer* to help my father. 'You go,' I'd say, and she would, dashing down the hill, like a young deer, leaping over snow tussocks and the great Scotch thistles that grew so tall around Dragonland.

It wasn't any fun up there on my own. After a while I'd trudge back down the hill, trying my best to sustain the magical circumstances of our ascent. But it was never the same. We never let on how dull Dragonland was in reality. Instead, we did our best to create a mystique about the place. We talked about it on the school bus so that the other kids heard us, slipping it into our conversation in a seemingly nonchalant manner. 'Oh, I can't do that,' I'd say, 'I'm going to Dragonland after school.'

It sounded exotic and mysterious. Its allure was fuelled by the fact that we refused to take anyone else along with us. We both knew any visitors would scoff when they saw it for themselves. It didn't take long for Arch to get sick of our mysterious comments. 'That's no dragon. That's just a dumb old rock.'

This remark made Lou bristle. 'I bet you'd be too scared to go to Dragonland.'

'Why? Scared of what?'

'Because ... because ... '

For once Lou was lost for words. Arch's face was beginning to slip into its usual sneer. I had a flash of inspiration. 'Because if anyone wants to enter Dragonland, the dragon breathes on them and their clothes smoulder off their bodies until they're naked,' I said quickly.

Nudity was sacrosanct. Everyone at school was simultaneously thrilled and terrified by it. That nudity was the rule at Dragonland caused ripples of excitement throughout the entire school and everyone regarded Lou and me with even greater respect.

The next time we went to Dragonland, we were almost

there when Lou announced that we were going to stand at the brink of the dragon's mouth and throw all our clothes off, into that ominous black hole. 'What?' I spluttered. 'That was just a story. Wasn't it?'

'It was your idea,' Lou replied sharply.

She strode on ahead, the very briskness of her pace daring me to challenge her. I knew whatever protest I made, she would overrule with some convincing argument. But I *had* to avoid it. There were several desperate reasons why it was inconceivable that I should shed my clothes, let alone throw them into that hole, from which I'd never dare to retrieve them again.

Things had changed. My body had become something I was ashamed of. I had gotten fat.

I hadn't noticed it happening, but the last time my mother and I had gone clothes shopping there were no sizes big enough in boyswear for me any more. That was shaming enough. But it wasn't just my belly that had swollen out. I'd developed these big blubbery breasts of sheer fat. They looked terrible. All the other boys at school had these perfectly flat little chests, punctuated by pale violet nipples, while I was all flabby curves and spare tyres. It was alarming. I knew that girls started to grow breasts at about this age and to my horror, I seemed to be doing the same thing. I was worried that I'd brought it on myself by dressing up too often. Now I was developing the figure to go with my grandmother's old clothes.

It was natural for Lou to presume that undressing in front of her wouldn't pose a problem. We'd seen each other naked hundreds of times before. We'd often taken our baths together and we also had this ritual of running round the house naked, to dry off, after a swim at the river. However, it was the middle of winter. We hadn't been swimming for over four months. Aunt Evelyn had outlawed us having our baths together round the same time. Since then, something else had happened, something that was even worse. I had sprouted a couple of hairs down below. I desperately didn't want Lou to know. Inevitably, she'd make a big fuss about it, tell lots of people and warn me I was going to end up like Roy Schluter. He was the new boy at school, who seemed to be developing hair just about everywhere: above his lip, all over his legs, under his arms and probably between his legs as well. Or at least that's what everyone speculated.

I desperately wanted to keep my clothes on. The thought of disrobing was making me sweat and pant more than ever. I wondered if I might simply expire on the spot. It would be fatal but it would be my salvation. Lou was well ahead of me. I stopped. Perhaps I could merely pretend to expire. I collapsed with an elaborate sigh and rolled under a nearby matagouri bush, getting badly scratched in the process. I waited for Lou to come and rescue me. She didn't. She was so intent on getting to Dragonland first, she hadn't noticed my collapse or bothered to check that I was still following her. It was at least five minutes later before I heard her coming back down the sheep track looking for me. She was calling out to me by my real name, instead of Judy. That was a bad sign.

'What are you doing under there?' she demanded when she came upon me.

My eyelids fluttered. I could see her standing over me, hands on her hips, an impatient grimace on her face. I moaned as if in agony, trying to win a bit of sympathy. But instead she kicked me. 'Get up,' she said, 'or I'll shoot you. That's what they do in the movies to horses that give up the ghost.'

'I'm not a horse. I've sprained my ankle, John.'

That was an inspiration. I didn't actually know what

spraining your ankle entailed but it was a common occurrence in *The Famous Five* adventure series. Anne was always spraining her ankle at inopportune moments near the climax of the adventure.

'John,' I moaned. 'Help me, John.'

Lou loved being called John.

'Come on then,' said Lou a little more gallantly. 'The dragon's waiting for his sacrifice.'

'John, I can't walk any further.'

Lou sighed. Though she grumbled and complained, she loved coming to my rescue. She bent over me and helped me to my feet. 'Come on,' she said, 'lean on me.'

I leant upon her heavily and together we hobbled a few steps up the sheep track. Suddenly, I sprang away from her, laughing, and started running down the hill. Lou yelled after me, protesting, but I called back to her that I'd race her down the hill. That was one thing Lou couldn't pass up, a challenge to a race. She always had to come first. She dashed past me effortlessly and had soon disappeared from sight into a gully. I stopped running and began to plod down the hill instead. The moment of revelation had been averted. But I knew it was likely to arise again and prove just as difficult to avoid. It wasn't easy keeping secrets, especially from Lou. I was going to have to become good at it.

5

Aunt Evelyn gave me the nickname that plagued me throughout my last months at primary school. She bestowed it quite unwittingly and would've been horrified if she'd ever realised what she'd precipitated. But she failed to realise. As the days passed and the name calling showed no sign of abating, my faith in Aunt Evelyn dwindled away, leaving a rancorous blame to mount up in its stead.

I drew away from her. I avoided her Shakespeare recitals. Refused her invitations for duets on the piano. I made a show of not listening to whatever she said, whether it was one of her theatrical anecdotes or a command to do a chore for her. I derived a malicious pleasure that she seemed hurt and bewildered by my behaviour. I began to treat her the way Lou treated her, as a pest who was best ignored.

She knew I was brooding over something. She *had* to realise she had done something wrong. I waited for her to ask what the matter was but she never did. Instead she remarked loudly to my mother one day that teenagers were awfully moody.

By estranging myself from Aunt Evelyn, I deprived myself. I had adored our play-acting times together and she had always encouraged me. But there was another, even greater loss. I never had the opportunity to ask Aunt Evelyn my burning question. What was *acting the poof*? She had been the person most likely to provide the answers, but after what she started, no matter how much I wanted to know, I couldn't bring myself to ask her. I felt betrayed.

She said it at Lou's twelfth birthday party in front of the entire school. That sounds like a lot of guests to invite to a birthday party but the school roll was actually only eighteen. It wasn't because Lou was friends with everyone that the whole school was invited. In fact, Lou had such a fearsome reputation that she couldn't truthfully be described as popular. It was Aunt Evelyn who had insisted on inviting everyone. She liked to 'set the standard' and for everybody to recognise her accomplishment.

I'd heard my mother discussing the party on the telephone with Velda Pile. 'I can't believe that Evelyn has to prove something with a child's birthday party as well. She already has the newest house, the biggest garden, her own car, the most frequent hair appointments, to go with Arthur having the biggest farm in Mawera. Where will she draw the line?'

Aunt Evelyn was famous for organising innovative party games that culminated in the eating of something sweet. The first game that particular year was the licorice strap race. Everyone was commanded to pair off into boy-girl couples. Lou rebelled, declaring that all the boys were too dumb. She insisted on choosing her best friend Susan Scott instead. Aunt Evelyn smiled grimly but was forced to demur. Being Lou's birthday, she was entitled to flout the usual etiquette of obeying when being told what to do.

There were equal numbers of boys and girls, so Lou's rebellion ruined the obvious symmetry of things. It meant two of the boys had to pair up as well. I being Aunt Evelyn's nephew and more subject to her authority than anyone else, was instructed to pair with Roy Schluter. He was the new boy at school who everyone was still wary of, on account of his outlandish name, his strange clothes and the damage adolescence was wrecking upon his face and body. He was older than me by six months. His recent arrival had stripped me of the honour of being the oldest pupil at school. Strange things were happening to Roy. He had the vague shadow of a moustache above his mouth that everyone at school was always whispering in awe about. All over his forehead, he had what Arch Sampson described as 'a crop of pimples', with additional plantations threatening to sprout down the planes of his face. It was also rumoured that his penis was as big and as hairy as anything our fathers possessed. Arch claimed to have seen it after rugby practice the previous week. He'd offered Roy a look at his *Penthouse* if he'd show him, but Roy had told him to go away and that he had nothing special to display.

I had a particular aversion to being paired with Roy. I didn't want to get too close to his pimples. They looked contagious. Unfortunately, I had to do as I was told.

The licorice game was always over in a flash. Each couple had to stand facing one another with a licorice strap connecting their mouths. When Aunt Evelyn shouted 'go', the idea was to chomp through as much licorice strap as possible until you couldn't go any further, unless you were game to stick your tongue into your opponent's mouth to retrieve what they'd already claimed.

Roy Schluter and I faced one another. I was something of a champion at the licorice game but on this occasion when Aunt Evelyn shouted 'go', I nibbled forward tentatively. I'd only claimed about an inch when Roy's face seemed to loom horribly close. I bit through the licorice, surrendering the game. I loved licorice but those things on Roy's face were enough to make you lose your appetite. I waited for Roy to suck the strap up into his mouth triumphantly. He didn't. He just stood there with it dangling, like he didn't understand what to do next. He looked up at me quizzically. 'You won,' I said, wishing he'd just eat it and stop staring at me.

But he didn't eat it. Instead, he tore the licorice strap in two and held out half to me, his eyes wide, watching me, waiting. The way Roy stared made me uneasy. I snatched the licorice and stuffed it in my mouth all at once. As I chewed, a slow satisfied smile spread across Roy's face. There was something about that smile that made me stop chewing for a moment. It seemed to intimate something. I had the sinking feeling that he thought we were friends now.

There was no way I wanted to be friends with Roy. He was already the most mocked kid at school. To even be associated with him would mean inviting ridicule upon oneself. Luckily for me, no one noticed Roy's overture of friendship. Everyone was watching Lou and Susan. The game was over but Lou and Susan's mouths were still locked together furiously. 'Susan and Lou are kissing,' squealed someone.

'No, they're not,' said Aunt Evelyn coldly. 'They're merely being overly competitive.'

Aunt Evelyn quickly announced that it was time for the treasure hunt. Lou abruptly broke away from Susan. She'd spied on her mother as she'd laid out the clues. Aunt Evelyn gave Lou a handkerchief. She had licorice all over her chin. The treasure hunt wasn't a success. Lou and Susan Scott disappeared at the start of the hunt and weren't seen again until fifteen clues later, sitting where the treasure was supposed to be, but wasn't.

Aunt Evelyn banned Lou and Susan from the next game. The chocolate game. This was a particular favourite of mine as it involved my two favourite things. Dressing up and eating. The object of the game was to roll a six on the dice, once that was achieved you earned the right to throw on some silly dress-up clothes and then eat as much chocolate with a knife and fork as possible, before someone else threw a six on the dice and foisted you out of the clothes and away from the chocolate.

Luck was on my side. I threw five sixes, though only actually got the knife and the fork to the chocolate three times. Resplendent in Uncle Arthur's gumboots, an old church hat of Aunt Evelyn's and a pair of Lou's witches britches, I lopped off a whole row of chocolate, speared it with the fork and got it into my mouth, two seconds before Gina Turner threw a six. It was always a very exciting game and soon everyone had forgotten the disappointment of the treasure hunt. Aunt Evelyn had generously allowed two king size blocks of chocolate and also kept a few squares in reserve for those children who missed out altogether.

After the chocolate game, it was time for birthday tea. Lou had devised the menu in unsolicited consultation with me. There were Cheerios with tomato sauce, sausage rolls, fairy bread, potato chips, two whole pavlovas and a two-tone jelly. Lou sat at the head of the table and I made sure I sat in close vicinity to one of the pavlovas, which were lavishly decorated with chocolate chips and sliced Chinese gooseberries. Aunt Evelyn hovered about, making sure everyone was helping themselves and not feeling shy. She saw me take my second piece of pavlova and promptly moved the plate down the other end of the table. Luckily, I'd had the foresight to take the largest piece on the plate.

Once everything had been eaten, Aunt Evelyn turned off the lights and dashed into the kitchen. A few seconds later she reappeared bearing the birthday cake with twelve candles burning tentatively. She set the cake down in front of Lou and kissed her on the cheek. Then she began to sing 'Happy Birthday' in her commanding voice. Everyone else was so in awe of Aunt Evelyn's volume that they all just mimed their way through the song.

I could see Lou cringing. She hated it when her mother sang. She always complained that she sang too loudly and drew too much attention to herself and that it was showing off. I could see what she meant. After all it was only 'Happy Birthday' and not the finale of *The King and I*.

When Aunt Evelyn had finished, everyone chorused for Lou to make a wish. She blew the candles out so forcefully that several of them were ejected from the sponge cake. It was a lamington cake. I had advised Lou on this. Aunt Evelyn miscalculated cutting it up and ended up with three extra slices. After everyone had disposed of their first pieces, she offered around seconds. I was first to stick out my plate. I had been waiting for her to offer.

Aunt Evelyn looked at me doubtfully. 'No, Billy,' she said firmly, 'I think one piece is plenty for you. You don't want to go putting on even more weight.'

I was stunned. I had never been refused food before. No one had ever told me in my entire life that I shouldn't eat something. In fact, it was quite the opposite. I was always being told I was a growing boy and urged to eat as much as I possibly could. I was so surprised. Then someone giggled and the first flush of humiliation began to creep into my face. I put my plate down and stared at the table cloth. Luckily, everyone was so busy jostling for the last pieces of cake that no one was paying any attention to me. By the time the commotion had passed, I had stopped crying and wiped my eyes on my party hat.

After the cake, Arch Sampson pulled me aside. 'You gotta help me, Fats. We're gonna ambush Roy an' pull his pants down an' find out what he's got down there.'

I didn't like the new name that Arch had come up with for me. I knew I should refuse to help him if he was going to call me names but I was curious to see this man-sized thing between Roy's skinny legs. 'Okay,' I said.

Everyone ran outside to play a game of kiss-tig as the sun went down, before the mothers arrived to collect their sons and daughters. Roy loped along with the others. 'You lure him over near the drive, behind the hedge,' instructed Arch. 'Then I'll grab him in a headlock an' you sit on his chest an' I'll pull his pants down.'

I sidled up to Roy and told him I'd saved some chocolate for him. 'Come over by the hedge, so no one else sees and grabs it,' I said.

Roy grinned and I quickly looked away. I felt so treacherous, seeing him so easily pleased and knowing it was a trick. But those finer feelings were a mere twinge, quickly overcome by a more urgent emotion, the thrill of anticipation at what we were going to find. As soon as we got near the hedge, Arch sprang out from within it, tackling Roy rugby style who crashed heavily to the ground. 'Sit on him Fatty, sit on him,' Arch yelled.

I plonked myself down on Roy's chest. I was relieved I didn't have to look at his face registering this betrayal. Arch pulled down his grey shorts. Underneath he was wearing pale blue briefs, with an iron-on transfer of a leaking tap over his crotch. 'Water works' it said. I studied his underwear, wishing my mother would buy ones like that for me. There did seem to be a fairly sizeable bulge in them too, though I couldn't see any tell-tale hairs creeping over the top of the elastic.

At first Roy struggled and kicked, but Arch told him to knock it off and surprisingly, he did. I was intrigued. Roy was older than both of us and bigger and shouldn't have done what two younger boys told him to. It went against the natural hierarchy of things. But it seemed Roy didn't understand that. Or perhaps because Mr Schluter worked for Arch's father, maybe he thought he had to obey Arch the way his father obeyed Old Man Sampson. Roy lay still and

Arch yanked down his briefs and let out a whoop. Sure enough he did have a man-size one and a real thatch of pubes. I couldn't believe that a thirteen year old could have pubes like that. Even Robert Sack, the centre for the Glenora rugby team who everyone was scared to tackle because he was so big, only had a few wispy ones he proudly displayed in the changing room after matches.

Arch jumped up and ran off to tell everybody. I could hear him yelling, urging everyone to hurry up and come and take a look. We were alone. Roy didn't push me off or punch me. As I stared at what he had down there, I realised I wanted to touch it. I grasped his cock. It lolled there in my hands. I was impressed by its size. It didn't seem possible that it could get even bigger when it was stiff. I patted it encouragingly and Roy whimpered, a sad little cry.

Suddenly, there were lights upon us. Dazzled, I jumped to my feet and plunged into the hedge to hide. It was the first of the mothers' cars. Luckily, it was Mrs Turner, a keen gardener, who was so preoccupied peering jealously at Aunt Evelyn's exotic shrubs up the roadside, that she barely looked ahead of herself. Roy plunged into the hedge after me and I couldn't resist giving his cock another good feel before he eased his underpants up, covering himself.

Arch and the rest of the school arrived just as Mrs Turner drove past us. She got a terrible fright. She glanced back at the road to find she was about to run the entire school population over. She stopped the car, got out and told everybody off on the spot for being so stupid as to play on the driveway. She sent them all back to the house in disgrace. Before climbing back into her car and continuing up the drive, Mrs Turner snapped a cutting off one of Aunt Evelyn's shrubs.

By this time, Roy had his shorts up round his waist again. 'Let's go back to the house,' I said in a friendly manner, to make up for the doublecross.

Roy mumbled that he'd follow me later. It seemed he was sulking. I felt a pang of regret. I'd wanted to get him to show it to me again. In a farewell gesture, I gave his crotch one final squeeze before slipping out of the hedge. Amazingly, his cock was even bigger than before. My hand lingered, marvelling at it. Then I realised. Roy had a stiffy and was staying put in the hedge, waiting for it to subside so it wasn't so obvious.

I left Roy to shrink and hurried back across the lawn to the house. When I got inside, everyone started asking me if it was true about Roy. 'Go on Fatty,' said Arch. 'Tell 'em what we saw, how big and hairy it was.'

I blushed. I hated this new name Arch had invented and I hated Arch even more. Everyone was staring at me and snickering, whispering my new nickname amongst themselves. I wished I'd stayed outside in the hedge with Roy.

'Come on Fats, tell us,' said Peter Hammer.

I hesitated. It occurred to me that by confirming Arch's story, I could probably deflect this attention away from myself and focus it all on Roy. Surely, this revelation about Roy was big enough to make everyone forget about me and how fat I'd become. Just then Roy himself sidled into the room. Everyone was staring at me so no one else noticed him. He looked beaten and weary, like one of the farm dogs after they'd been shouted and sworn at for chasing the sheep the wrong way. It was that look on his face that made me change my mind.

'I didn't see nothing down there and you know that, Arch,' I said. 'It's just a story you decided to make up and told me to back you up.'

Arch stared at me in disbelief. Everyone started jostling him and punching him for making up stories. His protests were lost in the jeers of the others. I couldn't see Roy any more. I was beginning to worry as to whether I'd done the right thing. Undoubtedly I'd made an enemy of Arch.

Then Mr Schluter appeared in the doorway. 'Arch, I've come to collect you and Roy,' he said.

Mr Schluter wore strange clothes too, just like his son. He had on dirty khaki overalls and white gumboots. I'd never even seen white gumboots before. All the farmers round the Styx wore hobnail boots or black gumboots. I'd heard my mother on the phone saying that he'd never worked on a farm before and that he had a few funny ideas about what it entailed. 'I guess city folk often have naive ideas about country life,' she'd said in a wistful kind of way.

Arch stamped up to Mr Schluter. 'I'm driving home. My father always lets me.'

Mr Schluter looked at Arch doubtfully. 'Roy,' he called, and Roy glided out from the crowd to stand beside his father.

'Thank Lou for the nice party,' Mr Schluter instructed.

Roy and Arch mumbled a thank you in unison. 'Be seeing you all,' said Mr Schluter to no one in particular and turned to go back outside.

Arch raced ahead of Mr Schluter to beat him to the driver's seat. I watched them from the doorway. Mr Schluter was having a hard time getting Arch to move over to the passenger's seat. Finally, I heard him raise his voice, and Arch slid across. Meanwhile, Roy had climbed up on the back of the jeep and was crouching there beside the dogs, patting them, though Mr Schluter was insisting he get in the front. Roy didn't want to. He didn't want to have to sit beside Arch.

Eventually, Mr Schluter gave up, slammed his door, started the jeep and set off down the drive. It was obvious he hadn't got the hang of driving it. He had trouble getting from second gear into third. I could imagine Arch telling him how he could drive a whole lot better than that, and he probably could. Old Man Sampson had taught Arch to drive when he was eight years old. According to a phone conversation of my mother's that I'd overheard, he'd only hired the Schluters because Mrs Sampson was going to have another baby and had refused to help with the feeding out any longer.

Lou came up beside me. 'That Roy didn't give me a present. Everyone else in the school did, except him.'

'Perhaps he didn't know. Maybe it's different in the city, where they come from,' I said.

'Maybe,' said Lou. 'But the least he could've done was show me his dick, if it really is so big and hairy. That would've done as a present, having a squeeze of it.'

I didn't confide, even to Lou, that I'd usurped that particular birthday privilege. It was our secret, Roy's and mine. The fact that he'd gotten hard when I'd touched it, made me feel pretty confident that he'd want to fool around again just as much as I did.

6

The day after the birthday party, when I climbed into the school bus, I was greeted with a chorus of my new nickname. Fatty Fernando. Fatty Fernando. Fatty Fernando. 'Zorro' had just begun a new series on television and was being eagerly watched and discussed by everyone at school. Fatty Fernando was Zorro's bumbling opponent. From the delight everyone was taking in the new name, I could tell it had the resonance that was going to make it stick.

I shuffled to the back of the bus, ashamed that Babe and Lou were witness to my humiliation. They sat right up the front, gazing out the window, pretending not to hear or not to know me. I couldn't tell which. They stared at their feet when Arch started singing the theme song from 'Zorro', and everyone else joined in. Except them of course, and Roy. He turned those big moony eyes of his on me to emphasise that his silence was a mark of friendship. I looked away. I hated him and cursed myself for being stupid enough to feel sorry for him. I'd spared him and sacrificed myself to the worst that Arch could think up.

I blamed Roy. But it was Aunt Evelyn who was my real nemesis. It had been her drawing attention to the fact that I had put on weight that had made everyone take notice.

Adults were authoritative. Especially Aunt Evelyn, the sometimes school teacher. No one would have thought of calling me fat until she opened her big opera-trained mouth. All the kids at school were so used to seeing me every day, that they just accepted me as I was. They were accustomed to me and no one thought to comment because no one had really noticed the change.

Of course, there had been occasional comments on my weight, but none of them had made me feel embarrassed or alarmed or even made me stop to consider my shape as a problem. Instead, the remarks had usually made me feel dubiously pleased with myself. 'You'll be like your uncles,' my mother insisted. 'They all grew out, then up and look at them now.'

My mother's three brothers were all monsters, six foot three and big solid men without being at all fat. It was reassuring to think I'd end up the same way and that being fat was just a phase that would effortlessly work itself out into proportion. That my father wasn't tall gave me a few uneasy moments. In fact, he was decidedly short. So were Uncle Arthur and Grampy.

My father noticed my weight increase too. 'You'll be an asset round the farm now you're starting to get so big and strong,' he remarked kindly one day. Not that I liked helping round the farm, but it was nice to be praised and told I'd be an asset to someone.

About the only thing I could find to enjoy about working on the farm were the smokos and meals in-between jobs. My mother often baked something special for morning tea, like pinwheel scones or muffins, especially if it was a frosty morning. The tins were always full of fresh baking for afternoon tea; usually yo yos and afghans and belgium biscuits because they were Babe's and my favourites. Practically every night there'd be a roast dinner. Or at least that's how it had been until my mother began to rebel, and place the future of those roasts in doubt.

My mother had developed some strange new ideas about food. They complemented her strange new ideas on a variety of other matters. She renounced meat. To be a vegetarian on a farm was simply unheard of. Generally, meat featured on the menu three meals a day, seven days a week, a fact my mother pointed out. 'It's ridiculously excessive,' she said and promptly served up a meatless meal, that none of us could identify or felt particularly inclined to eat.

We all nibbled politely in silence. My mother was the only one to clear her plate. After the meal, while my mother was clearing up, my father went to the fridge and made himself a cold mutton sandwich and sat back down at the table to eat it. Babe and I were urged to go and watch television. From the lounge room we could hear my parents arguing in low voices. The upshot was that my mother cooked two meals from that day forward: one with meat and one without. Neither Babe nor I dared show too much interest in what our mother ate. Our father had a word to us on the sly, warning us that the future of the nightly roast dinner was at threat if we showed any inclination for 'vegetablerism'.

My mother's new diet coincided with my own realisation of how fat I had actually become. I weighed myself when I got home from Lou's party and was horrified to find that I was over ten stone. In fact, I was closer to eleven stone. I was only twelve years old, not even five-foot tall, and I weighed practically *twice* as much as my contemporaries. It was alarming. Embarrassing. I didn't want anyone to know how much I weighed. As I stood there on the scales, unable to believe the evidence before my eyes, I resolved to go on a diet. A *secret* diet.

It was bad enough being teased about being fat. I didn't want to be teased about being on a diet as well. As far as I knew men never went on diets. There were never diets for men in any magazines. I'd never heard of a man not eating something because he was concerned about his weight. It just didn't happen. Practically every man I'd ever encountered had a beer gut swelling over his belt.

That night, after the party, I went to bed with a stack of Babe's *Pink*s to research possible diets. Our mother had treated both Babe and me to a magazine subscription a few months previously. She'd said that we could choose whatever we wanted. Babe had already made up her mind before we even got to the newsagent in Glenora. She knew exactly where *Pink* the new British girls' magazine was on the magazine stand. She thrust a copy of it at our mother who examined it sceptically, then tried to persuade Babe into something more worthy. '*Look and Learn* is very interesting,' she suggested.

Babe was adamant. 'You said I could choose for myself,' she whined loudly so that the shopkeeper would hear.

My mother sighed and was obliged to agree. 'Well, that means you can have *Look and Learn* then, Billy-Boy,' she said, turning to me.

Her smile was tightly strained. I knew better than to argue.

The only thing I ever bothered reading in *Look and Learn* was the comic strip in the back. But the magazines that Babe and my mother had subscribed to fascinated me. For my mother had taken out a subscription to *Cleo*, the shocking new women's magazine that featured nude male centrefolds.

Cleo was never left lying around the lounge room. Babe and I pestered my mother for weeks to show us the centrefold. Finally one day she took us to her bedroom, retrieved a copy of the magazine from under the bed and opened it to the centre page. 'There,' she said, thrusting the naked man's torso beneath our noses. 'Satisfied?'

I was more than satisfied. I was tremendously excited. It

was a strain to act blasé for my mother's benefit. I actually felt tremulous from the thrill of seeing the centrefold. Now that I knew exactly where my mother kept the magazines, I resolved to return and study the centre pages of every issue much more closely at the first possible opportunity. Next golf day.

I was also intrigued to notice that my mother didn't offer her *Cleo*s to Aunt Evelyn. Usually, the two of them swapped their magazines with remarks like, 'This has a great recipe for a six tin sausage casserole,' or 'This one says shocking things about Princess Anne and her horses.' But the *Cleos* remained discreetly under the bed. I couldn't decide whether my mother was too embarrassed to offer them to Aunt Evelyn, or whether perhaps Aunt Evelyn already subscribed herself.

Pink was rather tame by comparison, though still a lot more interesting than *Look and Learn*. It was full of tips on all manner of important subjects such as how to sew tartan onto your clothes Bay City Rollers style, and competitions to win a date with David Cassidy. It also offered dieting advice. That night, after the scales had revealed the sorry truth, I read every *Pink* article on dieting. They all seemed to advocate the same basic strategy: munching on carrots, celery sticks and crispbread thinly spread with cottage cheese.

This was all rather foreign and not particularly practical to me. Carrots were the only thing on the *Pink* diet that were familiar. Unfortunately they were also the preferred nourishment of the rabbits who regularly raided my mother's vegetable garden. These rabbits infuriated my father who had wasted many of his evenings, hiding behind the raspberry bushes with his shotgun, waiting for them to appear. When they failed to, he laid poisoned carrots around the perimeter of the vegetable garden. The inevitable happened. Somehow, one of those carrots ended up in the salad my mother served to the local Wrightson's agent. The poor man had to be induced to vomit and then rushed to Glenora hospital. My father blamed my mother and my mother blamed my father, but the upshot was that the vegetable garden was abandoned to the rabbits.

Carrots became a word fraught with highly-charged significance in our home. My mother decided it was best not to serve them again until the incident became a distant memory. Wrightson's became extremely inflexible with our credit account after 'the attempted poisoning' much to my father's chagrin. I would wander out to the vegetable garden and look longingly at the carrots. They were my possible salvation according to *Pink* magazine, but they were all either half-nibbled by the rabbits or potentially lethal.

So I turned to celery. I had a vague idea it was a vegetable but no idea what it looked like. The range of vegetables I was familiar with was rather basic. My father insisted on potatoes, carrots and frozen peas and would eat nothing else. When carrots became an unmentionable, they were tactfully supplanted by cauliflower on our dinner plates, which no one ever ate, except my mother. Celery was another enigma for me.

Whenever we went to the Crayburn Superstore or to the more extensive Glenora Four Square, I would always rush straight to the vegetable section. My mother was terribly impressed by this behaviour. She presumed that I too longed to forsake meat but was too scared of my father to suggest it. But I was only in search of celery and I never found it in either of those two shops. I didn't dare ask for it either. Celery was renowned as excellent for dieters. I didn't want my secret intentions to be deciphered and mocked.

The only dietary option left to me was crispbread and cottage cheese. These at least were slightly more familiar. I interpreted crispbread as a bizarre British name for toast. Cottage cheese I assumed to mean homemade cheese. Toast was of course easily obtainable, and I began to eat it at every opportunity. I even demanded that my mother make my sandwiches out of toast. Homemade cheese was more of a challenge. The old dairy where Nan used to make cream, butter and cheese when she lived at the farmhouse was disused. Over the years, it had become a dumping ground for various tools and odds and ends that my father couldn't be bothered putting away properly or throwing out. I knew that one day I would end up being instructed to clean it out and put everything in its proper place. It was another of those tasks my father was saving for a rainy day.

I investigated the contents of the dairy and tried to work out what was used for what. But with all my father's junk in there I couldn't be certain if the object I had discovered was a churner or some new device for mixing sheep dip. I gave up. I hadn't been able to find a recipe for cheese anyway. I had gone through all my mother's recipe books and even written to the most famous cook in New Zealand, Alison Holst.

Alison had her own cooking show on television and had written a virtual library of recipe books. I couldn't believe none of her books had a recipe for cheese. I wrote to her care of the television show, asking for one. I got a letter back pointing out that we were living in the 1970s and busy mothers preferred to buy cheese ('there are many different varieties now available') from supermarkets and spare themselves the extra work. So I wrote to New Zealand's other celebrity cook, Tui Flower of the *New Zealand Women's Weekly* cooking column. She tersely replied that homemade cheese was before her time and was I making insinuations about her age?

The one person who could have solved the problem for

me, Nan, was dead. So I approached Grampy, who did have a very sharp memory for 'the old days'. My request set him off on a long story about how when he was my age, he'd had to milk the cows at six every morning, whatever the weather. He claimed that one day the snow was so deep that he'd had to shovel it out from beneath the cow's udder to get at her teats. He reckoned that by the time he got the buckets of milk back to the dairy that morning, the milk had frozen solid.

'So how did Nan turn that frozen milk into cheese?' I persisted, trying to get him back onto the topic.

Grampy stared at me with his good eye. Then he cleared his throat. Clearing his throat was always a prelude to one of his famous maxims. Grampy was one of the oldest guys around. He commanded a certain respect in the community and was always offering advice to people. It was only natural that he would have something authoritative to say about cheese-making.

'Eat hearty, my boy,' he instructed. 'Because you never know when you'll eat again. You might get yourself lost on a muster or stuck in the tractor down the swamp or just be too damn busy to break for lunch. Eat hearty, lad, always.'

The prospect of having to carry out such vile tasks, let alone getting stuck or lost while doing so, gave me some food for thought. Maybe Grampy was right. Homemade cheese and toast wasn't much of a meal. I also liked the idea of heeding his advice, to make up for my father, who never did. He was always complaining about Grampy and his endless advice which he ignored as a matter of principle. He'd do things his own way, and if it proved unsuccessful he'd swear so much the dogs would all run and hide from him. I felt someone had to make Grampy believe his wisdom was appreciated. I liked the way he'd tell me things, even if it was for the umpteenth time. He always said it like it was top secret, eyes wide and expression dead serious. So I abandoned the idea of dieting, out of respect to Grampy.

A week after I'd made that decision, Babe announced that she was going on a diet and would only eat raw carrots and celery and crispbread thinly spread with cottage cheese. My mother was terribly excited by Babe's new plan. It was, after all, a vegetarian diet, albeit a rather drastic one. My mother decided to make a special trip to Dunedin to buy the essentials for the new diet. She cursed the inadequacies of the local shops for my father's benefit. Secretly she was always eager for an excuse to visit Dunedin and call upon her friends from the university yoga society that she only got to see occasionally. She took Babe with her and together the two of them spent a frivolous hour, and almost a month's worth of her housekeeping budget, in Sanitarium. My mother bought all sorts of foodstuffs, not approved by *Pink*, which she hoped to tempt Babe into trying.

For the entire day they were away my father complained about my mother and her whims and the dangers of the diet she so passionately desired for herself and everyone else. Finally, he conceded that it might be alright for women to eat 'that muck' but to expect a man to was nothing short of 'bloody stupid'. My fate was sealed. It should have been the easiest thing in the world for me to simply announce that I too would join in the new diet, but now I realised to do so would be an act traitorous to my entire gender. My father would never forgive me if I was to break rank at the nightly roast dinner.

He was prone to hoarding particularly nasty farm chores until Babe or I did something to annoy him. For instance, I knew that all the manure under the gratings at the woolshed hadn't been cleaned out for well over a year. It was beginning to ooze through the cracks. Lou, who was always hanging around my father and trying to be helpful, had even been so foolish as to point it out to him. 'I know, I know,' said my father, in a voice that sounded particularly malevolent to my expert ear.

There was no way I wanted to cop that one.

So that night when my mother arrived home, the boot of the Holden piled up with boxes of foods and vegetables I'd never even seen before, I pretended not to be interested. My father and I sat in the lounge and watched 'Zorro', which was now of particular torment to me. He didn't send me, as he usually did, to help my mother up the path with her parcels. He had, however, dispatched me off earlier in the afternoon from the woolshed to get the roast on. This was a welcome reprieve from helping him trim the stud ewes' feet.

So when my mother staggered into the kitchen with her plastic bags of eggplant and zucchini and broccoli, a copy of *The Creative Vegetarian* tucked under her arm, she was greeted by the smell of roasting leg of mutton. Babe followed at her heels, dubiously clutching a small sack of wheatgerm. She sniffed the air appreciatively. My mother noticed and handed Babe the recipe book. 'Pick out whatever you fancy, dear,' she said. 'And I'll make it for you tonight.'

Babe flicked straight to the desserts section. It looked as though she had been converted during the course of the Dunedin excursion to fully fledged vegetarianism. 'I would like,' she finally decided, 'banana buckwheat pancakes with homemade apricot ice-cream.'

My mother looked alarmed. 'Is that in there?'

Babe nodded and held up the recipe as proof.

'I thought you were wanting to diet, dear, and be more conscious of what you were eating,' my mother said.

'Then I'll have my crackers and lumpy cheese,' snapped Babe.

That, I discovered, was what crispbread and cottage

cheese actually was. I was relieved that I'd decided to support my father in his masculine meat-eating fraternity. As we tucked into our roast dinner, Babe miserably nibbled at a cracker. My mother, too, had opted for crackers after she had discovered that the recipe for bean stew required overnight soaking of the beans. When my father maliciously asked Babe to pass the gravy for the third time, she finally burst into tears, and ran off to her bedroom, detouring via the oven and snatching two roast potatoes as she went. My father had instructed me to make sure that I cooked plenty of roast vegetables that night, just in case Babe and my mother could be tempted.

After dinner I went to find Babe, but she was in bed with the lights turned off, pretending to be asleep. I pinched her latest issue of *Pink* and retired to my own bedroom. There was a 'Would David date you?' quiz, and I discovered to my delight that he would, if I told a few sneaky lies. Alongside was a photograph of him shirtless which I wanted to rip out, but I knew Babe would notice. Even though she professed to loathe David Cassidy, it didn't mean she would let anyone else enjoy him semi-nude. I would have to wait a few weeks before I stole it and added it to my 'private collection' of cuttings from magazines of men in their togs or with their shirts off. They were mostly Bullworker advertisements from *The Listener* of men who had once been nine-stone weaklings but had been transformed by Bullworker into 'rippling brutes'. I undid my shirt and examined my own body. I had ripples, but they weren't of the Bullworker approved variety.

I went to the bathroom and weighed myself. I had put on two pounds since the previous night. I felt terribly guilty for having eaten such a big roast dinner. I decided to have a very hot bath in the hope that it might melt the extra two pounds off. I had seen a program on television where people got into tubs of hot water with only their heads poking out the top, and emerged later, half the size of what they had been before.

I ran the bath from the hot tap only. The entire bathroom became enveloped in steam. The water was ferociously hot. It took forever to slowly ease all of me into the water. The heat was almost more than I could bear, but its intensity reassured me that it must be doing something. It was only when I was completely submerged that I remembered that the program with the sauna sequence had been a cartoon. People also got blown up or fell off cliffs in cartoons and came out of it looking just fine. I lost faith in the idea and clambered out.

Then my father barged into the bathroom. 'Hurry up in there,' he growled. 'And you better not have taken all the hot water, or there'll be trouble.'

Trouble usually meant some unpopular task around the farm that he didn't want to do himself.

I dried myself off and hopped onto the scales. It was difficult to read because of the steam, but it looked as though I'd lost the two pounds. I didn't peer too closely, in case I was proved wrong. I scampered across the passage into my bedroom, put on my pyjamas and jumped into bed. The *Pink* magazine had disappeared from beside my bed. Babe had retrieved it while I was in the bath, which was a shame. I had wanted to look at the photo of David Cassidy, one more time, before I turned off the light and went to sleep.

I reached for my cow's tail instead. I kept it coiled in the drawer of my bedside table. I held it up high, admiring its glittering blondness in the light of my lamp. With my other hand I reached for the hairbrush that I kept alongside it in the drawer. Slowly, reverently, I began to brush 'my hair'. With every stroke of the brush, I whispered under my breath 'fabulous'. I had mastered about fifteen different ways of saying it, though I wasn't sure how distinctive each of those fifteen ways was. Fifty different ways just seemed inconceivable.

I heard my father go into the bathroom. I switched my light off, arranging 'my hair' so that it rested upon my chest. I lay there in bed, tensing, waiting for my father's roar, when the hot water ran out. It didn't come and I fell asleep. It wasn't until the next morning that I learnt he had gotten engrossed reading *The Farmer* on the toilet, and so by the time he came to run his bath I was asleep and deaf to his curses and commands for me to boil water in the kitchen and bring it through to him.

My father left a note on my bread and butter plate that next morning. 'I have a special job for you after school today over at the woolshed.'

7

Aunt Evelyn developed something of a knack for launching new nicknames upon me. She was responsible for one even worse than Fatty, and for marring my looks for life. It was Aunt Evelyn who decided I needed glasses.

The world had become a blur. I realised, one day at school, that I was having to strain to see the blackboard. I didn't think anything of it, dismissed it as another curious development in the process of growing up. Like what was happening down below. Turning twelve had brought with it so many mysteries and complications and things I didn't fully understand. Having my vision fail me was just something else to endure. I tried to pretend that none of it was happening.

Aunt Evelyn was relieving at school the day she made her discovery. She would probably never have noticed if she hadn't been making such a special effort with me. I'd been doing my best to avoid her since Lou's birthday. My days at school had become a torment and I blamed her. No one called me Billy anymore. I was now Fatty.

But I couldn't avoid Aunt Evelyn that day. She sat at the teacher's desk, right in front of the class. Every time I looked up, she'd be staring at me intently with a concerned smile on her face. Her smile got on my nerves. I tried to keep my head bowed, but I could sense Aunt Evelyn's eyes were still upon me. That smile was relentless. It haunted me. Mocked me with a sympathy I no longer trusted.

When I was obliged to look at the blackboard, I stared right past her. Suddenly, she snapped to her feet and swooped down on me. 'You're squinting,' she crowed. 'You're squinting at the blackboard. You need to have your eyes examined.'

She led me into the staff room and rang my mother. 'Your son needs to go to an optician,' she declared, as if she was some sort of doctor delivering a diagnosis. 'I'm surprised no one's noticed before. *I* noticed immediately.'

I hated Aunt Evelyn anew. She seemed to consider it such a triumph to have observed what my mother had failed to. When the truth was if she hadn't been staring at me so much she probably wouldn't have noticed a thing. But what really irritated me was the undertone of criticism in Aunt Evelyn's voice. She was prone to this sort of manner. It wasn't exactly criticism. It was more subtle than that—she possessed this attitude of being assured of her own superiority.

Which is not to say that Aunt Evelyn wasn't also outspoken in her opinions. Particularly when she got on the phone and was being goaded from the other end by the likes of Velda Pile. She always talked loudly on the phone, just as she sang 'Happy Birthday' too loudly. Lou and I hadn't been able to avoid overhearing her talking to Velda recently, about my mother. 'She lives in a world of her own,' Aunt Evelyn had said. 'And it's a weird sort of world I'm telling you.'

Lou and I didn't discuss it. But I could tell from Lou's face that she was ashamed of her mother, her loud voice and her disloyal remark. Aunt Evelyn seemed to be making a lot of careless and rather cruel comments. Perhaps she'd always done so and I'd failed to notice. I'd never been the victim of one of them before.

Despite this disenchantment with my aunt, when the topic of my future career came up, I was tempted to overlook her betrayals. She started to bring it into conversation all the time, and I soon realised why. In the past, discussing my career had established an affinity between us. She'd ask me what I wanted to be and I'd say 'an actor or a singer, just like you Aunt Evelyn'.

But I noticed, for the first time, something smug in the way she asked that question. As if she'd already anticipated both my answer and how she in turn would respond to that answer. She would play the supportive aunt, a contrast to my mother 'who was in a world of her own', and my father who was always telling me that I'd be a farmer and that was that.

That morning, as we stood in the teacher's staff room, Aunt Evelyn's hand lingered on the telephone that she had hung up, as if she still relished the recent conversation. She glanced at me, her triumphant smile softening a little. 'You can still be an actor with glasses Billy,' she said, 'a character actor.'

I hesitated before replying. It was the moment when I might have confided my new aspiration, 'I want to act the poof'. I could imagine how Aunt Evelyn would smile and nod her head encouragingly, then start talking nineteen to the dozen about how I might go about accomplishing my goal. But as I was mulling over this possibility, I looked up into her self-assured smile, already gloating its victory at winning me back. My confession shrivelled on my tongue. I was overcome by a greater urge. A desire to hurt her. For I knew exactly how to do it.

I curled my own mouth in an imitation of her same smile and lied. 'I want to be a farmer,' I said, 'like Lou.'

Aunt Evelyn gasped. She would not hear of Lou's ambitions for the farm. She literally refused to hear them. Long ago, it had been deemed a taboo subject. Lou claimed it was the one thing that could reduce Aunt Evelyn to tears.

Her face had dissolved into disbelief but once she registered that I had actually said what she thought I'd said, she struggled to regain her composure. A stiff expressionless mask slid over her features. Only her eyes betrayed her, larger than usual, slightly shocked and blinking furiously.

'I don't believe you'd make a success of that,' Aunt Evelyn snorted, with a short, cruel laugh.

'But I'd have Lou to help me and she's an expert,' I said. 'We'd get along okay.'

Aunt Evelyn turned and walked away from me, pretending not to have heard. For a moment I felt my own brief surge of triumph. Had I made her cry? The thought of Aunt Evelyn in tears was almost impossible to contemplate, and for me to have purposefully induced them was a victory of sorts, but one that ultimately left me feeling guilty and uneasy. It was no longer Aunt Evelyn's smile that haunted me. It was those eyes. Blinking. Struggling to keep back the tears. Aunt Evelyn ceased her special-effort campaign after that and I began to fret and wonder if perhaps I had made a mistake.

My mother took me to Dunedin the week after Aunt Evelyn's diagnosis to have my eyes tested. I was excited by the prospect of getting glasses. I'd convinced myself that they'd improve my appearance which always dissatisfied me whenever I looked in the mirror. I wanted a *big* change. Ideally, I would've liked to have been slim with long, sleek dark hair like David Cassidy, instead of being fat with wispy blond hair. But if I couldn't have that, then having glasses would be a major new cosmetic flourish. It could only be an improvement.

I had so set my heart on having glasses, that when I was sat up in the optician's chair and told to read off the letters of the alphabet way down the other end of the room, I deliberately made mistakes. I could read the letters quite well if I closed one eye, but I made up entirely different sequences. Once, I made the mistake of reeling off seven letters instead of six, and I thought the optician realised what I was doing. But instead he gasped, 'Double vision as well'.

My mother squirmed in her seat guiltily. How had she failed to notice that her son was half-blind?

Meanwhile, I was doubly delighted with myself. I would get my glasses, and I had also realised how easy it was to deceive grown-ups, people I had always perceived as superior and quite infallible. It was a revelation that my mother could be so easily duped. When the time came to choose the frames, my mother took charge and selected a pair of heavy black frames. 'They look lovely,' the optician assured her.

Which wasn't what the kids at school said when the glasses finally arrived in the mail a week later and I got to wear them for the first time.

'Yuck.'

'Revolting.'

By playtime, I had a new nickname. Fatty Four-eyes.

When I got home from school that day, I told my mother I didn't want to wear glasses any more. 'But you have to, so you can see properly,' she said.

'But they give me a headache,' I complained. 'And I don't see any better with them.'

'You just need to get used to them,' she said.

I couldn't confess what I had done. It would mean another new pair of glasses and another trip to Dunedin. Petrol was expensive and everyone had been urged to try to conserve it. My father would have a fit. So I took my glasses off at every opportunity, or let them slip down my nose so that I didn't have to look through the lenses. I hoped these tactics would help the kids at school forget about the glasses and stop tormenting me.

They didn't. Everyone loved the way the new name glided off their tongues. Wherever I went, it was chanted, 'Fatty Fatty Four-eyes'.

I was crushed after that first day at school in my glasses. When I got home, I studied myself critically in the bedroom mirror. I looked nothing like David Cassidy and a lot like Billy Bunter, a resemblance I hoped no one else would notice. I couldn't believe how much I'd changed. A year ago, I'd been a normal eleven-year-old boy with blond hair, blue eyes, and a skinny frame like everyone else. Friends of my mother had declared me adorable and ruffled my wispy hair. Slowly, over the next year, their compliments petered out. Those same women said nothing to me, just looked at me, and I could tell they were thinking the same things that the kids yelled at me at school.

My body had betrayed me. Degenerated into a shape I was deeply ashamed of but which I felt powerless to alter. I sneaked my mother's appetite suppressants for a while, but they didn't seem to work. They tasted okay, a bit like chewy caramels. Some days I'd gorge on them, eat a handful in despair, willing them to save me and take me back to how I once had been. My mother must have realised what I was doing but she said nothing. Instead she bought another packet in chocolate flavour, which were even more tempting than the standard vanilla.

The clothes I was having to wear depressed me even more. They always looked strange because my mother had to buy trousers big enough to go around my waist from the menswear department and then lop about a foot off the length and rehem them. It was humiliating having to shop in menswear when all my contemporaries went to boyswear and could buy clothes that fitted perfectly and didn't need any adjustments.

My mother would try to cheer me up. 'You're becoming a real little man,' she'd say. 'Already shopping in menswear, just like your father.'

It wasn't consoling. I didn't want to become a man. I had seen what it was doing to Roy Schluter and I didn't want to start growing all that hair and getting pimples. I looked bad enough as it was, I didn't need anything else to mar my appearance. I prayed that I would be a late developer, but in the back of my mind, I knew I wouldn't be spared. My body was having a huge joke at my expense. It was like the way kids disfigure faces in magazine photos, drawing moustaches and glasses over beautiful women—someone was doing the same thing to me. Was it God? Or had God abandoned me altogether? If so, for what reason? I brooded on this God matter for several weeks, then suddenly one afternoon I realised where I had erred.

My mother was at golf, and I had taken advantage of her absence to sneak into her room and scrutinise the centrefolds in her *Cleo* magazines. My cock got hard through my jeans (an old pair of my father's, rehemmed) and I started rubbing it. Unexpectedly, a glorious sensation began to stir within me, emanating from my crotch but rising up so that my entire body seemed newly sensitised and aglow. I soon realised that the harder I rubbed, the better it felt. I increased my pace, and the sensations correspondingly intensified, building to a peak of such rapture that I flung myself at the magazines, burying my face in the pictures, heaving against the bed, moaning. Then, abruptly, the feelings ebbed away, leaving me limp and groggy, and slipping off my parents' bed.

I was shocked at myself. I felt as if I'd been possessed. I had been making sounds I didn't know I could make. What had happened? I stared at the magazines. One of them was a little crumpled with a dribble of saliva upon it. I wiped it off with my sleeve, praying that it wouldn't stain. I slapped the magazines shut, carefully arranged them in the exact order I'd found them and stowed them away. I smoothed out the bed. Everything looked as it should.

I darted out of the bedroom and into the lounge, turned on the television and settled into a chair, trying to look as if I'd been there for hours, in case someone should suddenly appear. But I couldn't concentrate on the television. I was so puzzled by what I had just managed to do, I couldn't think of anything else. As I sat there, I unzipped my jeans to look at myself. My stiffy had shrunken away and offered no clues. It wasn't until I gained my boarding school education in all things sexual that I realised I must have had a dry orgasm, all the sensations without the ejaculation. I was totally bewildered. Even though the experience had been pleasurable, I felt awed and almost frightened by the frantic urge it had whipped up in me, the way I had humped against the bed to keep the sensation building, my desperate belief that at that moment nothing else mattered.

When in fact it did. I had been in a situation fraught with the danger of discovery. What I'd been doing was utterly nefarious, yet I had lost all sense of caution. All reason. I had completely given myself over to sensation. Now my commonsense flooded back. Guilt sank its claws into me and shook me. I began to shiver at the thought of my foolhardiness and the risk of discovery I had run.

Quickly, I put my cock away. What I had been doing was absolutely taboo. Looking at pictures of people in the nude was bad enough, but to want to look at pictures of men, instead of women, was perverse. I knew it, from the way all the other boys at school behaved and talked. It was *Penthouses* that should have provided my illicit thrill. That was what the daring boys at school like Arch Simmons and Peter

Hammer were always bragging about, the *Penthouses* they had at home.

Sometimes they'd sneak some cut-out pictures to school and show them round at playtime in the privacy of the old tennis pavilion. They charged a twenty cent admission to come in for a look. But when I looked at those pictures I didn't feel the same excitement that they seemed to generate in the other boys. My interest was curious but utterly dispassionate. The only time I felt like I'd actually gotten my twenty cents worth, was when Arch had produced some pictures with a guy in them as well. That time, I got a stiffy. Arch had a full spread of photographs, five or six pages, which told a story set in outer space.

An astronaut had crash landed on a strange planet where women frolicked naked together, kissing and slapping each other playfully. Two of these big-breasted alien women pounced upon the astronaut with mischievous delight, stripped him of his spacesuit, leered over him, teased him with their bodies and their own provocative intimacy. The spread was called 'Lust in Space'.

I was fascinated by those pictures. I tried to buy them off Arch, but he refused. Later that afternoon, Arch seized me and pushed me up against the cloakroom pegs, threatening me with his fists if I didn't give them back. 'Give what back?' I protested.

'Those pictures. I had them hidden in the broken lining of my parka and now they're gone.'

I felt the loss as keenly as Arch. 'Really? Are you sure they're not there? That's terrible. Have you looked properly?'

Arch studied me suspiciously. He knew I had ambitions as an actor. But this was no act. I was genuinely dismayed. I had hoped to come up with a swap alluring enough to tempt Arch into parting with them. I'd even considered the cow's tail which he'd shown an interest in a couple of months back.

'You don't think the teacher's found them?'

'Nope. If it'd been the teacher, he'd have hauled me into the staff room and given me the strap by now. Someone snitched them. You sure it wasn't you Fatso?'

'Nope. Cross my heart, Arch. Honest.'

I cursed myself for not thinking of doing exactly that. 'Who else could it have been?' Arch mumbled. 'Maybe Roy the Freak. He's always doing sneaky things to piss me off and pretending he didn't do anything. It must've been him.'

Arch tore across the playground to where Roy was sitting, leaning against one of the rugby posts, staring out into space. I watched Arch circle him, accusing him. Roy just stared past him, ignoring Arch as if he was some pesky fly or something. If Roy had taken the pictures, I wondered if he'd consider showing them to me.

That afternoon, with the blaring television failing to distract me, I began to feel more and more alarmed. Why was it that all the other boys at school gloated and chuckled over pictures of naked women and I felt nothing, *nothing* but an almighty detachment from the spectacle, and from my peers? While my fascination with my mother's *Cleo*s was becoming more and more extreme. Every month I waited with increasing impatience, for the new issue to arrive in the mail. Once it had, I could hardly bear to wait for the next opportunity to arise when I would be alone in the house and be able to sneak a look. The anticipation was agony, yet it thrilled me to the core.

Then it occurred to me. I was being punished for coveting these pictures of naked men. It was a revelation. Suddenly, it all made sense. My physical degeneration had coincided with the blossoming of my fascination with men, wanting to see them naked and touch them. It had to be God punishing me for my evil thoughts. He'd become disgusted by what I was doing and had abandoned me to ruin.

It seemed a likely enough theory. But I wanted to know conclusively. I wanted it to be confirmed, to read it in a book or be assured by an adult that it was so. For the first time I wondered about being Catholic. I had seen in movies how Catholics could go to confession, spill out their troubles and be forgiven their sins. But even as the thought occurred to me, I knew that even if I was Catholic, I would never be able to confess to the desires that racked me. I didn't understand them entirely, but I knew enough to realise it was something that must be kept secret. These thoughts were shameful. No one must ever know.

My theory of punishment obsessed me. I decided to make some discreet enquiries and gather a few opinions.

I tried my mother first. She was embroiled in a spiritual quest of her own, which most of the Serpentine county considered thoroughly bizarre. She had renounced the Presbyterian church in Clayburn and was consulting clairvoyants in Dunedin and buying strange books with titles such as *Cosmic Lover* and *Crystal Pleasure*. She had also taken to practising yoga on the sundeck, much to my father's horror. 'Everyone can see you,' he protested.

That wasn't strictly true. Our nearest neighbours were two miles down the road and cars rarely drove past our house, maybe three or four a day at the most. Probably my father was concerned about the families living over the other side of the valley, with their high-powered binoculars. But my mother ignored him, and continued to entangle herself in complicated positions, frowning at the manual she had open by her side. Sometimes Babe and I joined her, but I was too fat and inflexible to mould myself into even the most basic of positions.

It was while she was out on the sundeck practising, that

I approached her with my question. 'Mum,' I ventured. She struggled to maintain her position, gave up, collapsed and sat up looking irritated. 'You know I don't like being called that,' she snapped.

My mother and Aunt Evelyn had recently decided that they would no longer be called Mum now that there was a deodorant frequently advertised on television called Mum. Of course, it had been Aunt Evelyn's idea to boycott Mum. 'I will not share the same name as a deodorant,' she told my mother, who had agreed.

Lou was supposed to call Aunt Evelyn 'mother'. It sounded so formal and cold that Lou had refused and declared that she was boycotting 'mother'. Meanwhile, my mother insisted that she be called Reebie, which neither Babe nor I could manage to say. The upshot was that we had no name for our mothers and had to clear our throats or tap them on the arm to get their attention.

'Um . . . I have a question,' I said nervously.

'Yes?' said my mother.

'How would God punish someone if he didn't like them for some reason?'

My mother stared at me. 'What an odd question. Do you mean, the Christian god?'

'Isn't He the only one?'

'It depends what you believe.'

'Oh,' I said, considering this. 'So is there a sort of choice of gods?'

'Not in the Serpentine there isn't,' said my mother. 'But certainly in a large city, there are lots of different religions with their own gods, as well as people with beliefs that aren't governed by any religion as such.'

This answer was extremely puzzling. 'And are some of the other gods nicer than the one we have here?' I asked.

My mother pursed her lips. 'There are some that aren't so

obsessed with guilt. What makes you think God is punishing you anyway?'

'I'm not talking about me,' I said quickly. 'I was just wondering.'

I turned away from her, not wishing to continue the conversation. I felt too transparent. But my mother persisted. 'If I was having a difficult time in my life,' she said loudly, demanding my attention, 'Rather than interpreting it as a punishment, I'd try and look at it as an experience I could learn something from, a bit like a lesson in school. Does that make sense?'

I nodded, not daring to look at her and began to walk away. 'I have some books on this sort of philosophy if you want to read them,' she offered.

'Okay,' I said, walking away as quickly as I could.

I knew her eyes were following me, trying to work out what had inspired my concern.

That night, when I went to bed, I found a couple of her new books stacked on my bedside table. Over the next few nights, I flicked through them, but found it difficult to accept them as authoritative. How could you compare a book published last year with the Bible that had been around for centuries?

I decided to ask my father for his opinion. 'If God wanted to punish someone? He'd give them a wife like your mother and a son that can't play rugby, that's what He'd do.'

And my father went off to grease the tractor.

I was reluctant to try Aunt Evelyn, but my father's answer had been so inadequate and my mother's new ideas so dubious. As soon as I'd asked her, I wished I hadn't. That same superior smile spread across her features, reminding me of her past betrayals. 'Whatever you do,' Aunt Evelyn said urgently, 'don't ask your mother a question like that. She's got strange ideas on that subject and she'll fill your head with nonsense. Come to me and I'll set you straight.'

Aunt Evelyn claimed that God didn't punish people, but that He might make things difficult for them so that they came to a deeper understanding of their sins. 'But how can you be sure what's a sin and what isn't?' I asked.

'You can ask me,' said Aunt Evelyn, waiting expectantly.

I said nothing.

The silence drew out for so long it became embarrassing. I could feel myself blushing. Even Aunt Evelyn began to look awkward, and then doubtful, as if she'd begun to change her mind. Her expression seemed to say that if my sins were so unspeakable, perhaps she didn't want to hear them after all. Finally, I screwed up the courage to excuse myself, thanking her for her advice. I was surprised that she let me go without demanding a confession out of me. I started to run, in case she called me back.

Grampy was my last chance. He snorted at my question. 'God,' he spat. 'There's no such thing in my opinion. People are always wanting to blame their own mistakes and problems on fate or God, instead of facing up to them and doing something about them. Listen to me, boy, if you want to get on in this life, you'll forget about God and do what has to be done.'

I was shocked by Grampy's forthright advice. It only made everything even more confusing.

After days of wrestling with all these different theories, I finally decided to conduct an experiment. I resolved not to look at the next *Cleo* when it arrived. In return for this sacrifice, I expected my weight to plummet. I laid all of this out to God one night, kneeling down beside the bed, hands pressed together in the approved position for divine communication.

After the *Cleo* had been delivered, it took all my resolve

not to peek at it. Frustratingly, there were ample opportunities for me to do exactly that. My mother was away so often that month, always finding an excuse to go to Dunedin. I seemed to be alone in the house so often, yet time and time again I resisted. I had made my pact with God and I was determined to reap my reward.

A second issue of *Cleo* arrived. That night, after my bath I climbed onto the scales. I hadn't weighed myself for a month and was confident of a substantial loss. I couldn't believe it when the needle on the scales finally registered its verdict. I had put on a quarter of a stone.

I was furious. I had resisted temptation for an entire month and that was what I got for my sacrifice. It was all the proof I needed. Grampy was right. There was no God.

Later that night, I sneaked into my parents' bedroom when they seemed safely settled in front of the television and Babe was in the bath. This was an act fraught with risk. I had never dared to look at the *Cleo*s unless I was sure I was completely alone in the house with no prospect of being disturbed.

My hand trembled when I reached for the magazine on the top of the pile. Already I was hard at the mere thought of what I would see. The magazine fell open at the centrefold and I spread it out. Then I reached for the previous month's issue and opened that out as well. I drank in the sight of the two new centrefolds. Double the pleasure. And double the guilt.

All I could think of was the prospect of being caught in the act. Yet my cock seemed to thrive on this very fear. It had never been so hard. It ached with desire. My heartbeat resounded through me. It seemed to throb in my head. For a moment I felt dizzy. That terrified me. If I fainted, discovery would be certain. I stuffed the magazines under the bed and ran to my bedroom.

That night I dreamt of the male centrefolds. They rose up in my mind, gloriously naked, revealing everything. I knew I could touch them if I only dared and although I longed to more than anything else, I never managed to. Some circumstance in my dream would always nonsensically intervene, or I would simply fail to steel my resolve and the moment would slip away. Even my dreams were confined by my guilt.

The next morning these frustrating fantasies would haunt me. I cursed myself for not doing in the sanctuary of my dreams—where I could never be spied upon—what I was too scared to do in reality. I raged against my own restraint. I explained it to myself, over and over in my mind, trying to convince whatever was holding me back how unnecessary it was. But I couldn't dissuade my own guilt. It was buried much too deep for that.

8

Sport was the lifeblood of the Serpentine. It was a passion that was both universal and compulsory. Even if you weren't good at any sport in particular, you played and you got good.

I was not the sporting type.

I possessed little natural inclination for it and certainly none of the ardour that sport, and rugby in particular, inspired in all the other boys. Nevertheless, I was obliged to play. I had the legacy of a father who had been the captain of his high school first fifteen to live up to. Rugby was sacred to him. It inspired a reverence and fervour nothing else could ever approach. The one time my father would actually stop work (which meant everybody else could stop too) was when the rugby was on television.

He would even get up in the middle of the night to watch rugby, when the All Blacks played overseas test matches against the Lions or the French. I would be rudely roused awake to watch it with him, though I'd never expressed an interest in rugby at any hour of the day or night. He'd switch my light on and gleefully crow, 'Footie's about to start.'

It was another of the trials I suffered for being born a boy.

He always gave me rugby books for my birthday and at Christmas. It was the only time he ever bought anyone a present. I probably should have felt privileged. My mother bought the birthday and Christmas presents for the rest of the family. She chose. He paid. Yet he insisted on buying those books for me. Biographies of All Black greats. Grant Batty. Bryan Williams. Graham Meads. 'Hardbacks are expensive Billy-Boy,' he'd say, 'but they're worth it for the ambition they inspire.'

I didn't even pretend to read them. I'd unwrap the book and hand it straight to him, mumbling that I'd read it after him. When he gave it back, I'd look to see if there were any photographs of those sporting heroes semi-nude in the changing rooms. Usually there was one or two.

It was never my decision whether or not I played rugby. It was my father's. Watching me play rekindled all the glorious memories of his own triumphs on the field. There was nothing he adored more than dissecting a game I'd just played, in the car on the way home afterwards. Telling me how he would have played it and won. He got very excited when he realised how much weight I'd gained over the past year. He began plotting possible position changes for me on the team. 'Pull you in off that wing. Get you in the forwards. Maybe lock. Or prop. Somewhere right in the thick of it.'

I had no desire to be promoted into the thick of it. I decided I quite liked playing wing, once he'd recited off these other possibilities. At least out on the wing, the odds were strong that the ball would get dropped or the boy in possession of it tackled, before it made its way out to me on the end of the line. That was why I'd been put there in the first place. So I was out of the way. But my father rang up Mr McTaggart, the rugby coach, and told him to put me in the forwards. He described me as if I was one of his cows he was trying to sell. 'Bob, he's beefing up at a helluva rate. He's carrying a lot of weight. He'll be an asset to you in the forwards.'

Mr McTaggart then had the gall to enquire as to my

weight and my father was insensitive enough to answer truthfully.

'Christ, he must be gettin' onto ten stone. He's a whopper, I'm telling you. You won't know him from last season.'

I couldn't believe it. Could not believe what my father had just said over the phone. He might as well have had it announced over the radio. People were always listening in on the telephone party line. Everyone in Mawera had to share a line with three or four other families. Evenings were a particularly popular time for eavesdropping entertainment. Our neighbours would lift the phone to see if it was busy and then if something interesting was being said, they'd only pretend to put it down again. How much I weighed would be all over school the next day for certain.

I dreaded the rugby season. I schemed to come up with an excuse good enough to avoid it. But I knew unless something really major (and very painful) befell me, like a cow charging me and battering me half to death or falling off my bike and breaking my leg, there was no escape. I wasn't prepared to suffer physical agony to escape rugby. So I developed strategies to avoid playing, even when I was obliged to be in the middle of a game.

I was extremely unfit. For most of a game, I'd be loping a good twenty yards behind the action. My aim was to never touch the ball during a match, though my father would thwart these plans by yelling insistently from the sideline for other boys to pass it to me. Sometimes they would. They were used to obeying adults. I always dropped it smartly, so I didn't get tackled. I loathed being tackled.

I also had the excuse of having to take my glasses off to play. This meant I spent the entire game in a hazy state of not being able to see properly. I always made out that I was more visually impaired than I actually was, in the vain hope that someone would declare me useless and order me off the field. Sometimes, I'd wander off of my own accord, pretending not to know where I was. But my father always kept a very close eye on me and would rush over and push me back in the direction of the ball. 'Seize the ball, son, seize it and make a run for it,' he'd instruct me. 'For my sake.' I had no intention of seizing the ball, although I would have liked to have seized Stuart Hale.

Stuart Hale. Thirteen years old, the county sprint star, tall dark and leggy, with a smile that *Pink* would have described as 'dreamy'.

Unfortunately, being the county sprint star, he was also very fast around the field. He was the one person I would have been prepared to tackle and risk the mud and potential damage, but there was no way I could ever catch him. Occasionally I'd amble after him earnestly, and my father would urge me on ecstatically from the sideline, but it was hopeless. Stuart was too fast, too elusive, swerving, darting and dashing about, which made him all the more desirable to me.

I eventually realised that even though I couldn't see or keep up with the ball, there would be no getting out of playing. There were barely enough players for a team. We had to combine with the Crayburn school to make up the numbers. No matter how inept I contrived to be, they would still make me play because they had to have fifteen players on the team.

At the start of the season my father bribed me, offering me a dollar for every try I scored. It encouraged me for about ten minutes into our first match. I actually kept up with the ball and received a pass, only to be tackled immediately and thrown down into the mud. That experience quelled any desire to touch the ball again that season.

The changing room meant further tortures. I was torn two ways. I was curious to see the other boys naked under the shower, but I was reluctant to allow them to see me. I was self-conscious about my size and the fact that instead of a chest, I had a bosom. I knew my breasts would provoke unprecedented ridicule if they were noticed. So I always dawdled off the field, and let everyone else get there ahead of me. Once they'd all been through, I'd slink into the showers with my arms firmly crossed over my chest, so nothing could be seen. If I did end up in the shower next to someone else, I'd ignore them (though I was dying to peek) and pretend to be washing my hair. Keeping my hands above my head made things look more streamlined.

I was lucky that at our first tournament game that season there was a distraction in the changing room. Roy Schluter. Arch was determined to prove to everyone what Roy had between his legs. Everyone formed a circle around Roy, waiting for him to get undressed. Roy just sat there on the bench, staring at the concrete floor, saying nothing. Meantime, I enjoyed the luxury of a hot, solitary shower. I was out and dried off with my shirt back on, when Arch finally tried to pull Roy's shorts off. Roy gave an awful sounding scream and punched out wildly at Arch. The next thing, Arch was crouching on the floor with a bleeding nose. Roy refused to get in the shower. When Mr McTaggart questioned him about it, he said he'd forgotten to bring a towel.

Roy neglected to bring a towel to rugby for the next few weeks. Arch tried a new tack, taunting Roy that he was dirty and that he stank. He even complained to Mr McTaggart about Roy, hoping that he'd order him to have a shower like everyone else. Mr McTaggart did have a quiet word with him, but Roy must have had a good excuse, because he wasn't made to shower. He stopped coming into the changing room after practice or games. He'd sit outside on the bench, until it was time to go home.

I was disappointed that Roy never came back in the changing room. Not that I wanted him to be humiliated in front of everyone, but I would've liked to get another peek at his cock. I often thought of that evening, when we'd been huddled up in the hedge together, and I'd reached out to find it hard and swollen. Just the memory of the moment was enough to make me feel the way I'd felt that night: as though my heart was beating in my head and as if I might faint and as if I should go to the toilet, all at the same time. It was a muddle of all sorts of sensations with fear and guilt churning round in there too. I got hard myself remembering that evening.

Not that I ever thought about Roy the way I did about Stuart Hale. Physically, Roy repulsed me. I wondered if he'd been better looking before adolescence started in on him. Not that I was great looking myself, but because that fact was only reinforced when I made the mistake of looking in a mirror, I tended to forget it. In my own mind, I was Judy with her beautiful blonde hair and slinky spacesuits. I was ravishing.

I was fairly sure that if the circumstances were right, Roy would permit me another squeeze. The fact that he'd cracked a stiffy last time seemed to indicate he'd enjoyed it. We hadn't spoken since that evening. Our eyes had met on a number of occasions and we'd stared uncertainly at one another. Roy was so difficult to read. I couldn't tell if he was angry over what had happened or whether he was just shy and loath to smile.

I tried to avoid him at school. Arch had been suspicious of me ever since I'd lied to protect Roy the night of the party. I didn't want to attract his attention any more than I already did. He'd single-handedly established my identity as Fatty. Occasionally he came up with inspired variations on that name, such as Billy-Boy Bunter and Tubby Titanic. They were bad enough. Allying myself with Roy would have tainted me with the same label as him: the Freak. If there was one name that was worse than Fatty, that was it. What's more, Fatty and the Freak had a certain resonance when said together aloud, which I didn't want anyone else to discover.

Roy was a loner. Everyone reckoned he was weird and it wasn't just that he looked different. He never really spoke unless he was asked a question. He didn't seem to understand the natural order of things either. He was the oldest boy in the school and by rights, should have been the natural leader and voice of authority. But he never showed any initiative in that direction. He would meekly do what just about anyone told him, with the exception of Arch, who he completely ignored.

I kept my distance from Roy and wondered.

When we played rugby I couldn't avoid him. We were forced to get as physically close as two guys usually ever get. Mr McTaggart had taken one look at me and declared me a prop. This was in the front row of the scrum. There was no use protesting. I would only have been sent to run around the field three times for presuming to know better than him. Roy, he decided, would be a lock because of his height. Every time we went down for a scrum, he was there, slotted in against my hip, his hand up between my legs, gripping the hem of my jersey.

My father was delighted with my new position. 'Go into the mauls hard Billy-Boy,' he'd say, his eyes sparkling with excitement. 'Just like Big Ken Grey. Show no mercy.'

I was more inclined to stand off to the side and watch the mauls, though Arch as halfback often gave me a malicious shove into the thick of it. Yet, for all my reluctance, everyone seemed to consider me a great asset to the team because of my superior weight. Mr McTaggart told me I was a certainty for the county representative side, the overweights division. I was horrified. Firstly, to actually be playing in a grade called the overweights and secondly, that it would mean even *more* games of rugby against bigger, fiercer boys.

There were two teams in representative rugby. The underweights (under six stone seven) and the overweights (over six stone seven). At the trials, I knew the showdown would come. I would be weighed in front of all the other boys. Everyone was going to learn exactly how much I weighed. I couldn't see any way of avoiding it.

Naturally, Mr McTaggart mentioned his ambitions for me to my father, who became terribly excited and insisted that I begin a training program in readiness for the trials. He started giving me jobs to do across on the other side of the farm and told me to run there and back, carrying a spade or a sledgehammer. He claimed this was how Colin Meads trained. 'He used to run up the hill on his farm with stacks of waratahs balanced on his shoulders. Maybe in time you'll be doing that too. Run up the hill to that hide-out you've got up there.'

There was no way I was ever going to do anything other than stagger there, but I said nothing. The fence up the hill was shot and my father knew it. I didn't want to be sent up there lugging replacement standards.

When the day of the trials came I felt sick through. But it wasn't vomiting sick—a visible excuse to stay at home—I was sick with dread. I tried to get my father to leave early, so that we would arrive at the grounds first, and I could get on the scales before anyone else arrived. But of course, he had little jobs for both of us to do first. We ended up leaving late. It was a typical winter's day. Hard frost and a weak sun. The ground was frozen solid. It would feel like rock if I got tackled. In the car, my mind raced with avoidance tactics. If I went last and dawdled, maybe I could avoid everyone else hearing. Or perhaps I could simply whisper my weight to Mr McTaggart and avoid getting on the scales at all. I had little faith in either plan. I felt doomed for further humiliation.

When we arrrived at Glenora, everyone was milling around Mr McTaggart and Cracker Watt, the Glenora coach. Cracker had been a trialist for the All Blacks twenty years ago and had earned his nickname because he tackled his opponents so ferociously that on several occasions, he left them with broken bones. My father parked and walked me over to join the others. My reluctance must have been obvious as he put his hand on my neck to guide me forward. The scales were positioned on the frosty grass between Cracker and Mr McTaggart. One by one, the boys were getting on. To my enormous relief, Mr McTaggart wasn't actually calling out the weights. He simply said 'over' or 'under', then sent the boy to join the appropriate team. I was so relieved. I noticed with pleasure that Stuart Hale had been assigned into the overweight division.

When my turn came, I didn't feel nervous at all. Mr McTaggart would call out 'over' and I would trot over and stand near Stuart. I got on the scales. Conversation dwindled away. All eyes suddenly turned in my direction. Mr McTaggart was taking his time pronouncing me 'over'. He was scrutinising the scales, bending down even closer. 'Christ Cracker,' he finally said, 'we've got an over the overweights here.'

I felt cheated. No one else had attracted any remarks on their weight. It was so unfair. I was deeply mortified. Some of the other boys tried to edge forward to get a look at the scales. They didn't need to. Cracker came over to take a look and announced my weight to the world. 'Eleven stone,' he said in awe.

Everyone was staring at me and whispering. My father rushed over. 'What's the problem?' he asked.

'He's too heavy,' said Cracker. 'He's over six stone seven

of course, but he's over the upper limit of nine stone seven as well. There's no division for him.'

I digested that information. Was I actually going to be pronounced too fat to play? All of the indignity would be bearable if that was the case. Then I noticed Arch Sampson. His grin was jeering. His eyes gloating. My brief flare of hope curdled. It would never be worth it. Arch was going to torment me mercilessly.

'But you're short of players in the overs,' my father started to argue, much to my horror. 'No one'll know anyway. There'll be no scales about when you're playing matches. No one's going to think twice about it.'

'That's true,' Cracker nodded vigorously. 'We shouldn't let the boy miss out when he's keen.'

I wanted to protest, but my father was nodding as vigorously as Cracker. 'Oh, he's keen as mustard. Been in training for the trials for weeks.'

I felt like crying. But knew it would only make things worse, become another source of ridicule for Arch and his cronies. I squeezed my eyes tight to hold the tears back. I couldn't believe that salvation had come so teasingly close and then been so brusquely snatched away. I'd managed to check my tears, but a fury of emotions were seething within me. My father placed an encouraging hand on my shoulder and I wrenched away from him as if I'd been stung. I caught a brief glimpse of his bewildered face, surprised at my sudden reaction and what he saw burning in my face. Hatred. He, who was always trying to cajole me into killing something—an old ewe for dog tucker, the vegetable-garden rabbits—had finally succeeded in arousing the killer instinct in me. At that moment, I hated my father with a murderous intensity.

My father had stepped back from me in surprise. It was Mr McTaggart who guided me in the direction of the overweight team. 'Off you go, son,' he said kindly.

With that, the flame of feeling faded as quickly as it had sparked. 'He's got a bit of spirit in him after all,' Cracker remarked to my father as I plodded over to join the other boys.

There were only thirteen of us over six stone seven. It was a foregone conclusion that all of us would be selected for the team and two more players scraped up from somewhere. Nevertheless, Cracker and Mr McTaggart insisted we still had to go through the formality of the trial. They stood on the sideline bellowing instructions at us, trying us out in various positions. I began to feel like one of my father's dogs after a while.

Going into a scrum, close to the goalposts, Stuart approached me and put a hand on my shoulder. 'Push hard this time,' he said, 'I want this ball.'

For the first time, I actually saw some purpose to the game. Trying to push our opponents back off the ball, so Stuart could scoop it up and dash through for a try. I heaved, the ball disappeared and when I finally emerged out of the scrum, Stuart was diving for a try. A tremor of excitement pulsed through me at the sight of him. I felt uplifted for a moment by the thrill of our victory. I could hear my father cheering. I jogged modestly back down the paddock, anticipating that Stuart would come leaping after me, jump on my back and rub up against me, like they did in British soccer matches on television.

But he did none of that. When I looked back for him, he was preoccupied lining up the ball for the conversion. And after that, he ignored me. He didn't thank me or even acknowledge me with a grin or a glance. After a while, I realised he must've been brooding over his conversion and forgotten me. It had been a disaster. The ball had veered off to the left and missed the rugby posts completely.

Stuart scored all the tries. No one could catch him. With his reputation as a sprint star, no one on the other team even tried to. After half an hour, Cracker called us off the field and announced the team. I was prop. Roy was my lock and Stuart was centre and captain of the team. We were sent off to shower. I went to find my father to get my glasses back from him. I wanted to get a good look at Stuart under the shower. After I'd retrieved them, I actually ran across to the changing rooms. I didn't want to miss anything. Roy was sitting morosely on a bench outside. 'I wouldn't go in there if I was you,' said Roy.

I stared at him in surprise. It was the first time he'd spoken to me directly, but I had no time for Roy or anything he had to say. I plunged on into the changing room. It was dark and steamy. One of the lights had blown. The other boys were yelling over the sound of the showers. My glasses fogged up instantly and I couldn't see. Someone yelled, 'Here he is, the one-man scrum,' and there were whoops and cheers all around, coming closer, encircling me.

At first, I thought they meant to congratulate me. I had pushed hard and Stuart had scored a try. I stood there, smiling shyly, trying to wipe my glasses so that I could see. I wanted to see Stuart smiling his gratitude. Then someone seized my hands and pinned them behind my back, his fingers pinching into my wrists. I realised I'd been mistaken.

My vision was a blur, yet I knew I was surrounded. I could feel the hot breath of my team-mates all around me. One of them gave me a shove and then they all started to push me, so that I swayed back and forth between them. I lost all sense of direction. I couldn't think where the door was to escape. Everything was strange and surreal. Shapes moved in front of my eyes. Insults echoed around me. Liniment fumes choked me so that I could hardly breathe, let alone call out for help. Slowly I crumpled downward. I huddled there on the cold, concrete floor, while they panted above me, hesitating for a moment. I realised my hands were free and hastily I wiped at one of my lenses so that I could see.

A glimpse of muscled leg. A mud splattered boot. A flash of steel in the dim light, descending upon me.

I screamed and as if that was the signal they had waited for, they all set in on me, the studs of their rugby boots raking at me, as if I held the ball or had something else clutched to my chest, something to hide.

Later, they threw me under the shower. I'd lost my glasses at some point, but even without them I could see that there was blood dripping from somewhere onto the tiles, before it was swirled down the drain.

Roy was holding my glasses when I emerged from the changing room. He handed them to me without a word and walked off. I limped over to the car. Not that my leg hurt particularly, but because I wanted someone to notice the damage that had been done to me. But the fathers were all having a beer out of the back of Cracker's station wagon. No one even glanced my way. I felt battered, dazed and bewildered. I had aches and pains, but they were almost vague and unreal to me, compared to the sharp misery of feeling suddenly so alone and vulnerable. What had I done to provoke the attack? I didn't understand why.

When my father finally joined me in the car, he glanced at me quickly. 'I don't know how you got that cut on your forehead,' he said. 'You were hanging off the mauls for the whole game. You should have been in there with your boots, rooting for the ball. That's how I would have played it . . . '

I let the words wash over me and leaned back in the seat. I wept silently and my father failed to notice as he instructed me in the ways of rugby and men, a world in which I was hopelessly at sea.

9

Even now after all the years that have passed since that afternoon in the changing rooms, the memory of it still makes me wince. In the days and weeks that followed, I tried my best to repress what happened. But I was bewildered. I couldn't understand why. That made it impossible to forget. It tormented me. There had been such malevolence in that casual brutality. What had I done to inspire such intensity of feeling?

They were boys I only knew in the vaguest way because our mothers played golf together or their fathers ran businesses in Glenora that we patronised. The attack hadn't been incited by Arch, the closest person I had to an enemy. He'd still been out trialing for the underweights. He bore a grudge against me, but he would never act upon it in such a way. We were 'Mawera men' and that was an unmistakeable bond, a reason even to protect me from outsiders. These were strangers compelled for some reason to shame me.

At first, I thought it must have been my appearance. My physical grossness had been enough to provoke them. They had flung the usual names at me. Fatty. Fatso. But there had been another name too. For a moment, I'd felt a fond recognition. Poof. Poofter. But the name had been reinforced with the raking of their sprigs and I screamed when the steel tore at my skin. Those boys knew the meaning of that word. They'd chanted it at me, leaving me with no doubt that it was the gravest of insults. There was venom in their voices.

That afternoon in the changing room destroyed my sense of joy in my ambition. *Acting the poof* lost all of its allure. No magic remained in those words. For a fortnight afterwards, whenever I took a bath, the hot water would sting, reminding me, and I'd swear to myself that I didn't want to be 'that' when I grew up any more. I didn't even want to know what it meant. It was loaded with shameful connotations and that was enough to know.

But there was something else about that incident, something even more hurtful than the violence, something I tried *never* to think of. Largely, I succeeded. Nights were my downfall. There in my bed, I was alone in the dark with no distractions. It was then that what I had seen came back to haunt me. Loomed large in my mind. Insinuated itself into my dreams, where, monster-like, it transformed, growing in its malignancy, exaggerated and distorted into even crueller scenarios. I would wake grasping my pillow as if it were him.

Stuart. Stuart Hale.

In that brief moment before that first boot came down on me, I had caught a glimpse of a muscular leg. Only one boy had legs like that.

Stuart Hale had been the first to kick me with his boots. He was the natural leader in all things from being captain of the rugby team to setting an example with girls. The assault on me had been no different. He had gone first. But why? Had I been unsubtle in my admiration? Had he noticed me staring at him? I couldn't see how. I had worshipped him from afar. But he must have sensed something to lash out at me in such a way. My anguish at such an unmistakeable rejection lingered long after the scratches and swellings he and his mates had inflicted.

I refused to go into the changing room after the first of the three county matches that the team played. My father ordered me in there but I wouldn't answer him. It was the first time I had disobeyed him, not done exactly as I was instructed. To my surprise he didn't insist. He didn't say anything. For once we drove home in silence. Finally, when we were drawing close to home, he turned to me and asked, 'Do things go on in the changing rooms . . . things you don't like?'

I was too surprised to say anything. I nodded. My father stared at me gravely for a moment and then turned his attention back to the road and said nothing more. I was puzzled that he did not try to prise further details out of me. I glanced at him. He was staring fixedly at the road. This was also out of character. Usually his eyes were everywhere at this point on the drive home, appraising the state of our neighbours' farms and what a poor comparison they made with our own.

I realised my father found the subject awkward, though I wasn't sure what the subject actually was. What illicit activity did he imagine went on in the changing rooms? I was intrigued. I had rebelled, refused to do as he said and hadn't been interrogated or even reprimanded. I knew he hadn't guessed at what had actually happened. He had never even remarked upon the bruises on my arms and legs.

The end of the rugby season helped the memory of the incident fade. I would never have to play rugby with those boys again. I was to go to boarding school in Dunedin the following year. It was the school where both Grampy and my father had gone, and reportedly distinguished themselves with various honours and accolades on the sportsfield. I was expected to emulate their success. My father had even gone so far as to enrol me as a boarder a few weeks after I was born, to ensure me a place. He was a vigorous supporter of the Old Boys' Society, taking even more delight in their occasional newsletters than he did in reading *The Farmer* magazine, the only reading material permitted to remain on the windowsill by the toilet 'for the whole family to enjoy'.

With rugby over and my father engrossed in the sport on the television, Saturday afternoons became my own again. Lou always came over and we'd amuse ourselves in one of our make-believe games. But one weekend Aunt Evelyn made Lou stay home to measure her for new summer dresses. Lou was furious, but had to do as she was told.

I was restless and bored without her, but didn't want my father noticing. He always thought I'd be eager for a job to do. Finally I decided to go for a bike ride to avoid him, setting off with no real destination in mind. I still wanted to lose weight and a recent issue of *Pink* had declared that cycling was an excellent way of burning calories. I ended up riding all the way to the old gaol down by the river, a distance of at least five miles. I felt certain that it would've worked off pounds of excess weight.

The gaol was disused. To my mind it never looked much like a prison, more like someone's neglected home. It lacked bars on the windows, and had proper glass windows instead. Once you stepped inside it became more convincing. There were iron rings driven into the stone, with chains dangling off them. Just like what we tied our dogs up to. Those rings and chains always made me shiver. The walls of the gaol were covered with initials, and though I knew most of them had been scratched in by locals or tourists, at least some of them must have been genuine prisoners' initials.

That afternoon, as I cycled down there, I invented a grander reason for my solitary circumstances. I decided I was a conqueror returning from my journeys in foreign lands, come home to inspect the contents of my personal dungeon where I had abandoned my enemies (various rugby-playing local boys) to rot in chains years before. Only over Stuart Hale did I hesitate. Despite his treachery, I couldn't bring myself to consign him to the chains. Finally I decided upon the perfect punishment for his crimes: I would make him my personal slave, obliged to do anything I desired or he would be banished to the dungeon with his cohorts.

When I arrived, I left my bike at the road, slipped through the fence and wandered down to the gaol. It was tucked in beneath the willow trees that lined the little creek. Often there were campers or fishermen about, but there was no sign of anyone that day. It seemed I had the place to myself. By the time I'd reached the gaol, I was well into the spirit of my new game. I was surprised to notice that the bolt on the door was drawn. All the locals knew you were supposed to lock it after you'd been inside. It was an oversight I could incorporate very satisfactorily into my game.

I flung the door open.

'So you've been trying to escape while I've been away?' I bellowed.

My eyes adjusted to the gloom, and I realised with mounting embarrassment that there was actually someone there. For a moment I thought I'd somehow slipped back in time and this was an actual prisoner, for the person was slouched on the floor, one hand through one of the iron hoops, scratching at the stone wall with a stick. I'd startled him with my sudden entry, and he jumped to his feet. It was then that I recognised him. It was Roy.

We both muttered sorry at the same time and stared at the ground, lost for words. 'I was playing a game,' I finally said.

'Yeah, me too,' said Roy.

Neither of us knew what to do. Finally, Roy sat down again and went back to scratching his name on the stone wall. A nervous excitement began to stir in me. There hadn't been an opportunity for me to be alone with Roy since Lou's party. There was an expectant intimacy in our situation but I wasn't sure how to proceed. I didn't trust myself to speak. Tentatively I slithered down on the floor beside Roy, wrapping one of the chains around my arm.

The light was dim, and even sitting right next to Roy, I couldn't see his features properly. I was relieved. I didn't want to see that superfluous hair creeping up the planes of his face and the shocking smattering of pimples over his forehead. Side by side, propped up against the stone wall, I could almost imagine I was next to Stuart. Roy and Stuart were about the same height, similar build, both on the brink of adolescence, which had been kinder to Stuart. Stuart who was my personal slave. Stuart who I could do whatever I wished with. There was no need to ask permission. I sank my hand into the crotch of the boy next to me and felt the flush of his breath on my cheek as he turned towards me.

He didn't object. Instead he reciprocated, reaching between my legs for what was swelling in the confines of my underwear. We fondled one another, both of us growing hard. Abruptly he pushed my hand away and began tugging down his jeans until he had them round his knees. He took my hand, clasped it for a moment before guiding it back to his cock. Then his hand burrowed beneath the elastic waists of my trousers and my underwear, grasping my cock as best he could amongst the complications of my clothes. The touch of his fingers upon it was a revelation. My cock pulsed as if it had developed a heartbeat. I closed my eyes. Everything was sensation. I was in a drowsy, swooning state. It was easy to believe that it was Stuart pressed against me. Stuart ransacking my pants and murmuring his appreciation over what he had found there.

His breath was hoarse and heaving in my ear. Then

suddenly he gasped. I opened my eyes, turned towards the door, alarmed. Had someone silently entered the gaol and discovered us? But the door was still shut. There was no one there. I turned back to Roy, puzzled but also annoyed. The moment had been interrupted and ruined. I was disagreeably aware that it was Roy who was next to me, not Stuart. But before I could ask him what he'd seen, he pressed his face against mine, his mouth wetly seeking mine. Roy kissed me.

I resisted. I did not want to be kissed by Roy Schluter. I was worried his pimples would rub off onto my face and start growing there. But this was a kiss like no other I had ever known and there was no stopping him once he'd started. His mouth squirmed wildly against my own as if he was trying to get a taste of me. Then, suddenly, he stuck his tongue into my mouth. It was the creepiest sensation to suddenly feel it force itself between my lips and protrude there hot and heavy in my mouth. My own tongue retreated in alarm. Was it intended as an insult? Generally that was why kids stuck their tongues out at each other. I was relieved when Roy finally drew back.

His hot breath panted in my face, smelling of his mother's menthol cigarettes. He burrowed his face into my neck and pressed himself against me, clenching my cock even harder. 'Rub it faster,' he said in a broken voice, a voice that didn't even sound like Roy. 'As fast as you can.'

I obeyed. This didn't seem like the Roy I knew at all. He was possessed by a forcefulness of spirit I could never have imagined of him. I matched the pace he was setting with my own cock, and he began to squirm against me and moan in my ear. Then, suddenly, he let out a cry like he'd been shot in a game of cowboys and Indians. He abandoned my cock, grabbed his own and rubbed it furiously. But not before I felt a warm liquid explode between my fingers.

I had no idea what I had done but I didn't like the feel of

it. Surely Roy hadn't gone to the toilet on me? Gingerly, I rubbed my fingers together. No, it was too heavy and sticky for that. Could it be blood? Had I pulled too hard and somehow burst a vein in it? Is that why he'd howled? Yet he didn't seem in pain now or even concerned about checking for damage. He was on his feet and stuffing himself back into his underwear and doing up his jeans. The next thing he was out the door without a word or even a backward glance.

Hastily I rearranged my own pants before I followed him. My panic was mounting. What if I'd injured him seriously and he had to go to the doctor and explain what had happened, and everyone found out? I stood in the doorway of the gaol, dazzled for a moment by the afternoon sun, looking round for him. But there was no sign of him. He had vanished.

It was then that I thought to look at my hand. Sticky white stuff clung between my fingers. Gingerly, I touched it with my other index finger. What had happened? It looked like pus. Did Roy have some sort of sore on his cock? I knew about such things. There had been some frightful pictures in the sealed section of an issue of *Cleo* some months back. Photos of sores and rashes and discharges that had frightened me so much, I never again looked at that particular issue. I was convinced that Roy must be infected. With dread wrenching up in me I hurried down to the creek behind the gaol to wash my hands. But even as I plunged my hand into the water, I knew the odds were that it was probably too late. I was undoubtedly infected too.

The stuff on my hand didn't wash away easily. In fact, the water only seemed to adhere it more stubbornly than ever. Frantically, I tried wiping my hand back and forth on the grass, which shifted some of it. Finally, I got rid of the last of it by intertwining my fingers and rubbing them back and forth vigorously in the water. I scrutinised my hand. It looked just the same as usual. There was no sign of a rash or any other visible manifestation of infection. I prayed that my swift action had saved me from whatever disease it was that Roy was suffering from.

I ran up the hill to my bike. I wanted to get away from there. I jumped on and pedalled as fast as I could. Then it occurred to me that if I rode too fast, I might catch up with Roy heading home. I didn't want to have to talk to him. I slowed my pace. Once I'd reached the school, where Roy would take the turn-off to the other side of the valley, I trod down hard on the pedals again. I wanted to get home, have a hot sterilising bath and forget the afternoon had ever happened.

But that proved not so easy to do. I might have been able to ignore Roy successfully through the week at school by not looking at him, but my cock would have none of it. Just being in the same room as him was enough to cause it to stiffen beneath my desk. Despite my resolve to have nothing to do with him, I couldn't help sneaking the occasional glance at him. Each time Roy was staring right on back at me with an intensity that made me blush and bend my head back over my exercise book. His gaze was bold and inquisitive. I knew what Roy's eyes were spelling out and what my stolen glances were saying in reply. I felt engulfed by that same quivering giddy sensation, that same delicious tension that had thrilled me that afternoon as I'd realised that we were alone in the gaol together, with the same thing on our minds.

Every night when I had my bath and every morning before I got dressed, I examined myself for manifestations of the disease I was terrified was going to develop. But as each day drew closer and closer to Saturday, my paranoia began to subside and a more urgent compulsion enthralled me. I could not resist what the afternoon promised. By Friday, I could think of little else but how it had felt to hold Roy's cock in my hand.

But that Saturday had a complication which had been absent the previous weekend. Lou. She stayed Friday night as she always did, helped me Saturday morning with the feeding out and then after lunch announced an expedition to Dragonland. I always agreed to Lou's plans. She made the decisions and I obeyed. I didn't know how to say no to her but I tried.

'Um . . . last Saturday I went for a bike ride,' I said in what I hoped was a casual manner. 'I . . . enjoyed it.'

Lou's eyes narrowed suspiciously. She began to grind her teeth, almost as though she were sharpening them. I looked down at the ground and continued the little speech I'd rehearsed the previous night. It had seemed plausible enough then, but faced with Lou all my optimism abandoned me. My voice seemed clogged. I felt flushed and short of breath. 'Um . . . I was thinking . . . of maybe doing it again. A . . . bike . . . ride.'

I glanced up at Lou. Her expression was severe. 'I think . . . it's good for my weight to go for a long ride,' I added nervously.

'Boys don't worry about their weight,' Lou said firmly. 'That's a female obsession.'

I was crushed. I didn't know what obsession meant. It was another of these words that Lou had picked up from Aunt Evelyn. But her tone was plain enough. I was teased my nostrils about being girly and a sook, but neither Lou nor Babe ever acknowledged those taunts and certainly would never fling one at me themselves. This was a betrayal. I felt tears threatening to slip over the rim of my eyes.

I looked at Lou. She was staring on back at me grimly,

her arms crossed over the beginnings of the breasts she denied were there. I was sure she must be regretting her remark, though she'd never own up to it. She'd made the decision years ago to be not just as tough as a boy but as tough as a grown up man, and if being tough meant being cruel, Lou would be that too. Her mouth was a tight line. No apology would be permitted to pass those stern lips. I wondered if I could make her feel bad by allowing myself to cry? But there was another emotion stirring within me, something defiant and mean rising up, something urging me to hurt her back. She became awkward as the silence between us drew out, and began to fidget with her hair, ensuring her ponytail was well and truly stuffed down the back of her tee-shirt. Suddenly I knew. I knew just as I'd known with Aunt Evelyn, exactly what to say, the words that would wound her the most viciously.

'And what sort of girl stuffs her hair down the back of her tee-shirt and swaggers round calling herself after her dead brother?'

It was the worst thing I could ever have said.

I got scared, too scared to even look at Lou and see how she reacted. I turned and fled. Down to the garage, jumped on my bike and sailed down the driveway and out onto the road, away from her, pumping the pedals, saying over and over to myself, in time to the rhythm of my feet, 'she deserved it, she deserved it'. But I couldn't make myself believe it. Gradually the rhythm of the words died away and I began to cry.

I felt so guilty that I forgot about Roy and the gaol for the moment. It was only when I noticed I was passing the school that I remembered what had precipitated the whole awful clash. I was halfway to the gaol. That was the point when I might have hesitated, might have thought of turning back and seeking Lou out to apologise. But I rode on.

There was an erection straining in my pants, cramped by my posture. I raised myself off the seat and cycled harder, straining forward into the breeze. I was breathless but it wasn't from fatigue. I realised my guilt had gone, slipped away without a fuss some miles back, like a rabbit clipped by a car, left to rot, forgotten, at the side of the road.

I dumped my bike in the same place and hurried down the hill. There was a car parked down by the bridge over the creek. I stopped. There was no sign of any people. Probably fishermen, safely out of the way, down by the river. I approached the gaol stealthily. Would Roy be there? My mind began to doubt but my cock was hard and confident. I felt a little faint as the door loomed before me. I was almost scared to look at the bolt, but sure enough, it was shot free, with the door open a fraction, as if in invitation. I looked around. There was no one in sight. Slowly the door creaked open, pulled from within, beckoning, just wide enough for me to slip inside.

I could smell Roy's breath before I could make him out in the dark. That acrid menthol cigarette breath. Slowly, my eyes adjusted to the darkness. Roy materialised out of the shadows, like a pale ghost. He was already naked. His clothes in a little pile by the door. He had pulled them off as he watched me approach. I turned back to close the door firmly. There had to be absolutely no light. I didn't want to see his face. I only wanted to feel him.

He came up behind me as I fumbled with the door. His hands made straight for my fly, popping the dome, releasing the zip, pulling my underwear down. I was relieved his hands didn't stray over my body. I didn't want him feeling how fat I truly was. But he was intent on playing with my cock. His own was pressed up hard against the small of my back and he began to move himself against me. Gently at first, slowly building a rhythm, until he was rocking against me with such force it took all my strength to stand my ground and not topple onto the dirt floor. He didn't cry out like the previous time. Merely shuddered against me and moaned my name in my ear. I felt the wetness explode against my back and then slowly trickle down. Roy wiped it off me with his hanky before pulling on his clothes.

Cycling home that afternoon, I rode past Aunt Evelyn and Uncle Arthur's house. It reinforced the fact that I had renounced Lou for what I'd just done with Roy. For a moment I forgot to pedal. It was such a gross betrayal. Lou and I had been so close, had spent so much time with each other. She had been my best friend and protector. I felt a sudden awful ache for her. I missed her. I contemplated stopping and going in to find her and apologising, but then the bike began to wobble and I had to pedal quickly before it toppled over. Too soon, the house was behind me. The moment gone. I could've easily turned back, but I didn't. I resolved to apologise at school on Monday instead.

I took a bath as soon as I got home. I hated looking at those first hairs that had sprouted down there by my cock. They made me think of Roy. I wanted to be rid of them. They were dark and coarse and took a great deal of effort to pluck out. In the end I had to use my mother's tweezers, as my fingers couldn't get a decent grip. There were only about five of them, and I prayed that they had been a mistake, like a lamb born out of season.

In the night I awoke, pitched out of sleep by a strangely familiar sensation. I was too scared to turn on the light. I tried to turn over and go back to sleep, but that was impossible. All my senses were straining, confirming what I feared. I could feel it on my skin, slowly slithering down over my hip. Gingerly, I extended my fingers, confirming the sticky dampness splattered over my belly.

Roy had done it to me. I was convinced. I had been

dreaming of him before I woke up. For the rest of the night, I didn't sleep. I lay on my back, my knees in the air, trying to save the sheets, while the stuff dried on my stomach. With the first hint of light, I got up, stripped the bed and took my sheets to the wash-house. It was a few days before they were due to be changed, and I hoped my mother wouldn't notice.

She must have. A few days later, when I went to bed after an evening's television, I found a slim pamphlet on my pillow. It was called *Becoming a Teenager: The Agonies of Adolescence Explained*. The corner of one of the pages had been turned up and the little book naturally fell open there. Two subjects were explained on that page. Wet dreams and homosexuality. My mother had surely sought to reassure me with this book, and spare us both the embarrassment of a face-to-face discussion. But I had trouble sleeping that night. Much had been explained, some of my anxieties had been eased, but another fear had crept into my mind.

I was haunted by the corner of that page, creased and upturned. What did my mother suspect me of? Wet dreams or homosexuality? I was guilty of both, but did she realise that? The paragraph on homosexuality had been both alarming and reassuring. It had described it as 'unnatural', 'perverse' and 'aberrant' all in the same sentence. I'd had to look some of those words up in the study dictionary. However, the pamphlet had then practically given permission to do this dreadful thing. It said that it was common for adolescent boys to experiment with each other and that this was only a phase they would quickly outgrow. This seemed to excuse me fooling round with Roy.

However, my fears were revived the next time I visited my mother's bedroom to flip through her *Cleo* magazines. There was another new book on her bedside table and I glanced at the title as I knelt down to delve under the bed. *Developing your Clairvoyant Self*. I ran out of the room, without even looking at the magazines. What was my mother doing? Was she trying to become like 'The Tomorrow People' reading people's minds? Had she started practising on me?

I was careful from that point not to look her in the eyes. I didn't want her trying to probe into my secrets. We went on in this manner for several days, until finally she came to my bedroom one night, where I was in bed reading Babe's *Pink*. 'Is there something you want to talk about? You seem a little nervous lately. Something you read in that book that you'd like me to explain?'

'No.'

'Did you read it?' she persisted.

'Yes.'

'And you understood everything?'

'Yes.'

I put the magazine aside and snuggled further under the blankets, hinting that I wanted to sleep and for her to leave me alone. 'If you're too embarrassed to ask me something, you can always ask your father,' she said.

We both knew I'd never do that. 'Or you could write me a note, leave it on your pillow and I could write the answer. That is, if you feel awkward . . . and embarrassed.'

My mother was sounding very awkward and embarrassed herself. I realised then and there that she couldn't be much of a mind reader if she didn't comprehend that I just wanted to be left alone. Finally she departed and I felt reassured by her apparent psychic incompetence.

Yet the incident left me wary. I had secrets that no one must ever learn. I turned off the bedside lamp and automatically my thoughts turned to Roy. After my wet dream, I'd been convinced that he'd contaminated me. I swore I'd never return to the gaol. But once the pamphlet had explained what had happened to me, I was restless to return.

The next Saturday he was there, lurking in the shadows, tossing off his clothes as I closed the door behind myself. His hands grabbed at me but there was something I wanted to bring up. 'My mother gave me a book explaining things,' I whispered, 'I don't know if we should be doing this or not.'

His hands ceased their grappling. 'It's alright if it's in the dark,' he whispered back finally. 'You can pretend whatever you like in the dark and just enjoy it.'

I was taken aback for a moment. I wondered if Roy suspected that I pretended I was with Stuart. But if he did, it didn't seem to bother him. He was intent again on pulling out my cock. Then it occurred to me for Roy to make such a comment meant he probably imagined I was someone else. I began to feel a little indignant. But Roy's hands were stirring me so expertly, that feeling of affront quickly ebbed away.

I don't know if it was reading the pamphlet and understanding what the upshot of our manipulations should be or whether I was just ready biologically, but whatever the reason I had my first real orgasm that afternoon, shooting all over the dusty stone walls of the gaol. We didn't try wiping it off. It seemed like a monument of sorts.

10

Spring came though the winter temperatures persisted. It was a time of year I dreaded. There was always so much work to be done. Bloody and dirty work, which often involved getting up before it was light. Shearing, lambing and calving, then lamb-marking, followed by hay-making from late November through January. So it was a great shock when my father asked my mother to give a hand over in the wool-shed when the shearers were due and she refused. It shouldn't have been such a surprise. She'd been showing less and less inclination to help out since she'd developed her other interests.

'Well, if you won't help, then I'll have to hire someone who will,' my father fumed. 'And pay them.'

'That's a good idea,' my mother replied.

My father stared at her angrily. 'You'll have to cook meat for a worker, lots of it . . . and clean up after him . . .' My father began scrambling to think of drawbacks.

'That's alright. I have to do that for you anyway. One more won't make such a difference,' my mother responded coolly.

I admired my mother's style. I longed to follow her example, rebel and have whole days to myself uncluttered by tiresome chores. But her defection doomed my own yearning for escape. My father relied on me more than ever. He gave me new responsibilities, acting as if they were something I should feel honoured and grateful for. I made a point of making a mess of these new chores. My father never complained outright to me about these disasters—he wanted to encourage me for the future—but his expression was eloquent enough. One day I heard him moan to my mother how 'bloody useless' I was.

'You're demanding too much of him,' she said. 'He's only a boy.'

My father had to grudgingly agree and mumbled something about advertising for a worker.

The prospect of a farm boy aroused mixed feelings in me. I was thrilled that he would relieve me of my new chores but I was wary that he might mock me, like the boys in Glenora had. I knew that Lou would hate the prospect of a farm boy. She'd been hoping that Uncle Jack might let her drive the hay baler that summer.

But she no longer came over to help me with my chores. We were estranged. My obligation to apologise had hung heavily upon me from the very moment of our clash, but with every passing day that I procrastinated, the more impossible a reconciliation began to seem.

I'd planned to apologise that first Monday at school. I saw the expectancy in her eyes when she climbed onto the school bus that morning. But there was Roy slouched in his seat, just along from her, staring at me too. The way he looked at me made me grow hard in my pants. I looked out the window, away from both of them. To apologise to Lou would've meant denying myself another meeting with Roy. I couldn't have found a plausible excuse for not spending Saturday afternoon with her. She was suspicious and insistent. She would guess that I was up to something and go out of her way to find out what it was.

I truly didn't know what to do. It was such an impossible decision. So I did nothing at all. I avoided looking at Lou throughout that day at school—which doomed me in her eyes—but I couldn't bring myself to meet her gaze. I felt so guilty. I was convinced that she would only have to look me in the eye and I would be powerless. She would wheedle the reason for my betrayal out of me.

The most awful moment of that entire day was the bus ride home. Our house was the stop before Lou's. Babe hopped off the bus and I hurried after her, not daring to look back to see if Lou was following. The door shut behind me and Babe began to wail when she turned to discover Lou still sitting in her seat, framed by the window. Babe sprang forward and pounded on the glass, calling her name. The bus began to edge away and I had to pull Babe back, writhing and screaming. I looked up and caught a glimpse of Lou, her bewildered face looking down at me, a study of exquisite sorrow. But Lou wasn't one to show vulnerability for long. The next day at school, her gaze was cold and unseeing. She barricaded herself from me with a brittle silence. My few timid attempts to speak to her were imperiously ignored.

There was no question of where Babe's allegiance lay. She sat alongside Lou on the school bus, aping her disdaining attitude. The two of them looked straight through me when I got off the bus and Babe accompanied Lou home to Aunt Evelyn's. If Lou was around, Babe would ignore me. But at home, when it was just the two of us, she would gleefully recount all the wonderful things Lou and she now did together and how they had become 'bestest friends'.

The days turned into weeks and still Lou and I didn't speak. The silence between us seemed insurmountable, laden with unspoken accusations.

Naturally our parents noticed and remarked upon the change. I overheard my mother discussing it with Aunt

Evelyn on the telephone. Aunt Evelyn was jubilant. She had interpreted it as a sign that Lou wanted to renounce her tomboyish ways.

My mother was unconvinced. 'I think it's more likely that they've argued over something.'

The worst part of continuing to meet Roy at the gaol was having to ride past Lou's house to get there. Once I'd passed her house, I kept glancing back all the way there to make sure she wasn't following.

But despite my anxiety and guilt, there was never any doubt that I would meet Roy. Especially once he'd introduced me to my own orgasm. I wanted him to show me how it was accomplished. I had tried at home without the same spectacular result. I wore my cow's tail, the next time, tucked under my cap. Roy didn't even seem to notice my 'hair'. At least, he didn't remark on it. But it was so dark and he was intent on other things. After a few minutes I tugged the tail out from beneath my cap and let it drop to the floor. I didn't want him to be startled and interrupt what we'd begun if his fingers happened to brush upon it. An explanation would've been awkward. I was no longer sure why I'd even worn it. Suddenly it seemed a childish prank.

'Can you do what you did to me last week?' I whispered in his ear.

He said nothing but his hand gripped me with authority.

Afterwards, when we'd finished and he was dressed, about to walk out the door, for no reason, he turned back to face me. 'I'm too young to shave,' he said plaintively. 'Thirteen is too young to shave.'

I said nothing. I didn't want to encourage him to linger and chat, even though the topic of his facial hair was one that the entire school was obsessed by. Arch reckoned that if he didn't start shaving soon he'd end up with whiskers like Santa Claus. The Hammer brothers were always hiding disposable razors where Roy would come across them: in his desk, in his school bag, in the pocket of his parka that hung out in the cloakroom. Yet Roy managed to ignore all these subtle hints and the more blatant enquiries and insults.

'When you gunna shave your mo off?' Arch had finally demanded one day.

Roy simply looked through him as if he hadn't heard the question.

That afternoon was the first time I'd known Roy to even admit knowledge of his moustache. It was a rare moment. His hand was on the door knob as he shyly turned back towards me, mumbling a little as he spoke. His vulnerability demanded a sensitive response, but I failed to recognise that. I said nothing. I stared at the dirt floor, wishing him gone. Roy hesitated, pulled the door open and I felt a rush of relief that he was leaving. Yet he continued to linger. He stood there, framed in the doorway, his profile spotlighted by the afternoon sun. The hairs above his lip glittered in the sun. They had never seemed more prominent. A shiver of revulsion flickered through me. It was too dark for Roy to see my expression, but he may not have needed to. For suddenly he was gone, slamming the door after himself. I was surprised he slammed the door. We were supposed to be discreet. Not draw attention to ourselves. Anyone could be about. Quickly I slipped my clothes back on.

Walking up to reclaim my bike, I felt a pang of guilt. It wouldn't have cost me anything to spare him some kind words. Even if I didn't mean them. Five minutes earlier, as we'd strained against one another, I felt as if I would've done anything for him. It intrigued me that my feelings towards him could sway so greatly. But then, in the dark, when we were touching one another, it wasn't as if I was touching Roy. My mind was filled with the faces of other more handsome boys. That vivid glimpse of his face as he left cruelly reinforced the fact that it was only Roy I'd been with. Roy Schluter. Roy the freak. Roy who was far too hairy, much too young. The thought disgusted me. I told myself that I'd never come to the gaol again.

But that was a resolution I'd made and broken many times before. I always felt that way afterwards. Early in the week it was easy enough to maintain my resolve. When I saw Roy at school, the sight of him repulsed me. I felt ashamed at what we did together. But by the time Thursday and Friday came round, Roy's blank stares had become highly suggestive. My resistance crumbled. I couldn't deny myself. I would get hard on and off all day Friday, just knowing what the next day meant.

Those encounters with Roy never developed into a friendship. I told him that we should avoid each other at school, so that no one should ever suspect us, and he agreed. That was partly true. I did occasionally feel guilty about the illicit nature of what we were doing, and nervous of being found out. But those fears also added to the thrill of our meetings. It had to be managed so sneakily, so stealthily. It had the elements of an adventure about it, like the ones in my books and on television, adventures that never materialised in real life.

My real reasons for resisting a friendship with Roy were complex. He provoked such contradictory feelings in me. I found him both repellent and alluring. I loathed how adolescence was ravaging his face, yet I was fascinated by how it had transformed what he had between his legs. I found him physically unattractive, yet in the dark would do intimate things with him. Most telling of all, I noticed physical changes in Roy that I wished I hadn't. Roy was a symbol of my own fate. A reminder that puberty lurked on my horizon. Inevitably, it would claim me and render a cruel metamorphosis upon me too. The awful truth, the truth I couldn't bear to contemplate, was that I feared it had already begun.

Riding home from the gaol, these confusing feelings swirling around in me, I came upon Lou and Babe, doubling on Uncle Arthur's black mare. I stopped and dismounted from my bike, and held up my hand in greeting. But as soon as she saw me, Lou kicked the horse up into a canter and they flashed past me, without any greeting, without even a glance from up high. I ambled home half-heartedly, pushing my bike. There was nothing for me there except chores and more chores that I now had to do on my own.

That night I felt devastated. Ready to say anything, fulfil whatever penance Lou demanded of me. But the next day, everything changed.

It was a typical Sunday afternoon. I was in the lounge reading while my father watched the sport on television. My mother was on the balcony in some complicated position. A car tore up the drive, a black Torana, stirring up a fury of dust, sending the farm dogs into a frenzy, barking and darting out to bite the car's tyres. The commotion was enough to provoke my father's attention away from the rugby match.

'That boy drives too fast,' he said. 'I'll have to have a word with him about that before I let him loose in my vehicles.'

'Who is it?' I asked.

I'd forgotten about the farm boy arriving. I hadn't paid much attention when my father announced he'd hired someone to help through the busy spring and summer period. There had been other farm boys in the past. Lou, Babe and I had always found reasons to criticise them. We disliked them as a matter of principle. We were the boss's family and that endowed us with a haughty superiority. We scrutinised everything they did, eager to find faults, which we would then discuss in front of my father.

'It's the new farm boy. Now run down, Billy-Boy, and show him the hut and help him carry in his gear.'

I reluctantly abandoned my book and the beanbag.

'Hurry up,' snapped my father, 'before he wanders round and finds your mother on the balcony in one of her weird moments.'

I was sliding my feet into my gumboots when I glanced up to see him for the first time, on the other side of the glass door. *David Cassidy.* I knew it was impossible but it looked so much like him—the hair, the smile—I couldn't help but believe what my eyes were insisting was true.

His hair was exactly like David's. Long and dark. Centre parted. It hung glossily round his jaw with a fringe that swept down to his eyes. And his smile. He had David Cassidy's exact smile. Dazzling. Dreamy. So full of joy. It simply transformed his face and made you feel transformed too, just from basking in its radiance a while. I was helpless in the face of that smile. All I could do was grin inanely back. If he'd been wearing a skintight satin jumpsuit the resemblance would have been absolutely undeniable. He was dressed casually. Cowboy boots, jeans and a checked cotton shirt, only half-buttoned up. It afforded a glimpse of his chest, which was as tanned as his face, even though it was only September.

I forgot to open the door. All I could do was stare and smile.

Jamie had to open the door himself. 'Hi there,' he said. 'You must be Billy. They told me I'd have a young helper and wouldn't have to be doing everything by myself. I like having company.'

He winked at me and I was enchanted. It suggested complicity and intimacy, which at this point was what I wanted with him more than anything else. I was staring but I couldn't help myself.

He stuck out his hand. 'I'm Jamie,' he said. 'They probably told you that.'

I grasped his hand and we shook. I clung on a moment too long, relishing the feel of his skin against mine. He stared at me expectantly and I felt giddy with pleasure. Then I remembered what I was supposed to be doing. 'I've come to show you the hut where you'll be staying.'

I was sorry that Jamie wouldn't be sleeping over in the house. I liked the idea of having him under the same roof as me, and in the same room even better. But the boys that my father occasionally employed always slept over in the old railway hut that he'd bought cheaply when the trains stopped running from Dunedin. He didn't want them in the house cluttering up his evenings. Babe and I were banned from entering the hut, though we used to peek through the window. The last boy there had confirmed all my mother's reasons for making the hut out of bounds. When we'd peered into the room we'd seen overflowing ashtrays, cartons of beer and pin-ups from *Playboy* magazine all over the walls. All three of the most illicit pleasures in one place. Lou and I were fascinated by the hut, though not by its occupant, a surly, pale redhead called Dean, who kicked the dogs and was always showing off riding the motorbike. We loved it when he fell off.

I ambled alongside Jamie back to his car. Jamie opened the back door and handed me a guitar. This seemed to confirm everything. 'You're a singer?' I gasped.

'I'm not much of a singer but I can strum along okay,' said Jamie, tugging out two large suitcases. 'Now, where am I going to be sleeping?'

I led the way, the dogs padding after us, sniffing around Jamie's heels. He didn't kick them away. The hut was beyond the dog kennels. Dean had always complained that the dogs woke him up in the middle of the night barking at possums or the full moon. I hoped Jamie was a heavy sleeper and not going to complain and leave. When we reached the hut, I opened the door and Jamie strode in. It was simply furnished. An old double bed of my parents, a dresser and a small black and white television in the corner. It had always seemed more than adequate for any of the other farm boys. But for the first time I felt ashamed of the hut. There was only a long-drop toilet in a tin shed out the back. The shower was over in the wash-house.

'The toilet's out the back,' I said vaguely, hoping he wouldn't go and inspect it, find it inadequate and leave.

But Jamie was smiling as he always seemed to be, and showed no inclination to fault anything. 'I've never had my own place before,' he said. 'This is really something.'

'How old are you?' I asked.

'Nineteen,' he said. 'How 'bout you?'

'I'm twelve.'

Jamie raised his eyebrows. 'Betcha you're your dad's best helper.'

I couldn't lie, but I also wanted to impress Jamie, who obviously liked farm work, the only dubious quality about him. 'I'll be your helper. I'd like that better,' I said, which was both ingenuous and true.

Jamie grinned, and that was the beginning of my change of heart in regard to the farm. I discovered that all those chores could be tolerable if you had the right company. Previously, just about any job my father assigned me left me with a sinking feeling and a desperate desire to try to get out of it somehow. But all those jobs I detested became enjoyable once I had Jamie to joke around and talk with. I loved the careless masculine way he tossed his shirt off while we were working, showing off his smooth tanned chest. Sometimes the sight of him shirtless was just too entrancing and I'd find myself leaning on my shovel or a fence, doing nothing but stare.

We drenched sheep together, repaired fences, shifted the irrigation water, crutched sheep, even cleaned the sheep shit out from underneath the gratings at the woolshed, the most vile task of all. I found myself enjoying these things, even looking forward to getting home from school so I could join Jamie at whatever he was doing. My favourite moment was pressed up against him on the motorbike, with him letting the throttle out and tearing across the paddocks. I would encourage one of the old dogs to jump up on the bike's carrier, so that I had an excuse to press even closer against him, feel my legs hard up against his, my face crushed into his back.

My father was amazed. I heard him talking on the phone to Grampy about me. 'Billy-Boy's come right,' he said. 'We'll make a farmer of him yet.'

My mother recognised that it was Jamie's company and not the farm work that had motivated me, but she didn't bother disillusioning my father. She liked Jamie too. He was very diplomatic and always insisted on sampling her latest vegetarian concoction as an 'entree' before launching into his massive plate of roast dinner. He didn't stick *Playboy* pin-ups all over his walls either, which she was grateful for when she vacuumed over there.

Jamie's arrival was uncannily timely for me. He filled the void Lou had left in my life. What's more, I was secretly pleased not to have to share him with her. From the moment I first met him, I was spellbound, too distracted to give Lou more than a fleeting thought. Whenever the two of us were obliged to be in each other's company, I acted as downcast as possible. If our eyes met, she would give a brash, nasty smirk. She was so confident that I was suffering without her, struggling with all the chores around the farm that she used to relieve me of. I did nothing to correct this impression and prayed that neither Babe nor our parents would disillusion her. I wanted Jamie all to myself.

Right from our first meeting, he treated me as an equal, even though he was seven years older and in a league of his own in the looks department. A few days after his arrival, he started inviting me over to his hut in the evening. I was thrilled and asked my mother if it was alright. 'As long as he invited you and you didn't invite yourself,' she said. 'And if he offers you a glass of beer, say no. You're too young for that sort of thing.'

I adored those evenings with Jamie. We never did all that much, just sat around talking or watching television which was nowhere near as good as the colour set over at the house. But we were away from our parents, who represented authority for both of us. Over at the hut we were free. One night after a couple of bottles of beer, Jamie looked around the hut and grinned with appreciation. 'It's good to have a place that's all my own, that the old man can't poke his nose into and tell me what I should and shouldn't be doing.'

Jamie had fallen out with his father. He was vague about the actual reason for their big fight. 'It was bad,' was all he'd say. 'Real bad.'

Jamie had left home straight after, packed his belongings into his car and driven off. 'Left right in the middle of shearing. Pissed him off no end I bet. Busiest time of the year. But perhaps he'll come to realise how much work I do round his pissy farm without much in the way of thanks or remuneration.'

I couldn't imagine Jamie ever fighting with anyone. He was always so affable and even-tempered. His father I decided must be a real mean old bastard, even worse than Old Man Sampson. 'Does he know where you are?' I asked, worried for a moment that this tyrant might suddenly turn up and reclaim him.

'I rang and told Mum. She reckons it's the best thing for both of us. Have a bit of time apart. She's had enough of us fightin' all the time. Glad to get some peace I reckon, though she misses me. I promised to write to her. Billy, make sure I write to her.'

I nodded gravely. I loved it when he asked me to do things for him. His expression was so earnest, like he couldn't do without me. He was stretched out on the bed. I was on the floor alongside, as there were no chairs. I leaned my head back against the bed and Jamie tousled my curls affectionately. I preened into the touch of his hand, wishing he'd run his hand through my hair forever.

I was always trying to provoke some life into my fantasies about Jamie. When he shot outside to use the toilet or grab a beer from the creek, where he left them to cool, I'd claim his bed. I loved lying there. The smell of his sweat rising in the sheets when I sniffed them, the thought of his naked body lying between them at night. I had checked under the pillow and there were no pyjamas. This excited me tremendously. I often imagined some emergency, a fire or a flood, where I would have to sprint over to the hut, and rouse Jamie out of bed, and urge him into his clothes. I longed to see him naked.

Stealing his spot on the bed became like a game between us. He'd wander back in, half-expecting to find his position supplanted and it always would be. He'd act surprised, bellow his protests and then proceed to throw me off, back onto the floor. I loved this tussle. The chance to grip onto him. Feel his skin beneath my fingers. The firmness of the muscles in his arms. I always fought hard, trying to prolong those playful wrestles for as long as possible. Of course, Jamie was much stronger, but I was also more determined about staying there on the bed with him than I was about just about anything else. I was also a significant weight to shift. I wanted nothing better than for Jamie to simply declare me the victor and curl up alongside me on the bed. Unfortunately, this never happened.

There was only one time when he did give up trying to dislodge me. He merely slumped to the floor himself and sat there, withdrawn, silent for the rest of the evening. I crowed my victory until I realised he wasn't going to bite back. The mood had changed. Something was wrong. Later, when I'd gone back over to the house, I fretted that he had felt my cock, hard against him, during the heat of our tussle and had been repelled.

Jamie had Saturday afternoons and Sundays off. For his first few weeks he'd been content to hang around at home. But the Saturday after that unsettling evening, he rushed out to the wash-house after lunch and took a shower. I ambled after him and peeked through the window once the shower started running. It was impossible to make much out through the double camouflage of the steamed-up window and the shower curtain. I positioned myself outside the wash-house, playing with the dogs on the lawn, waiting, wondering what he was up to. When he emerged, hair wet and tangled, he was dressed in his favourite outfit, the jeans and shirt he'd worn on the day he arrived. 'Goin' somewhere?' I asked.

'Yeah. Into Glenora. Have a look around.'

I waited for him to ask me along. He didn't. He strode down to the spare garage, started his car and set off down the drive, tooting the horn, giving me a salute of farewell. The dogs deserted me to bite his tyres and I willed one of them to take an almighty mouthful of rubber so he couldn't go anywhere. I was left marooned, desolate on the lawn.

Eventually, I drifted off on my bike, down the road to the gaol. There was nothing better to do. I hadn't been there since Jamie arrived and I wondered if Roy would've given up on me. He hadn't.

That afternoon, I tried to pretend it was Jamie I was with. It was impossible. There were too many things that reeked so unmistakably of Roy. The awful smell of his mother's menthol cigarettes clinging to his breath. The feel of his wispy facial hair brushing against my face and neck. The paleness of his skin, so white that even in the gloom of the gaol, the shadows failed to shroud him. I had always felt guilty afterwards. That time, I felt uncomfortable before we even got started.

Jamie didn't get home until the early hours of the morning. I'd been drowsily waiting to hear him return, fearful he never would. My father heard his car too. The next morning at breakfast, he couldn't stop repeating the time he'd been awoken. 'Two o'clock in the morning. Two o'clock. What's he doing out till two in the morning?'

'Maybe the pub kept serving after hours,' my mother suggested.

My father frowned. 'That boy will get himself in trouble with the policeman. Mark my words. He's too young to be in the pub and old Hubble isn't going to know who he is and let him off with a warning. It's not like he's one of the locals yet.'

My father stopped for another mouthful of sausage. 'And he drives too fast. Drives too damn fast. I'll have a word with him about that.'

Jamie didn't appear until midday dinner. He looked just the same as ever, no trace of the ravages of the night before. My father tried to wheedle exactly what he'd been up to out of him, but Jamie neatly side-stepped his questions by launching in on the latest stories he'd heard of what people were doing down the plain. My father prickled with interest at the latest gossip and forgot about Jamie and his exploits.

Jamie started getting phone calls the following week from some of the guys he'd met at the pub, urging him to come out again the following weekend. I eavesdropped on those conversations, furious at his pleasure in their invitations. The next Saturday, he disappeared off in his car again. My father watched, tut-tutting from his chair and I echoed his disapproval, wishing he'd forbid him from going anywhere. Of course, he couldn't. I began to hope that Constable Hubble would catch him in the pub and book him, ban him from ever venturing in there again.

Perhaps something like that did happen because the following Saturday he didn't go to Glenora, despite a flurry of phone calls during the week. He came and sat out on the grass with me in front of the wash-house, the dogs nuzzling around the two of us, and suggested we go for a swim down at the river. 'A swim? In October?'

'Sure,' Jamie grinned. 'Go get your togs and tell your mother. And ask Babe if she wants to come.'

I pretended not to hear the last sentence. I raced to my bedroom and eventually found my togs. My mother was on the balcony, her eyes closed, with her feet up behind her head. When I told her I was going swimming with Jamie, she didn't make any response, which I presumed signified permission. I raced outside. Jamie was already slouched behind the wheel of his car, waiting. It was only when I'd climbed into the passenger's seat, and Jamie had turned the stereo up, that it occurred to me. He would see me in all my blubbery shame.

I had been so excited at the thought of seeing him practically naked, and horsing round together down at the river, that I'd forgotten about the embarrassing state of my own body. But it was too late to back out. Jamie had set off down the drive. Even the excitement of having a ride in his car for the first time, couldn't obliterate the nervousness gnawing up through my guts. I was so shaken that I didn't notice until we were a couple of miles down the road, that we were going in the opposite direction to the top bridge, where we usually swam. 'Where are we going?' I asked.

'Down by the gaol,' said Jamie. 'Isn't that the best place?'

I couldn't believe it. Swimming down near the gaol. On a Saturday afternoon. Just as my mind was whirling through the awful possibilities that could arise from such a situation, Jamie remarked, as if on cue, 'You know, I wouldn't mind taking a look at this gaol, seeing as it's the local landmark. I've been here 'bout a month now. Should take a look, don't you reckon?'

'It's nothing special,' I said.

Jamie shrugged. 'I still wanna see it sometime. Might as well be now.'

My mind scrambled for some means of escape. 'I wouldn't mind a swim first.'

'Okay,' he agreed.

Jamie parked off the road down by the bridge and leapt straight out of the car, grabbing a pair of rugby shorts off the floor. I clambered out too, but stayed by the car, shielded by its door. Jamie stood with his back to me and began to slither out of his jeans. I was torn. I wanted to see what was about to be revealed so badly. I wanted to watch it in slow motion, commit every second of his undressing to memory. But I was terrified of being caught staring. I had already unnerved Jamie once. Twice would be utterly ruinous to our friendship. I had to content myself with swift constant glances. Tearing my eyes back and forth. Jamie pulled his singlet off over his head and glanced back at me. I pretended to be fumbling with my shoelaces. 'Come on,' he said impatiently. 'You said you were keen for a swim.'

He pulled down his underwear, and I lost all sense of

caution. I stared openly. A flash of white buttocks and then as he stepped into his shorts, a glimpse of it, dangling thicker and longer than I'd ever imagined. My own cock had instantly snapped to rigid attention. That was awkward. I couldn't step out in my togs, until it had subsided, something it was showing no inclination to do.

Jamie glanced back at me again but didn't bother to wait. 'Last in's a sook.'

'First in's a show off,' I retorted.

He bounded across the bridge and then stopped to peer over at the river below. 'It looks deep enough,' he yelled back at me.

'It is. I can't touch the bottom,' I said, reluctantly undoing the buttons on my shirt and wondering how I could manoeuvre myself into the water without Jamie seeing me.

Jamie clambered up onto the railing of the bridge, pounded at his chest with his fists, and then leapt forward off the bridge. The sight of him was exhilarating. Plunging forward into space. Then he plummeted out of view, and I started to feel anxious. I had never known anyone to dare jump off the bridge before. I ran over to the railing. What if Jamie had hurt himself? This could be an opportunity for me to save him, to be a hero and win his gratitude. I couldn't help feeling a pang of disappointment when I looked over to find Jamie treading water, whooping and waving at me. Not that I really wanted him to be hurt but the thought of him prone and pale on the muddy riverbank and at my mercy was an alluring one. I could investigate the contents of his shorts before I administered artificial resuscitation the way we'd learnt at school. 'Come on in. It's damn cold,' yelled Jamie.

I trailed back to the car. I'd managed to lose my erection during the distraction. I slipped out of the rest of my clothes and pulled on my bathing suit. In a sudden flash of inspiration, I draped my towel round my neck, which completely hid my chest. I ducked through the fence and hurried down to the river. Jamie had floated off downstream, so I quickly flung the towel aside and dived straight in off the bank. Usually, I was a terrible coward about getting into cold water and would procrastinate and dither until someone gave me a push. This time, all I wanted was to submerge my body, out of view, beneath the dark water as soon as possible.

When I bobbed to the surface, Jamie was swimming back in my direction. The water was so cold, I was tempted to get straight back out again but Jamie was drawing closer and closer to me. I didn't want him witnessing the sight of me trying to clamber out. 'Last in, gets ducked,' he warned.

I giggled in nervous terror and set off in my best freestyle across to the other bank with Jamie in pursuit. Once he'd caught me, I clung to him for all I was worth, equally determined not to get ducked and to maintain the feel of his wet skin against my own for as long as possible. But of course, he was stronger and my head was forced under. I came up spluttering and Jamie retreated, laughing as I spat out river water. I made as much noise as I could, splashing Jamie in retaliation, threatening him loudly, hoping it would warn Roy that there were people about.

Then some instinct compelled me to look up at the bridge. I started. There was someone leaning on the railings looking down at us. A boy. Was it Roy? I'd taken my glasses off to swim. The face was a blur to me. I squinted upward, trying to work out if it was him. It seemed like the right build. Jamie noticed me staring. 'Hey there, coming in for a swim?' he called.

'No,' said the boy, and I realised that it wasn't Roy.

It wasn't even a boy. It was Lou.

I felt a chill rise through me. What was she doing down here? Was she spying on me?

'Very wise,' said Jamie. 'Too cold for anyone with any sense.'

That was true enough. I began to shiver. How long had she been watching us? Her silence and the way she stood there, hunched over the bridge railings, seemed ominous.

'You're not from round here.'

Lou's voice was sharp.

'Nope. Just here for the summer. Helpin' this guy make some hay.'

'He needs all the help he can get,' Lou snapped and with that she turned, her footsteps clumping across the wooden planks of the bridge in her hobnail boots, an old pair of her father's. She needed to wear three pairs of her thickest socks to make them fit.

'Tough little chap,' said Jamie.

I was uneasy. It was no coincidence that she had turned up. But how had she known? Had she noticed me cycling past her house on Saturdays and finally decided to come down herself and discover what I was doing? It was very likely. People in Mawera liked to keep an eye on who was coming and going and speculate as to the reasons why. What if Lou came upon Roy while she was prying round? Where had she gone? It was impossible to tell from where I was. My heart began to resound so strongly I half expected it to cause the river water to stir around me. Surely she hadn't gone to inspect the gaol?

As this occurred to me, Jamie ducked me again. I was completely unprepared for it. I'd been so absorbed by the anxieties that Lou's sudden appearance had provoked, I'd forgotten Jamie for the moment. I screamed when I felt his hands clutch me, forcing me under the water. My mouth and nose filled with water. I couldn't breathe. I came up choking and spluttering, gasping for air. Jamie didn't seem to notice. 'Gotcha a good one that time,' he chuckled.

He was floating on his back, a careful distance between

us, in case I tried to retaliate. I had no intention of retaliating. Jamie's sense of horseplay was too brutal for me. I'd have preferred something along the lines of trying to yank each other's togs down. 'I'm getting out,' I said. 'I'm cold.'

'Yep. This water'd freeze your balls off,' Jamie remarked.

I'd have liked to have offered to give them a rub for him. Instead I dog paddled to the bank, clambered out and enfolded myself quickly in my towel. Jamie continued to splash about in the water. I marched back up to the car and grabbed my glasses off the dashboard. I put them on hastily, peering all around for Lou. There was no sign of her. I considered getting dressed quickly and rushing to the gaol to warn Roy, but it seemed pointless. She was probably already there. My sudden appearance would only be incriminating.

There was also Jamie to consider. I wanted to watch him getting dressed again. That reminded me that I didn't want him to see the state of my body. I quickly dried myself off and put my clothes back on. I arranged myself on the hood of Jamie's car, feeling bad for Roy but also admiring the image of myself draped across Jamie's car.

A few minutes later, Jamie ran up from the river, sleek and dripping. He failed to notice my resemblance to the temptresses in car advertisements and ducked straight into the back seat to pull out his towel. He began to dry himself off and I willed him to remove his shorts. He didn't. 'You gunna show me this gaol then, where they lock up the wild locals?'

I had hoped he might have forgotten about that idea. 'It doesn't even look like a gaol,' I said.

Jamie stopped drying his hair and looked at me. For once, he wasn't grinning. 'But I'll show you, if you want to see it,' I added quickly.

Jamie pulled his singlet over his head and left his wet

shorts on. 'Okay,' he said, 'let's go take a look.'

He nattered away as we walked and I mumbled agreement. I wasn't really listening. My mind was churning through 'what if' scenarios. Roy usually stripped off when he saw me coming. What if he mistook Lou for me in his haste? What if she came upon him naked and then made him tell what he was doing? Who he was waiting for. And what if she then told Jamie? The more I thought about it, the sicker I felt. 'There it is,' I said, when we could see the gaol through the willow trees. 'It's nothing much.'

'But aren't there old handcuffs or something inside?' asked Jamie.

He kept walking. I stopped where I was. Jamie turned back, puzzled. 'Aren't you coming?'

'I've seen it a hundred times,' I said.

I had noticed what Jamie had failed to. There was someone slouched against the stone wall. From that distance I couldn't tell who it was. I strained to see, cursing my useless glasses. I sidled forward, closing one eye, peering at the figure. Suddenly, I recognised the shirt. It was Lou. I broke into a run. I didn't want her talking to Jamie. I didn't trust her. I caught up with Jamie just a few steps away from the gaol. He glanced at me. 'Changed your mind?' he said before directing his attention to Lou. 'Hello again.'

To my surprise, I noticed that Lou was smoking a cigarette with some expertise. 'Hey you're too young to smoke. It'll stunt your growth,' said Jamie.

'Good,' said Lou. 'I'd smoke packets every day if I really believed that bullshit.'

I was doubly shocked at her behaviour. I'd never known her to dare swear in front of an adult, though Jamie wasn't exactly an adult. He was grinning, amused by her tough talk.

'Do you want one?' Lou offered the packet, flicking it open. Jamie nodded. 'Thanks.'

He reached for a cigarette. Then suddenly he stopped and drew back. 'Oh. Menthol. Thanks all the same. Can't stand menthol.'

Lou's face fell a little. She studied the packet and then tossed it aside. 'I'm not all that keen on them myself. I found them in the gaol. Seems like some kid's been sneaking down here and smoking cigarettes. *Menthol* cigarettes.'

She gave me a condescending look. It was an expression she had perfected from imitating her mother. I couldn't help myself smirking back at her. I was so relieved she had got the situation so wrong. But I regretted it. Instantly, Lou's face glazed over frostily. Then the expression was gone and she had turned her attention back to Jamie, smiling. 'By the way, I'm Lou. His cousin.'

'Oh right, Arthur's son.'

Lou grinned. She glanced at me and I opened my mouth to correct Jamie's error. 'Actually, I'm a girl,' said Lou quickly brandishing her ponytail. 'But I'm a better farmer than all the boys round here.'

'I bet you are,' said Jamie. 'Well you had me fooled.'

Lou grinned her satisfaction. I couldn't bear to see her so smug. 'Let's look at the gaol, Jamie,' I said quickly, marching forward and unlocking the door.

'Oh yeah, the gaol,' said Jamie vaguely, following me.

I opened the door and ushered him in, pulling it half shut after we'd entered in case Lou was planning to follow. I pointed out the chains, which was all there was to see and Jamie knelt down to examine them. 'They're warm,' he exclaimed. 'You'd expect them to be cold, but they're not. Feel them. It's weird.'

I didn't want to touch them, warm from Roy's bare skin. Not when I was here with Jamie. But he was holding them out to me, insisting, his brow creased, trying to explain this phenomenon. 'Perhaps the place is haunted,' I said.

'So that's why you didn't want to come here. This place has a reputation for ghosts?'

'Something like that. Gives me the creeps.'

I shuddered involuntarily. All those Saturday afternoons were echoing back at me. 'Let's go.'

I didn't want Jamie poking round too carefully. Was there other evidence of our presence, besides Roy's cigarettes, that could incriminate us? I could see where I'd ejaculated all over the stone wall. Luckily it looked remarkably like bird shit.

Jamie dropped the chain reluctantly. 'Strange,' he mused, before easing himself to his feet and walking back outside.

Relieved, I followed and closed the door quickly, snapping the bolt into place. I had hoped that Lou might have wandered off but of course she hadn't. She was still sitting in exactly the same place. 'Can we give you a lift home?' Jamie offered.

'Okay,' said Lou in a neutral voice, but her eyes were sparkling, betraying her enthusiasm.

'Didn't you bike down here?' I asked.

'No,' she said quickly, aggressively.

We walked back to the bridge, Lou showing off all the way, talking expertly about lambing percentages and wool prices and even about the weather, the classic farmer's topic. To Jamie's discredit, he seemed to find the conversation fascinating. I said nothing. In the car, it was more of the same. Lou talking non-stop, but now it was about cars and what model she'd be buying for her first car. Abruptly, Jamie braked. Both Lou and I were jerked forward. 'Sorry,' he muttered. 'Someone up ahead. I never expect to see anyone on this road.'

It was Roy. Trudging home. As we approached, it struck me anew what a strange looking creature he was. So tall and lanky, yet stooped about the shoulders as if he was trying to make himself appear shorter. He was wearing an old pair of grey school shorts that made his legs look even longer and more gangly than ever. They seemed hairier than usual too. I cringed back against my seat. Roy should never have worn shorts. He should have kept himself covered up. Jamie slowed down and turned to me. 'Who's that? Should we stop and give him a lift?'

I hesitated. I could feel Lou's breath on the back of my neck as she leaned forward, interested. Roy stopped walking and half-turned, squinting back at us, his head at a quizzical angle. Our eyes met but his betrayed nothing. There was that same deadness in his gaze that used to irritate Arch so much and drive him to bait Roy incessantly, trying to get a rise out of him. He stood there, waiting for something to happen. Slowly, the car idled towards him.

Jamie had turned to Lou questioningly. 'I'm not sharing the back seat with the Freak,' she said firmly.

Her window was down. Her voice was penetrating, just like her mother's. If Roy had heard he gave no sign. Lou's voice took on a different tone, almost wheedling. 'Maybe Billy will get in the back with him, and I'll come in the front with you Jamie. I'll drive if you like. This is exactly the sort of car I want when I've got my licence. How does it handle?'

Jamie chuckled, delighted. The car eased to a halt. 'Well Billy. Shall we let your cousin drive?'

I couldn't answer. I hated Lou for being there, for ingratiating herself with Jamie, trying so hard to act like a boy, saying all the things that I had failed to. I'd never heard Jamie laugh the way he laughed when Lou said something, like he was amused and impressed. For a horrible moment I felt that I might cry. I felt so frustrated. It should've been just me and Jamie, the two of us. Lou had no right to intrude.

I looked down at my lap, struggling to control my emotions. When I looked up I saw to my horror that Roy was approaching the car. He had assumed that we'd stopped to give him a lift. His blank expression was gone. His face was transformed by a smile which made him look goofier than ever. Involuntarily I half-screamed. '*No.*'

Jamie looked confused. 'But he seems to want a ride.'

'Drive on,' hissed Lou from the back. 'We don't want him in here.'

Jamie pressed down hard on the accelerator and the tyres gave a squeal, kicking up dust and gravel. For a moment everything was trance-like; the world had idled into slow motion. Roy loomed up by my side window, his hand stretching out to rest on the roof, grinning like a fool. I closed my eyes. I couldn't bear to look at him. The car whipped off and I heard the thud of Roy's hand against the metal of the car as he was left behind in the dust.

Lou let out a whoop. 'Make the Freak eat dust,' she crowed.

She thumped the back of Jamie's seat in approval and started complimenting him on his driving, quizzing him on how he made the wheels squeal, insisting he show her how it was done. I said nothing. I wished Lou would shut up, wished we'd left her behind with Roy. Now Lou's voice had taken on a threatening tone. 'The Freak better not have damaged your car Jamie. I'll give him what for at school on Monday if there's a dent.'

'What?' I said amazed.

'He punched the car,' Lou said. 'You must have heard it. Just before we drove off. You should have seen the look on his face. Evil. Even scared me for an instant.'

That set Jamie and her off on another topic of conversation, Jamie claiming he couldn't imagine that anything would scare Lou and Lou modestly agreeing. I would've liked to have challenged her, said bullshit back to her, but I didn't dare. It was dangerous to provoke her. I muttered it under my breath. I couldn't imagine Roy ever getting angry about anything. It seemed Lou would say anything to impress Jamie, even make up stories if it provided an opportunity for her to show off.

As we approached Lou's house, she continued to babble on to Jamie. Finally, I had to speak out. 'Jamie, you'd better slow down. This is where Lou gets out.'

I could feel Lou's furious expression without having to see it. Jamie eased off the accelerator. I half-expected her to talk herself into staying in the car, but she didn't. She hopped out, thanked Jamie for the lift and ignored me completely. 'See you soon,' she said, leaning towards Jamie's window, smiling.

I watched her in the rear-vision mirror as we pulled away, sauntering up the drive to her house. I felt uneasy. It wasn't like her to smile and to remember to say thank you.

It was only another couple of miles down the road to our place. Finally, it was just Jamie and me, alone together in his car. But I could think of nothing to say or nothing that would sound as confident and adult as Lou's conversation. We drove in silence. I glanced across at Jamie. With his white singlet highlighting his tan, his wet hair curling up into ringlets, he'd never looked more handsome.

I wished we had further to go and could keep on driving.

11

I did not like Belinda Pepper. I'd heard all the stories about her and like everyone else never thought to doubt them. I tried to warn Jamie but he wouldn't allow me to repeat a word. He said he already knew. Everyone in the Serpentine knew about Belinda Pepper. She achieved notoriety young. Expelled from boarding school in Dunedin at the age of sixteen.

It had begun innocently enough. She had complained of a sore throat and been sent to the boarding school doctor. She expected to be told to go to bed and take some time off school. Instead, the doctor took some throat swabs and suggested she wear a scarf outdoors. Several days later, she was hauled into the Mother Superior's office by Sister Josephine. The Sister couldn't contain herself and slapped Belinda across the face, declaring her a sinner who had brought shame upon herself and the entire establishment. Neither of the nuns could bring themselves to speak Belinda's crime aloud. Instead, the Mother Superior pushed the laboratory report across the table for Belinda to read for herself. She had contracted gonorrhoea of the throat.

Belinda was locked in the sick bay for the night. 'You're diseased,' Sister Josephine had hissed at her. 'Physically and morally.'

Sister Josephine insisted that she be quarantined until her parents could collect her. This suited Belinda perfectly. There was a telephone in the sick bay for the doctor's use. Belinda made quick use of it, arranging an assignation with the very boy who had infected her. For the first but final time, the two of them had the luxury of a proper bed with sheets. Previously, they'd been obliged to do it amongst soggy leaves in the densely-wooded town belt.

The nuns never thought to offer Belinda any course of treatment for her problem. Her mother was obliged to take her to the doctor in Glenora to obtain a prescription. Of course, everybody noticed. They all knew she had been expelled. The doctor's appointment only served to confirm what they'd all suspected. Belinda Pepper must be pregnant.

'She's not pregnant,' protested Tracey Ingham, the doctor's receptionist, at the pub on Friday night. Tracey had downed several Bacardi and cokes. She felt it was her duty to halt the spread of such a story as efficiently as her employer halted disease. 'She's got gonorrhoea of the throat.'

Everyone's eyes were on Tracey. 'Whoops,' she tittered into her drink, realising her mistake. But it was too late. By Monday morning, everyone knew. Including the doctor. Tracey was fired. A few days later Belinda Pepper called at the surgery to enquire if the position was still vacant.

Belinda had announced to her parents that she had finished with school. The only class she'd attended with any regularity was biology. She preferred to experiment with her clothes and make-up and discover which pubs would accept her as looking twenty one and serve her a drink at three in the afternoon. To her delight, most would. Belinda had a stature and assurance well beyond her sixteen years.

Even in her school uniform she had looked unbearably provocative, despite the regulation that the school kilt was not to be worn higher than three inches above the knee. Three inches was quite enough to tantalise those who stared and then imagined what lay beyond for themselves. Belinda was an authority on grooming and make-up. She wanted to be a model. Unlike most girls her age, this wasn't an idle fantasy, but a serious career plan. She had enrolled at Dunedin's only model agency at age thirteen when she was sent to boarding school.

Belinda put to practice everything that she learned there. She dyed her long dark hair jet black. She had an exercise program especially designed to accentuate her curves and maintain her body tone. She kept to a strict diet for fear of pimples, not that a solitary one ever marred her complexion. She was prone to them on her bottom, an unsightly problem, given that Belinda began sexually experimenting young.

It was her walk that posed Belinda her biggest challenge. Yvonne from the model agency had shrieked that she had a 'farmer's gait' when she'd attended her first class. It had taken Belinda three years to perfect the 'confident, elegant stride' that Yvonne demanded of her students. Her rural influence was almost entirely exorcised. It only resurrected itself if she drank too many glasses of Chardon.

By sixteen she'd had a number of older lovers. She treated these men as lessons. She was intrigued by what they could teach her. The girls in her dormitory were equally intrigued. Belinda used to breathlessly narrate her adventures to them after lights out.

Belinda was impatient, impetuous. She wanted to be twenty-one and wasn't prepared to wait six years.

When her mother came to collect her from school, Belinda asked to be taken to the airport. 'I'm going to Auckland to become a professional model,' she said dreamily.

'The only place you're going is back to the farm where I can keep an eye on you,' her mother replied sharply.

Belinda sulked all the way home and then pretended her

throat infection had rendered her speechless. Her mother forced Belinda's head under the bathroom tap and tried to scrub her mouth out with the brush she used on her own dentures. Belinda soon began to shriek.

Marcia Pepper felt totally humiliated. She could forgive her only daughter almost anything, except when it was illicit and everyone found out about it. Marcia couldn't bring herself to go to bowls and face the other lady bowlers for the rest of that season. She knew it was the talk of the clubhouse and would be lingered over for months. Marcia longed for some other girl to scandalise herself and seize all the attention.

Alf Pepper blamed what had happened on city living. He'd never trusted it himself and was almost pleased to be proved correct, even though it was at the expense of his daughter's reputation. 'Home on the farm's where you belong, girlie,' he said, and set Belinda to work.

Belinda had no choice. Jobs were scarce in Glenora. 'You've no skills, dear,' the doctor's wife had kindly told her when she enquired about the position.

'But I've got a helluva reputation,' Belinda retorted, executing a perfect turn on two-inch stilettos and stalking across the waiting-room linoleum to the door. From there she went to the hairdresser and had her long hair cut off into a pageboy style. Belinda felt so trapped. She had an urge to do something shocking. The locals had never seen such a hairstyle before. It was the latest fashion. The style accentuated Belinda's charms—the impish mischievous cast to her face, the eyes that couldn't resist mocking, and the mouth that constantly curled into a crooked bemused smile. Belinda was forever laughing off her own follies and misadventures. She seemed to be in a constant state of amusement at her own appeal and the haphazard consequences it provoked.

To everyone's surprise Belinda settled down and began

working for her father without any fuss. What they didn't know was that she had talked him into paying her an extravagant salary, which would shortly see her on her way to Auckland, if she could only be disciplined enough to save some of it. The other thing that kept Belinda content was Rodney. He was their neighbour's son. She had been meeting him in the hay barn near the border of their two properties since the age of twelve. Their liaisons had been resurrected whenever Belinda returned home for school holidays. Now that she was home permanently, they became a daily ritual. Belinda felt a fond attachment to Rodney. They had lost their virginity together, her on top of him, barking instructions as to how it was supposed to be done. Rodney was now twenty, engaged to the dentist's daughter, and had developed quite a penchant for doing it on the top of haystacks. His fiancée was scared of heights.

This arrangement between Belinda and Rodney was proceeding nicely, until one day, their bucking and squealing disturbed a duck who had burrowed a nest for itself inbetween a couple of hay bales. It flapped up out of its hiding place in alarm, startling Rodney terribly. He shot off the top of Belinda and fell backwards off the haystack, landing awkwardly. Belinda had enough good sense not to touch him but to run immediately to the house to call for an ambulance. By not moving Rodney, Belinda undoubtedly saved him from becoming a cripple for life. She didn't save herself from further disgrace. Rodney had to be carefully transferred onto the stretcher with his pants around his knees. No one needed to ask what had happened.

Rodney was confined to a wheelchair for six months. The dentist's daughter broke off their engagement as soon as the scandal hit. She expected that he would now marry Belinda. When it became apparent that Belinda had no intention of marrying Rodney or even visiting him with some homemade ginger crunch (his favourite treat), the dentist's daughter baked a batch herself and steeled herself for the visit. She placed the tin of ginger crunch in Rodney's lap (a little more forcefully than was necessary), but then broke down and began to weep all over his poor redundant legs. He munched away leaving a confetti of crumbs in her hair.

She emerged from the visit, triumphantly engaged once more and with a malicious vendetta against Belinda Pepper. Soon the ladies at the bowling club knew all the intimate details of the incident. It was discussed at a special meeting: was Marcia a suitable vice-president for the club? Meanwhile, Marcia was tearfully berating Belinda and claiming that she could never play bowls again.

It was at the height of this scandal that Belinda received the offer of a job. Julie, the manageress of the only ladies' boutique in Glenora, had shrewdly noticed that almost half the girls in town were now wearing their hair in the same style as Belinda's. The hairdresser had never been so busy. Julie wanted a piece of the action. She suspected that Belinda had the attitude and figure to make any old garment look something special. They were the only sales skills she would need.

Belinda moved out of the farmhouse and into her own flat in Glenora. Within a week, Julie was proved correct. All the girls from the Serpentine Area School flocked into the shop wanting a pair of jeans or earrings just like the ones Belinda was wearing. Belinda was notorious, with an image that was highly alluring to all those small-town girls. They wanted to emulate Belinda's style. They wanted to look like her. But that was as far as it went. They wanted nothing else to do with her. On the street, they'd ignore her. They preferred to talk about her, rather than to her.

The local boys had no such scruples. There was always

some member of the rugby team ambling into the shop on the pretext of looking for a present for someone. Julie recognised the potential of this situation and began stocking a range of men's underwear which Belinda sold to these browsing shoppers effortlessly. They all desired Belinda. The gossip fuelled her allure. In a town where a facade of respectability and virtue was expected, Belinda broke all the rules. In the city she would have been just another adventurous, wayward young girl. In Glenora, she was exotic.

Much to my annoyance, Jamie became fascinated by her. I told him that she was dissolute, a word I had heard Aunt Evelyn use to describe Belinda. Jamie had to look the word up in the dictionary in the study. He came back to me chuckling. 'Yes,' he agreed, 'she is dissolute, but that's what makes her irresistible.'

I refused to admit I was jealous of Belinda. I merely considered her unworthy of him. He was so handsome, so cheerful, so much fun to be with. He deserved better. There were several other local girls who were eminently more suitable. Even though Belinda was undoubtedly the sexiest girl on the Serpentine plain, everyone agreed that she wasn't girlfriend material. She came into a category all of her own, a category the guys snickered about over their beers.

It was the talk of the district when it became apparent that Jamie was 'going out' with Belinda and not merely after 'the one thing she was good for'. Diana Drake, captain of the Glenora hockey team and darling of the district, was inconsolable. She'd had her eye on Jamie ever since he first strolled into the milkbar where she worked and ordered a sausage roll. She was incredulous that she'd lost him to Belinda, who she considered to be in a league worthy only of contempt.

Even my parents were concerned. Or at least, my father

was concerned. They discussed it over Sunday breakfast one morning, when Jamie had failed to return home at all the previous night. My father hadn't been awoken by his car coming up the drive in the middle of the night, and had dashed out first thing in the morning, worried his alertness was failing him. But Jamie's car wasn't in the spare garage. My father came back inside and sat himself down heavily at the table. 'That boy is up to mischief,' he announced.

'Hasn't he come home? I hope he's alright and hasn't rolled his car,' said my mother.

My father grunted.

'Well you're always complaining about him drinking and driving, and now when he acts sensibly and stays down the plain instead of trying to drive home drunk, you make a fuss,' said my mother.

'Yes, but where's he staying? That's the point. Everyone's going to know about it. His car will be parked outside her flat, which I'm told is on the main road. That's where he'll be, with his car parked outside, plain as day, for everyone to see.'

'Well, people should be driving to church on a Sunday shouldn't they, instead of past Belinda Pepper's flat on the other side of town.'

There were no more excursions to the river with Jamie for me. As soon as he'd finished work on Saturday morning, he'd gobble down some lunch, dash into the shower, then into his car, and be off to Glenora to see Belinda. Usually, he'd come home late Sunday night. My weekends were desolate without him and there was nothing that could distract me from the fact that I'd lost him.

Sometimes I thought of biking down to the gaol. Once I even got halfway there, before turning round and coming home again. Somehow it would've seemed like a betrayal of Jamie. I harboured the conviction that I could win Jamie away from Belinda, if my dedication to the goal was strong and pure enough. Mucking around with Roy would spoil all that. It made me unworthy of Jamie. My theory was that I needed to be saintly and virtuous—the attributes that were wanting in Belinda. I also needed to be patient. It was taking a long time for Jamie to recognise my superiority over Belinda, but I was sure that ultimately he would. That was how it always worked out in books and on television.

I suffered on those Mondays when Jamie happily chattered about what a wonderful weekend he'd had with Belinda. I didn't want to hear it. I tried withdrawing from him, ignoring him. I wanted him to be concerned and gently ask me what was wrong. I wanted him to miss our old companionship, to miss me. But it was impossible to be cold with Jamie for long. His mood was always so buoyant, his company so beguiling, that he could always tease me out of my attempts at isolating him. I couldn't resist him.

I felt so lonely and confused. I spent my weekends redoing chores that I'd done with Jamie earlier in the week, reliving the memory. It was a huge relief to look up from the ditch I was transforming into a canal one Sunday afternoon and find Lou standing off from me, watching. She didn't say hello. Instead she marched up to me so officiously I worried she was going to punch me in the face. Instead, she apologised. I was astounded. Then I got suspicious. It was completely out of character for her to admit fault. There had to be an ulterior motive. It didn't take long for her to reveal herself. She didn't even wait for me to reciprocate with an apology for what I'd said. As soon as her quick, terse sentence was uttered, she insisted that we go and investigate Jamie's hut. Immediately.

I shook my head. 'We're banned from there. You know that.'

It wasn't my mother's warnings that restrained me but my

desire to keep Jamie to myself. There was no putting Lou off. 'You don't have to come if you don't want to. I'll go look myself,' she said, setting off towards the hut.

I wasn't having her poking round over there by herself. I hurried after her. 'We should only look through the window,' I said.

'Okay,' said Lou, in a voice that betrayed she wasn't really listening.

'I've been over there heaps of times before anyway,' I boasted. 'Jamie asks me over there all the time. In the evenings.'

Lou was impressed. Though the truth was that since he'd met Belinda, no invitations had been forthcoming.

'What do you do?' asked Lou.

'Oh, watch television. He drinks beer and smokes and I have a wee sip and a puff,' I said.

That wasn't strictly true either.

'Does he have any *Playboy*s?'

'I've never seen any.'

'S'pose he doesn't need them, going out with Belinda Pepper.'

I didn't answer. I didn't like to think about what Lou was insinuating. We came to the hut and Lou eagerly peered through the window. 'He's got a guitar,' she noted approvingly. 'And cowboy boots. What's that?'

'Where?'

'A photo, stuck up on the mirror. Who is it?'

There was a photo stuck to the mirror that hadn't been there the last time I'd been invited over. 'I'm going to take a look,' said Lou.

'Lou,' I protested.

'Look, I don't think they've got clothes on in that photo. All I can see is skin.'

I squinted. She seemed to be right. Lou yanked the door

open and I tried to push past her to get to the photo first. She tripped me up and coolly walked past me, grovelling on the ground, to examine the photo. I clambered to my feet and jostled her to the side so that I could see myself. She was too entranced to push back.

It was a photo of Jamie and Belinda. They weren't naked. They were in their bathing suits. Jamie in the same black rugby shorts he'd worn the day we'd gone swimming. Belinda was wearing a chocolate-coloured bikini with yellow polka dots. It must've been taken by the Red River down on the plain somewhere, one of the swimming holes close to Glenora. You could make out a bit of the river and a willow tree in the background. They were sitting on his Torana. Jamie had his arm around Belinda and she was squeezed up against him, looking up at his face and laughing in a protesting way. Jamie was staring at the camera, smiling confidently. Belinda had one hand on his chest in a gesture of possession.

There were huge emotions swilling around in me, threatening to erupt. I didn't know whether I wanted to steal that photo or rip it up. Quickly, I walked outside and took some deep breaths. I didn't want to cry but I felt as though I might. There had to be some spilling of feeling at such a visible display of betrayal. By the time Lou ambled outside, carefully closing the door behind herself, I had regained my composure. 'Well, well,' said Lou in her best Aunt Evelyn voice.

'He used to take me swimming,' I said quickly.

'Really?'

'Yep.'

We wandered back over to the house. 'I'd like a bikini like Belinda's.'

I was aghast at this traitorous act. 'You don't want to look like her,' I snapped.

Lou shrugged. 'Why not?' she said. 'Jamie likes the way she looks.'

There was no answer to that.

But her remark bothered me. It wasn't like Lou to express a desire to wear feminine clothes. She was usually trying to deny every trace of femininity she possessed. She folded her arms all the time to hide the beginnings of her breasts. Now she wanted to reveal them to the world by wearing bikinis. It was highly suspicious behaviour.

The next day, Lou attached herself to me after school and informed me she'd come home and do my chores. 'The way it used to be,' she said, with a smile that somehow didn't seem meant for me.

I couldn't protest. We had made up due to her overture of friendship. To have tried to put her off would have been a slap in the face of her initiative. But I wanted to. I wanted to tell her she wasn't needed any more. But the words she used—*the way it used to be*—held so much significance, spoke so succinctly of our shared history. I choked back my ignoble doubts and managed an uncertain smile of acquiescence.

I knew as soon as she greeted Jamie that I had made a grave mistake. From that moment onward, she took over. It was agony to watch the two of them together. But to allow Lou to have him all to herself would have been far worse. So I watched and suffered as she dazzled him. She was at her most audacious, her most daring. She was borne up by the thrill of victory, for she was winning Jamie away from me with every day that passed.

The two of them got along famously. Jamie was so impressed by Lou. She was a girl and yet was as tough and as willing to work hard as any boy. Lou was showing off. It was so blatant it made me cringe. But Jamie grinned and lapped it all up.

In particular she seemed to be trying to highlight the differences between the two of us and show herself in a more favourable light. Lou could skin a rabbit with a few deft flashes of her pocket knife. I refused to even touch the stiff furry corpse. Lou could whistle to the dogs, guiding them this way and that, rounding up the sheep. I couldn't even whistle. I had to yell at the dogs instead, though they never followed my instructions the way they were supposed to. Lou was faster and more efficient at anything we were doing, whether it was digging a ditch or hammering in staples on a fence. Lou always finished first and then made a point of having to come and help me finish off. Lou. Lou. Lou. She was ubiquitous. Always there. Always encroaching. Denying me the one thing I craved more than anything. For it to be just Jamie and me, *the way it used to be*.

Jamie started making remarks like, 'Your cousin is really something,' or 'Lou's a real asset to have about'. Sometimes he even made little jokes about the difference between the two of us, jokes that I didn't find funny and that I certainly didn't want Lou to hear. I began to feel disgruntled with him. Sometimes I refused to help with the chores at all. I'd stay at home, longing to see a flicker of disappointment or concern on his face that I wasn't coming. But it was in vain. All his handsome face ever did was crinkle into a grin. I'd be left behind to moon about aimlessly, wishing I had gone with them and willing Jamie to miss me.

It was equally frustrating when I did accompany them. I couldn't compete with Lou so I didn't even bother to try. I'd flop down on the grass and watch the two of them working and when Jamie tried to kid me into helping, I'd snap, 'Let Wonderwoman do it'. After a while I realised that I was doing exactly what Lou wanted me to. This strange smug little smile would come over her face whenever I acted temperamentally. I realised Jamie was gaining a worse opinion of me, and rather than missing me when I didn't go along with them, Lou was probably bad-mouthing me or at least emphasising her own superiority.

My one consolation was that Lou always went home to her own house for dinner. The evenings were the opportunity for Jamie and I to spend alone together. I waited and waited for an invitation to his hut. My appetite began to suffer. I felt so wrenched up through dinner, waiting for him to speak. But no invitation ever came.

As soon as dinner was over, Jamie would always ask if he could use the phone. I longed to scream 'No, no you can't'. He spoke to Belinda every night. Usually phone conversations were overheard by everyone because the phone hung on the kitchen wall by the front door. But Jamie overcame that problem. He would dial Belinda's number and then walk through the door with the handpiece clutched to his ear, closing it after himself. We couldn't hear a word, though Babe and I, and maybe even my parents, would've loved to eavesdrop. I'd sit there at the dinner table and watch him through the glass door, willing them to have a fight over the phone. They never did. A different expression would steal over Jamie's face when he talked to Belinda on the phone. That big grin faded into something more tender and hesitant. After a while, Jamie got wise to the fact that I was watching him and he started to turn his back on the glass door. As soon as his conversation was finished, he'd open the door, replace the phone and call out a quick goodnight to everyone. There was never a chance to speak to him. He wouldn't even let me catch his eye.

Finally, I couldn't bear it any longer. One night, after he'd finished on the phone, I ran out to him, before he had a chance to close the door and disappear. 'Do you feel like a game of cards tonight?' I asked hopefully.

We'd played a few hands of poker together during those

evenings when he first arrived. 'Not tonight,' muttered Jamie, looking at his boots.

'Maybe tomorrow then,' I said.

'Tomorrow? Um, no, I can't tomorrow either.'

I waited for Jamie to elaborate. Finally, he looked up at me and began to stutter out an excuse. 'Lately . . . I've . . . been going rabbit shooting after dinner.'

Jamie knew I hated any kind of shooting. I couldn't bear the sound of the gun going off or the suspense of waiting for that to happen. 'Okay,' I said and turned away.

I wandered back into the kitchen and sat by the window, watching for Jamie. If I couldn't be with him, I could at least watch him. He walked away from the house, but surprisingly, he didn't head over to his hut to get his gun. He walked in the opposite direction altogether, over to the woolshed. I watched him disappear from view, through the trees, and still I sat there, entranced, trying to work out what he could possibly be doing. We hadn't done any work over there in days. There was no reason for him to go there.

The next morning, at breakfast, I asked him how many rabbits he'd gotten. Jamie looked a bit startled for a minute. 'Oh, three or four,' he said.

I didn't believe him. 'Why don't you teach me how you skin them after breakfast?' I said. 'I'm sick of Lou showing me up.'

It was the last skill I wanted to acquire, but I was pretty certain there were no rabbits to be skinned. Sure enough there was a long silence before Jamie answered. 'I've already done 'em. Did 'em before breakfast.'

That was an absolute lie. Jamie never got out of bed before he had to. He'd told me a hundred times how much he loved sleeping in and what an agony it was to drag himself out of bed when he was called for breakfast. There was no way he'd have gotten out of bed early just to skin a few old rabbits that would only get tossed to the dogs.

I watched Jamie, his head bowed over his cereal plate, avoiding looking at me. I was intrigued by his lies. What could be the reason behind them? He had to be protecting some kind of secret and I was determined to find out exactly what that secret was.

12

That December, drought gripped the Serpentine county. Grampy claimed it was the fiercest summer he could remember. There had been no rain since the beginning of November. The lucerne wilted in the paddocks that had been shut up for hay. Reluctantly, the farmers cut it early before it shrivelled up altogether. Some paddocks were completely bare of grass, stripped back by the stock to nothing but dust. The sheep lost condition, their bones beginning to protrude through their close-cropped wool. Water in the Serpentine was as precious as the gold so many had clamoured for a century before.

The seriousness of the drought was reinforced when Mervyn Hammer, head of the local volunteer fire brigade, came and addressed us at school, stressing how important it was to conserve water and the need for care when burning any household rubbish. 'Those hills are parched, beggin' for water. Creates a high fire risk,' he said grimly.

He kept repeating that phrase 'a high fire risk', his eyes circling the room, staring into the eyes of us all.

We echoed Mervyn's solemn warnings round the dinner table that night and offered to forsake having baths till it rained. Everyone laughed, except Jamie. Usually, he was the merriest one at the table but that night he was withdrawn.

As soon as dessert was over with, he excused himself and walked straight out the door. None of us could believe he hadn't rung Belinda for once. 'Perhaps it's all over,' my father said, echoing my own silent hopes.

I felt triumphant. Had Jamie finally realised Belinda's inadequacy? I wandered over to the window thoughtfully, wondering if I dared follow him over to his hut, uninvited, to offer my condolences. I looked out the window. I expected Jamie to be strolling soulfully away, perhaps looking back, hopeful someone was watching and wondering about the pain of his misguided love for Belinda. But he was doing nothing of the kind. He was walking very purposefully indeed. When he reached his hut, he flung the door open and plunged inside without bothering to close it. A few moments later, he reappeared in the doorway. In his hand he held the bucket my mother left over there for when she cleaned the place.

I stepped back behind the curtain. Ever since that night when I first realised Jamie was hiding something, I had spied on him from the kitchen window. He always went over to the woolshed. Unexpectedly, Jamie gave a quick, intent stare towards the house. It felt as if he was looking straight at me. Even though I was hidden behind the curtain, I lost my nerve and dropped down below the window. When I dared to look again, Jamie had disappeared. I couldn't concentrate on the television that night. I kept puzzling over what he could possibly need a bucket for.

The next day, over Saturday lunch, my mother mentioned that she'd been thinking about Mervyn Hammer's warnings. 'I've had an inspiration,' she said. 'These are desperate times and I'm going to do something for the district.'

She paused for effect. No one liked to ask what she had in mind. 'I'm going to divine for water,' she announced.

My father groaned and went into the lounge to watch the

sport on television. Jamie slipped out of the room saying he was off to Glenora. But Lou, Babe and I were fascinated. 'Everyone has the ability to water divine,' my mother told us. 'It's instinct. Animal instinct. Like the way a dog sniffs the ground before it lies down. A dog will never lie over water.'

She had Lou cut her a forked branch off the willow tree, and began stalking across the front lawn, her hands stretched out in front of her, clutching the stick. We watched sceptically from the balcony, but even from up there, we could tell when the stick began to dip in her hands.

'It's here, it's here,' she shouted triumphantly. 'It's very strong. I can barely hold it.'

Lou jumped off the balcony, even though she was always being told by my mother not to do that. Babe and I ran around the long way. By the time we got there, Lou had thrown the stick on the grass in disgust. 'Can't feel a thing,' she sniffed.

I picked up the stick. 'It's pure instinct,' whispered my mother to me. 'Just surrender yourself to the instinct.'

I shut my eyes and concentrated. I longed for something to happen. I'd always craved telepathic powers for myself like 'The Tomorrow People' on television. Water divining could be the first step in my development. Then I could advance to reading minds, Jamie's in particular. Unfortunately the stick was lifeless in my hands. I handed it reluctantly to Babe who had been clamouring for it during my attempts to concentrate. As soon as she grasped the stick, it began to twitch. She stared at it in terror and disbelief, then began to cry. 'Make it stop,' she sobbed. 'I don't like it, make it stop.'

Lou grabbed the stick off Babe, irritated that she could do something she couldn't.

'Junior,' my mother called to my father. 'Are you coming down here to dig up this spring I've found?'

'No,' came the reply from the Lazy-Boy Recliner Rocker chair.

'This is a drought and we need more water.'

'We don't need a spring in the middle of our front lawn. If you want to be useful, go down to the ten-acre paddock and see if you can find a spring down there. It's a helluva problem that there's no stock water in there.'

'I think a spring on the front lawn might be attractive.'

'It'd turn into a bloody bog.'

Then the phone rang and he cursed it. Even from out on the lawn we could hear him muttering to himself as he went to answer it, how he was never left in peace on his afternoon off, how Grampy always rang purposefully just as the match was about to kick off. We all stood there, listening to him talk, trying to decipher if it was Grampy and wondering if my father would hang up on him again like he had the previous Saturday. We all heard his voice snap out of its gruffness into urgency. Then the phone was slammed down and my father ran out onto the balcony, his eyes wild, straining out at the horizon.

'What's wrong?' asked my mother.

My father was intent on the hills opposite. He didn't answer. I wasn't concerned. I presumed he'd heard a bad weather forecast and was getting dramatic about his hay. But the next thing he did made me think again. He jumped off the balcony, just as Lou had a few minutes before. 'Jack, what's going on?' asked my mother, concerned.

But he didn't pause to explain. He was off and running towards the front fence. He hurdled it. I had never seen my father behave so athletically. 'There's a fire out in the hills behind Sampson's,' he called back at us over his shoulder.

We all turned to look in the direction of Sampson's but the trees that ran up from the road hid the view. It was those trees my father ran towards. My mother began to clamber over the fence and that was the signal for us all to do the same and hurry after my father. I arrived last. I always did when something involved running. My parents, Lou and Babe all stood there by the fence, under the pine trees, silent and staring. Sure enough, smoke rose up from the hills. My father swore. 'Buckets. We never have any damn buckets.'

Buckets were a subject of contention in our family. My father was always stealing my mother's wash-house buckets and taking them down to the cowshed to calve a cow or perform some other equally bloody operation. Inevitably, the cow would stand on the bucket and break it, or my father would forget about it and just leave it there. My mother took to painting 'return to wash-house' on every bucket she bought. My father got the message and the buckets did come back eventually, usually splattered with shit and blood and the occasional afterbirth. My mother said she despaired of buckets. Sometimes I helped her hide them from him.

'Why are there never any bloody buckets?' my father demanded.

No one bothered to point out the obvious. He sighed. 'Well, we'll just have to take what we can. Reeb, pack some food, and something to drink. I could be out there for a while. Kids, run and grab as many sacks as you can find and soak them in water in the wash-house.'

Then my mother remembered the bucket over at the hut. 'Billy-Boy, run over to Jamie's hut and bring back the bucket I leave over there. It'll be under the sink. And don't touch anything else.'

It was perfect. Jamie had driven off while we were all out on the front lawn. I ran with all my might over to his hut. I went straight to the sink and opened the cupboard beneath it. No bucket. I scanned the room. Checked under the bed. It was nowhere to be seen. I wandered about the room, looking for anything different or new, took a good long look at the photo of Jamie and Belinda and was about to leave when I noticed Jamie's clothes, the shirt and jeans he'd been wearing the day before, lying discarded on the floor. I picked them up and went through the pockets. I was looking for any clues as to what he might have been doing the night before. But there was nothing unusual about them. If anything they were just a bit dirtier and smellier than usual. There was a distinctive smell about the shirt. I picked it up and gave it a serious sniff. There was that familiar Jamie smell but there was also something else. It smelled like smoke. I clasped it to my face and inhaled. It was definitely smoke. But it didn't smell like the cigarettes Jamie sometimes smoked. It was more like the incense my mother burnt occasionally and my father complained about. Jamie had been burning something with a fragrance. Perfumed letters from Belinda? Maybe it truly was over.

I felt delighted by the thoroughness of my investigation. Not that it explained anything but a clue was a clue even if it was an enigma. I almost felt like confiding in Lou but that was a fleeting thought. I would never share any secrets about Jamie with her. She would find a way to use it to her own advantage. Carefully I rearranged his clothes on the floor and stepped outside.

I walked briskly back over to the house. Lou and Babe were in the wash-house. Lou was explaining to Babe how the sacks she was soaking in the sink would be used to beat back the burning tussock. 'I'm going to ask Uncle Jack to take me to help,' she declared and Babe's eyes shone with admiration.

Then Lou noticed me standing in the doorway. 'Here, help Babe carry these down to the truck,' she commanded as if she was Mervyn Hammer and in charge of the whole fire-fighting operation.

I said nothing. I had half-expected her to question me as to why I'd been so long. Babe and I carried one dripping sack at a time down to the truck and heaved them onto the back. By the time we'd lugged them all down we were as wet as the sacks. Then my father charged out of the house, dripping wet as well. He had stepped under the shower fully clothed. We all stared at him. 'Just a precaution,' he grinned.

Lou changed her mind and didn't ask to be taken along after all.

My mother appeared in the back doorway and thrust a packet of sandwiches, a thermos and a bottle of lemonade at my father. She stood there, shrouded by the dangling plastic fly-screen, watching as we walked my father down to the truck. 'If you're not back by dinnertime, I'll bring some more food out to you,' she called after him.

'Okay,' said my father, waving.

He climbed in behind the wheel and started the truck, grinning at our serious faces. He reversed and then ripped straight into second gear and was off down the drive, a trail of water from the sacks staining the gravel as he went. We all stood there for a while, staring at that trail. Finally Lou said, 'Let's go and see if it's got any worse,' and bounded off.

Babe and I followed. For most of that afternoon, we sat out by the trees, watching the smoke rise up from the hills behind Sampson's. It was spellbinding. Once we saw some flames shoot up into the air, startling us all out of our trance. 'I hope Daddy's alright,' murmured Babe.

Occasionally, my mother drifted out to watch for a while and offered the news she'd heard from talking on the phone: that there were over fifty men fighting the fire and two tractors with ploughs trying to dig wide fire breaks in the difficult tussock land. When the sun began to sink lower in the sky, becoming lost in the smoke's haze, my mother hurried back inside to start cooking some dinner to take to the men. The smoke was beginning to choke up the sky. We could smell the ash in the air. The firefighters didn't seem to be making much of an impression.

There was the most magnificent sunset that night, the smoke fuelling its glory. The hills and clouds were stained a fiery orange. When the sun vanished from view, the hills continued to glow orange. In horror we realised they were alive with flames. We ran inside screaming to tell my mother. She was standing by the front door, the telephone still in her hand, staring into space. Our appearance snapped her back to reality and she hung up the telephone. She nodded distractedly when we told her what we'd seen. 'I know,' she said. 'Now, Aunt Evelyn and I are taking some dinner out to the men. We may have to stay out there and help. Okay?'

We all nodded. 'Your dinner's ready now. Serve it up for me will you Billy-Boy. And go to bed if we're not home by nine o'clock.'

She started to walk back into the kitchen, then suddenly she stopped and turned back towards us. 'By the way, have any of you seen Roy Schluter today?'

I must have blushed. I felt myself growing hot. Lou and Babe were saying no and somehow I shook my head as well. My mother's eyes seemed to be fixed on me. 'Why?' asked Lou.

'He's missing. His mother hasn't seen him since lunch-time and she's started to get worried that he's gone up to look at the fire.'

'He's always wandering off,' said Lou. 'We've seen him before wandering round on a Saturday, haven't we Billy?'

I mumbled a yes but my mother wasn't paying attention. She'd hurried back into the kitchen and was putting some last-minute things into a big carton. 'Lou, can you take this down to the car for me? And Billy, serve dinner up before it gets cold.'

Lou seized the carton and my mother followed her out the door. I served dinner but none of us felt much like eating it. Afterwards even the television couldn't distract us. Lou kept running out to the trees every quarter of an hour to check on the fire. On her third mission she came running back inside, shrieking that there was a car coming up the drive.

'Is it Daddy? Is it Daddy?' squealed Babe.

'It's driving too fast to be Uncle Jack,' said Lou.

I knew it must be Jamie. I ran outside to check. It was him. 'There's some dinner going if you want it,' I yelled.

'Okay,' he called back.

I went back inside. It was odd that he was back so early on a Saturday night. 'Have you come home to help fight the fire?' I asked when he strolled into the kitchen.

'What fire?'

I couldn't believe he hadn't noticed the flames, smelled the smoke in the air. I was speechless.

'Where's this dinner then?'

I took it to him and he seized his cutlery, ploughing into the food. He was behaving very oddly. I wondered if he was drunk. 'Are you going to fight the fire too Jamie?' Babe asked.

'Nah,' he said, his mouth full of mashed potato.

'Even Aunt Evelyn's gone to fight it,' Babe said in awe.

'Well I'm sure she'll have it under control in no time,' he said with a laugh that sounded vaguely mocking.

He had to be drunk. He wasn't himself. I took Babe away from him, back into the lounge room to watch television. 'Why won't he go and help?' Babe whispered fiercely.

I didn't know what to say. 'Because . . . he wants to stay here and look after us. In case we get scared.'

With that Babe did begin to get scared and started to cry.

'What if Mummy and Daddy don't come back?'

I had to get Lou, her hero, to come and calm her down. Jamie was slumped at the table, legs stretched out, the plate scraped clean in front of him. 'Do you want to come and take a look at the fire?' I suggested.

Jamie got to his feet, a little unsteadily. 'Naw. Maybe later. I'll just go and see if there's any rabbits about.'

My face must have shown my disbelief. A sheepish look stole across his face and he stared at the floor for a moment. When he looked up again, he had that endearing grin stretched across his face. 'Then I'll come back inside and we can have that game of cards you've been after.'

Jamie winked at me and wandered out the door. I started stacking up the plates, keeping an eye out the window to see where he went. Lou darted back into the kitchen. 'Do you reckon he's had a fight with Belinda?' she said.

I didn't want to discuss Jamie with Lou. I shrugged.

'He was acting weird,' she persisted.

Beyond Lou, out the window, I could see Jamie walking briskly over to the woolshed. I watched him until he disappeared out of sight. I decided to follow him. It was something I'd often considered doing, yet never actually dared to. That night was different. I relished the risk involved. Maybe it was the excitement of the day. The threat of the fire. Something had gotten into me. My confidence was high and it was a cinch to get away from Lou. I offered to do the dishes by myself if she'd keep Babe distracted. She agreed immediately.

Once she'd gone back into the lounge room, I sneaked out the front door, and started running towards the woolshed, congratulating myself on my deviousness. My sense of triumph quickly waned. The evening was so menacingly dark. There was a full moon but it gave out only a ghastly glow, smudged by the smoke in the air. The dogs howled as

I passed near their kennels. I hoped Jamie would put their outburst down to the moon. When I drew close to the woolshed, I stopped and hid by the trees, listening for any sign of him. I must've waited there several minutes, before I heard him. He began to whistle, then sing a few lines of some song. He was no David Cassidy. I crept forward, following the sound of his tune, eerie in the gloom of the night. There were a couple of fences I had to negotiate as silently as possible.

As I drew closer to the woolshed, I realised he wasn't actually inside, but was doing something out behind it. Cautiously, I approached the corner of the shed and peered around. There was a light emanating from the old long-drop toilet, glowing through the cracks between the weatherboards. I knew it must be a torch. That toilet was primitive. There was no light. No flush. No one had used that toilet in years. Even the shearers for whom it was intended, shunned it. Last time I'd looked inside there were thistles growing up out of where you were supposed to sit.

What could Jamie possibly be doing? The only thing I could think of was that he had a stash of dirty magazines in there. But even that seemed unlikely. It would be an unnecessarily awkward hiding place. Whatever he was doing, he wasn't using the toilet conventionally. Suddenly Jamie backed out of the toilet, his face revealed in the light of his torch, frowning in concentration. Hastily I stepped back round the corner of the shed. I heard the door of the toilet thud shut and then Jamie's footsteps retreating, his boots retorting on first one and then the second wooden fence as he heaved himself over. Satisfied that he was on his way back to the house, I crept forward to investigate.

The moon seemed sicker and dimmer than ever. I had to edge forward carefully. Behind the woolshed was the parking spot for various farm implements but despite my caution I tripped over a set of harrows. Getting back to my feet, I didn't feel so sure of myself. I began to wish I'd brought Lou along with me. Once I stood in front of the toilet, I began to feel downright scared. Anything could be inside. I cursed myself for not bringing a torch. Finally I crept away, feeling a coward but telling myself I'd return in the morning.

I was about to climb over the first fence when suddenly I had a change of heart. I tore back to the toilet, yanked the door open but kept on running away, too scared of what might possibly emerge to even glance inside. I only stopped running when I reached the safety of the shed. I pressed myself against the corrugated iron wall, panting, my senses all frantically alert. Everything was still. Nothing stirred from within the toilet. I waited a full minute, and then reassured I tentatively approached it, slowly drawing closer and closer until my toes brushed up against its crude foundations.

It seemed that the thistles had completely claimed the toilet. It was full of them. Then I noticed my mother's bucket on the floor. I picked it up. It was half full of water. I stood there hopelessly looking from the bucket to the thistles. It made no sense. The wind lifted, banging the door back against the side wall. Perhaps the wind also stirred the smoke clogging the atmosphere for as I peered into the toilet I seemed to be able to see a little better. I could make out a silhouette of the plants against the back whitewashed wall. They weren't thistles. I stretched out my fingers gingerly to check. There were no prickles. These plants had rough crinkled leaves. The dogs barked again. It meant Jamie was nearing the house. I slammed the door shut and began to run. I was disappointed. I had expected to find something forbidden. It seemed all I'd stumbled upon was some sort of dreary agricultural experiment.

Jamie was standing by the front door as I approached the house. It gave me a terrible start for a moment. Had he realised I'd followed him? Was he waiting to confront me? But as I got closer, I recognised his posture. He was using the telephone, calling Belinda. I felt a flare of jealousy which helped me march past him with more confidence. 'Just been checkin' on the fire,' I said, as I ducked to get under the telephone cord that barred the door.

'It's okay. I've finished,' said Jamie, replacing the phone. 'No answer.'

He followed me back into the kitchen. Immediately, Lou bolted out of the lounge room. 'Where've you two been?' she demanded.

'Just out to look at the fire,' I said.

I waited for Jamie to explain his absence but he said nothing. Instead he began stacking plates in the sink.

'You've been gone a while,' Lou persisted.

I shrugged. Lou continued to frown at both of us suspiciously. 'Well don't think I'm going to help with the dishes,' she finally said and flounced back into the lounge.

Neither of us spoke as we did the dishes. When we'd finished, Jamie muttered something about trying the phone again. But within thirty seconds he was back. Still no answer.

The game of cards wasn't a success. No one could concentrate and Lou kept running outside to check on the fire, holding up progress. At ten o'clock she could still see flames. 'Time for bed,' Jamie announced.

We all howled our protests. 'We can't sleep when the fire's still burning,' said Lou.

Babe began to whine. 'I'm scared. Why aren't Mummy and Daddy home?'

Jamie stared at her helplessly. Suddenly, I had an inspiration. 'Maybe if you sleep over in the house Jamie, Babe'll feel better. Knowing you're here if she gets scared in the night.'

'Would you like that Babe? How 'bout I sleep over here?'

Babe nodded and began to smile through her tears.

'I'll go and check if the bed's made up,' I said and sped out of the room.

I danced along the passage to my bedroom. I was so thrilled at the prospect of Jamie spending the night in the house. In the spare bed. In my room. My mind was dancing too, anticipating the night ahead. I would watch him get undressed. Completely undressed. I was certain he slept nude. I'd never seen any pyjamas under his pillow when I'd been over in his hut. My mother never seemed to hang any out on the clothes line for him. I imagined myself getting scared in the night and creeping into bed beside him. Would I dare to do it? Was I too old to do that sort of thing? If I'd been Babe's age it would have been easy to get away with.

The bed was made up. I hurried into the bathroom. It would be a disaster to miss out on Jamie undressing because I had to brush my teeth. I gave them a quick flick, rushed back into the bedroom and threw off my clothes. I didn't want Jamie seeing me undressed. I was fatter than ever. I pulled on my pyjamas. When Jamie finally knocked gently at my door, I was in bed, pretending to read. 'Come in,' I said.

Jamie edged into the room, looking a little startled at the posters all over my walls. A shirtless David Cassidy loomed over the bed he was to sleep in. 'I thought you were David Cassidy when you first arrived,' I confessed.

I wanted to establish an intimate atmosphere. Jamie grinned, raising his eyebrows. He took his shirt off and preened beneath the poster, flexing his muscles. 'You reckon?'

Suddenly, there was a quick knock at the door and before

either of us had time to respond, Lou had thrust her head into the room. 'Just checking you don't need anything,' she said, exiting again before either of us had time to reply.

Jamie closed the door firmly after her but the moment was lost. The atmosphere ruined. Typical Lou. Jamie sat down on the bed and began to pull his socks off. 'You're having a quiet Saturday night,' I said, trying again.

I'd worked out that if I was having a conversation with him, then I had a good excuse to be looking at him all the time, rather than sneaking glances. 'Yeah, I guess,' said Jamie.

He was browner than ever. I was growing hard beneath my bedclothes. 'How come you're not seeing Belinda tonight?' Jamie stood up and turned his back to me, undoing the button on his jeans and then unzipping them. 'She's busy.'

I wished I could've seen his face as he said that. He was wearing purple jocks. They slipped down on one hip as he stepped out of his jeans, exposing the beginnings of one starkly white buttock. I was desperate for something to keep the conversation going and for Jamie to keep undressing. 'Belinda's so pretty,' I said wildly.

Jamie seemed to hesitate, his fingers on the elastic of his jocks. He turned round to face me. I was aware of the bulge just slightly below my line of sight. We were having a conversation and I had to look him in the eye, although I longed to look elsewhere. 'She's dissolute, Billy. Just like you told me ages ago. Dissolute.'

I didn't know what to say to that. He gave a sad little chuckle and climbed into bed, distracted, *without taking off his underwear*.

'G'night,' he said.

I turned off the light. 'G'night.'

I had no intention of sleeping. I planned to lie awake all

night, imagining what *might* happen given our situation. Staying awake was better than sleep where my dreams twisted and turned nonsensically. Their outcomes always left me frustrated. To simply listen to Jamie's breathing as he drifted into sleep was the perfect accompaniment to the fantasies that began to stir in my mind.

I craned my face towards him, as close as I dared, and felt the sigh of his breath on my face. I closed my eyes, basking in the sensation. Warm and masculine. A sweet, smoky odour clinging to it. The regularity of his breath was hypnotic, lulling me, soothing me. It seemed to whisper messages. Enticing me. Inviting me to cross the small gap that separated our twin beds. I swooned forward, lost my balance and half fell out of bed. Quickly I righted myself and lay absolutely still. In the other bed, Jamie grunted, rolled over and turned his back on me.

I lay there willing him to roll back the way he was. He didn't. After a while, I decided I preferred him facing that way. It would be easier to fool him when I slipped into his bed. I would don my cow tail and creep beneath his sheets, alongside him. In the dark, in his drowsy state, the sensation of my ponytail brushing against his back would be evidence enough for him to mistake me for Belinda. He would welcome me, embrace me and by the time he realised his mistake, would be utterly lost in the sensation of my skin upon his.

Then I remembered that he had fought with Belinda. He might spurn her advances. Perhaps he would welcome comfort from someone else. I could pretend to have had a bad dream, a nightmare about the fire and need comforting. We could hold one another, each of us confiding our fears. Or I could pretend to sleepwalk, thrust my arms out in front of me as I'd seen it done on television and stumble into his bed. I could remain in my trance and he could do anything he liked with me. Or maybe I could go to the bathroom and then come back and get into the wrong bed 'by mistake'. Once I was there, Jamie would confess his own mistake in loving Belinda.

I must have been almost asleep. Those wild dreams cackled through my mind, sweeping me along, urging me to act. I was vaguely aware of my foot slipping out of the bed, compelled there by a rhythm of its own, as if engaged in a dance to which it knew the steps instinctively. My toes touched the cold linoleum floor between the two beds and a tantalising shiver ran through me.

At that exact same moment, reality exploded in my ears, shattering everything. The silence. The mood. The seduction which had seemed so assured. My leg dangled out of bed betraying my intentions but I couldn't will it back beneath the blankets. My muscles had crumpled. I knew I couldn't possibly have heard what I was certain I had. I must've been dreaming and spooked myself. But Jamie was stirring and muttering from the other bed. He had been startled awake. Which meant it couldn't have been a dream.

Then the second gunshot exploded, echoing through the rooms of the house, overwhelming any lingering doubts, destroying all reassuring explanations. There was someone outside. Concealed by the night. Stalking me, with a gun. I jerked my foot off the floor, clutched my blankets to my throat and began to scream.

13

Someone loomed over me in the dark. It was a presence I could sense rather than see. Then a hand clamped down over my mouth and a voice began to hiss in my ear. I couldn't understand a word. The gunshots still echoed in my head. They'd taken on a life of their own, reverberating again and again, as if the sound was somehow trapped between my ears, ricocheting back and forth, confounding my senses. Suddenly I knew this was what it must be like for Judy, lost in space. Utter darkness. The unknown. And fear rising up in her like an erupting volcano. I knew those gunshots had been intended for me. A warning. I must not contemplate sin.

I screamed the way Judy screamed when she was confronted by aliens. I screamed for help, screamed for Don and fought against those hands that tried to restrain me. They were the hands of an alien, cold and cruel. It had me gripped by one shoulder, the other hand over my mouth. Cold alien flesh against my lips. I bit the hand as hard as I could until I felt the bone against my teeth. The voice swore and the hands dropped away. I knew I had to get away but escape seemed impossible. Those hands were relentless in their pursuit, grappling at me amongst the confusion of the bedclothes. I wriggled and kicked and scratched. Alien breath panted in my face from the exertion of trying to contain me. Alien breath that smelled of smoke. I shuddered. It was the alien that could breathe pure bolts of flame.

Suddenly the door burst open and some sense of reason began to seep back into my consciousness. I was in my bedroom, in my own bed. But if this was the intruder bursting through my door, who was I struggling against? I squinted at the alien in the dark. Its grip weakened when the door opened and I pulled away, diving beneath the covers. I strained against the mattress, willing my bulk to disappear into it. The bedsprings were wrecked, giving the bed a considerable slump and I prayed that it might be significant enough to conceal me in the darkness of the room. Then I felt somebody tugging at my blankets, trying to wrench them up. I fought back viciously, even more frantically than before, kicking out with both feet. I had no doubt now that this was the person with the gun, who wanted to expose me, expose the evidence of my lust, the hardness between my legs, which despite my terror was refusing to wane. In fact, it seemed more excited than ever.

I fought until I recognised what was being said. Someone was calling my name, over and over. A familiar voice, a comforting voice, drowning out the echo of the shots. It was Lou. I peeked my head out of the top of the blanket and immediately Babe scuttled beneath the blankets beside me, clinging to me. Lou turned the light on. Jamie stared at me, dazed, sucking his hand. There were raised red swellings across his torso from my struggles with him. He looked at me with an expression torn between astonishment and annoyance. Of course, it had been him trying to quieten me down. Somehow I had forgotten him.

'He didn't realise it was you, Jamie,' Lou explained. 'He thought it was . . . '

She didn't finish the sentence. We all knew who she

meant. Jamie snapped the light off. 'Sshhhh,' he whispered. 'Listen.'

We huddled together on my bed, straining to detect any sound, any clue to the presence of the intruder in the night. But there was nothing to be heard, except the panting breath of our communal fear. Outside, ominous silence reigned. We crouched there in the dark, clutching at one another. The pressure of our fingers expressed our fear more eloquently than words. Finally, we heard the sound of a vehicle and everybody tensed.

'It's alright. It's your parents,' Jamie said with relief. 'It's a car coming up the drive, not going away.'

We all listened. It did sound like the family car. But despite his confident tone, Jamie didn't seem entirely convinced. He didn't rush out to greet the car but lingered by the window, peering out into the darkness. We all waited to hear it park in the garage. Then we would know without a doubt. But the car didn't glide into the garage. It stopped short of it, not quite at the top of the drive. The engine rattled off into silence but the headlights continued to loom out into the night, casting light up high on my bedroom walls.

Then the voice rose up, cutting through that dead silence. An unearthly chilling voice. Surely a voice that could not be human. A cry of anguish, desolate and mournful. Simultaneously, Lou, Babe and I lunged forward to cling to Jamie. I clutched his knee cap, weeping into his calf muscle. He bent over us, patting our hair, whispering for us to be quiet, but there was no hushing us. 'It's an alien,' I sobbed to Lou and she nodded her agreement.

It was only when our sobs had subsided, that I recognised there was a pattern to the sound. A word was being repeated over and over again like an incantation. But no matter how I strained to hear I couldn't make sense of it.

Then we heard the front door creak open. We all gasped

in unison, the fingers that had relaxed, clutching one another harder still, pinching. A light went on somewhere in the house and then, unbelievably, thankfully, we heard my mother's voice calling our names, plaintively, as if she was uncertain of where we'd be. Jamie hurried out of the room, calling out to her, reassuring her that we were here and alright. The three of us hurried after him.

My mother stood pale and dazed by the front door, which she had neglected to close. She had turned the kitchen light on and moths had swarmed inside and were flitting around the light bulb. My mother seemed oblivious to them. Usually, she couldn't bear moths. Ever since Nan died, she'd detested the sight of them. Grampy's house had been filled with them, the night Nan suffered her stroke. In his hurry to get her to the hospital, he'd left his front door open. The moths had streamed in. Seeing them now, in our home, made me shudder. I knew something was terribly wrong.

My mother had one hand on the telephone as if she was about to use it. She stared at us, her eyes distraught as we ambled forward out of the hallway shadows, blinking into the light. The sound outside hadn't stopped. Standing there, with the door open to the night, there was a horrible clarity, almost a familiarity to the sound. We were so close, it shivered across my skin. We were all waiting for my mother to say something, to explain, but it was as if she had been rendered mute.

Lou stared at her, frowning, struggling to comprehend. Then suddenly she was gone. Out the door. My mother's hands flailed hopelessly after her, as if to retrieve her but they clutched at nothing and though her lips moved, no sound escaped them.

'I'll go after her,' said Jamie in a low voice and he followed Lou outside.

I watched him disappear into the dark and felt a pang of

loss. I wanted to be with him. Not left there with my mother. I couldn't bring myself to look at her. Not when she was in this dishevelled state. It was too disturbing. She cleared her throat as if she was about to speak and I fled out the door after Jamie. The darkness and the unknown seemed preferable to whatever she was about to say.

The concrete path was cold on my bare feet. Jamie and Lou stood a few yards ahead of me on the path, obstructing the view. I could see the car. It was stopped almost at the top of the drive, abandoned, the doors wide open, the headlights illuminating something slumped in the driveway. I had to step onto the grass to see past Lou and Jamie, to see for myself what lay beyond. There was a dew. On my toes it felt like . . .

Blood.

There was so much of it, as if the entire driveway had been paved over in slick red asphalt. It flowed out of him where he lay in the centre of the driveway. Seeped out of the great gash in his throat. My father knelt beside him. The blood soaking into his pants as he cradled that great head, studying the awful wound there as if the explanation for how such a thing could have happened was somehow buried deep within. He was dead of course. Shot through the skull and then his throat slashed for good measure.

My father must have sensed he was being watched. He looked up, his eyes awash with tears and the wailing died in his throat. Now that I saw him stretched out there dead, I could recognise the word my father had been repeating over and over. It was his name of course. Dante.

There was utter silence for a moment and then the dogs chained up at their kennels burst into crazed howling.

'Come inside Jack,' a voice croaked behind us.

We all turned. My mother was standing by the door, her arms cradling herself. 'Come inside. We can't do anything until morning. Just come inside. Leave him be.'

In the end Jamie had to help my father to his feet. My mother hovered by the door as Jamie half-carried my father up the path to the house. 'It's the shock and the exhaustion,' my mother explained to Jamie, 'from fighting the fire. He's half-dead on his feet. Billy-Boy give Jamie a hand.'

I got on the other side of him though I was too short to be much use. My father seemed glad to have me there though. 'Poor old Dante,' he muttered to me.

I had to turn away from him. His breath was rank. I knew that smell, not that I'd ever smelled it so bad before, especially not on my father. He was drunk. My mother had walked ahead of us into the house. 'Have a bit of a celebration after putting the fire out, eh Jack?' said Jamie.

My father nodded, grinning sheepishly. 'Someone's killed me best bull, Jamie,' he slurred. 'Me best bull.'

We got him inside. 'Put him in his chair,' said my mother. 'Don't worry about the blood. It's vinyl. It'll sponge off tomorrow.'

We heaved him into his Lazy-Boy chair and he rocked back and forth for a few moments. We all stood round staring at him. He was filthy. There was black ash smeared all over his clothes and even across his face. He smelt of smoke and spirits and blood. My mother stared at him grimly for a moment and then beckoned us all into the kitchen. She closed the door after us. 'Leave him be. Maybe he'll doze off for a bit.'

'He's had a skinful,' said Jamie.

My mother frowned at Jamie. 'What happened here?' she asked.

It was the sort of voice Aunt Evelyn used on us in the schoolroom. Jamie seemed to recognise that tone too. He stared at his feet and shrugged. 'There was a gunshot.'

'There were two gunshots,' I corrected him. 'You didn't hear the first one. It woke you up.'

Jamie nodded. 'Okay, two gunshots. Someone shot the bull.'

'Then cut its throat,' Lou added.

Now Lou was the object of my mother's forbidding stare. 'I think you children had better all go to bed.'

That remark created a commotion. Babe began to cry, saying she was too scared, and Lou protested over Babe's noise, practically shouting. It stirred my father in the lounge who started muttering away to himself. 'Me best bull,' he said mournfully over and over. 'Me best bloody bull.'

My mother hushed us all. She smiled, a strained effort but still a smile. 'Let's all have some supper,' she said, 'and calm down.'

She brought out some lemonade from the fridge and a bottle of beer for Jamie. She even had a glass of beer herself out of Jamie's bottle. When we'd finished she had Jamie help her get my father into the bath. Then she insisted there was nothing we could do that night and that she would report it to the police in the morning. In the meantime, she had Jamie go over to his hut to get his gun. 'Just for peace of mind,' she said.

Jamie disappeared into the night. A few minutes later he was back, shivering from the night air, his eyes bewildered. 'It's not there. The door of the hut was wide open, banging in the wind, and my gun's not there.'

My mother digested this information. 'So he's used your gun to do this.'

'Or she,' whispered Jamie, his eyes wide and staring.

My mother's expression tightened but she said nothing. All of us were silent, thinking of Belinda Pepper and her wild impetuous ways. I considered this new possibility. It did seem more likely that Belinda could be responsible than some vengeful gun-wielding alien. Finally, my mother sent Jamie out to the workshop to get my father's gun. 'Put it under our bed. And make sure it's loaded,' she called after him.

Lou and Babe heaved their mattresses into my parents' room and stayed in there that night. Jamie opted to spend the rest of the night in my bedroom. As soon as we were alone together, I started to apologise for my hysteria earlier, but he hushed me, not giving me the chance to say it properly. 'I just wanta sleep Billy.'

His smile was the wannest I'd ever seen it.

He didn't sleep. His breathing never resumed that easy rhythm. He just lay there. I couldn't sleep either. My paranoia returned as soon as the lights were switched off. The longer I lay there awake, the more convinced I became that this menacing act had been directed at me. Finally, after what seemed like hours of lying awake, I recognised the feeling of unease that nagged me. It was the same way I'd felt after the scuffle in the rugby changing rooms. This was another act of senseless violence. Or was it? The more I thought about it, the more likely it seemed that there was a deliberate plan behind it. My parents were away at the fire. Jamie should have been in Glenora for the night as he usually was. I lay there, drowsy, my mind running through a line-up of possibilities.

I was almost asleep when I heard something that startled me awake. Instantly awake. Jamie had crept out of his bed. I began to tremble. He was coming to me. I had to concentrate with all my might to lie still. In all the scenarios my mind had conjured up, I'd never dared hope that he might come to me. I felt like throwing the blankets back in welcome, jumping up and down on the bed for joy. But I had to restrain myself. Such a response was far too forward. I lay there modestly, shyly, waiting . . . for the touch that never came. Jamie crept out the door instead of into my bed.

A few moments later, I heard the rattle of the plastic fly-screen on the back door as he walked through it. Jamie had gone outside. I got out of bed and went to the window. I couldn't see him. Cautiously, I tiptoed out of my bedroom, out to the back door and stared out into the night. He didn't seem to have gone to the hut. There was no light on there. Abruptly, the dogs all barked in unison giving me a terrible shock. I went back to bed. I knew where he'd gone. 'Rabbit shooting.' I fell asleep almost at once. I was vaguely aware of him slipping back into his bed, some time later, in the depths of the night.

I jumped when Lou shook me awake the next morning. Maybe I even gave a little scream because I woke Jamie up. He gave an exasperated grunt from the other bed. Lou was fully dressed. 'Get up,' she hissed. 'We're going to investigate the scene of the crime for clues.'

She tiptoed from the room, silently signalling me to get out of bed at once. I glanced across at Jamie but he had rolled over to face the wall, pulling the blankets over his head. Obediently, I got out of bed and dressed as quietly as I could. Lou was waiting impatiently by the front door for me. Babe stood beside her, beaming with pleasure at being included in such an important mission. 'Right,' said Lou. 'I'm Julian. Who do you want to be?'

Both Lou and I adored 'The Famous Five' books. We'd been pining for years to have adventures of our own. 'I'll be Anne,' I said at once.

'Okay. Babe, you can be Timmy the dog,' said Lou rather unkindly.

We both expected her to run away and complain to my mother but instead she looked up at us angrily. 'But we've got seven dogs, any of them could be Timmy.'

There was no answer to that. Babe got to be Dick seeing

as she'd made such a smart reply. Lou marched out the door, urging us to follow. We trailed after her, opting to stand at a respectful distance from Dante's stiff and sunken carcass. Lou insisted on inspecting him close up.

It was strange seeing Dante lying there. My father had always said he'd have to die on the place because he was too big to fit up the ramp to the truck. All the other bulls got sent off to the freezing works to be slaughtered once they'd passed their prime. Dante stayed even though he was the oldest bull on the farm and quite lame. It was Grampy who noticed he'd lost some condition and suggested he might now fit up the ramp. So he and my father tried. Grampy was right. Dante had lost weight and would've fitted up the ramp if he'd been inclined to walk up it. But he was too smart for that. No matter how much he was pushed, poked and electronically prodded Dante wouldn't budge.

'He's got hay in his mouth,' Lou announced triumphantly. 'Someone lured him out of his paddock with some hay. I bet we'll find a trail of it from the front paddock to here.'

Babe was sent to confirm this hypothesis. Lou circled the dead bull, rather like a bird of prey about to take a mouthful. She was examining his rear quarters when she gave an abrupt grunt and began pulling at his tail. She approached me, a grim expression on her face. She held her hand out in front of her, clasped tightly, something concealed within her grasp. She stopped in front of me and made me hold out my hand. I knew she was going to drop something disgusting into it, a turd or a bit of shattered brain. I closed my eyes, not wanting to look but not brave enough to refuse her. But it was something light and delicate that fluttered into my upturned palm. I opened my eyes in surprise. It was a piece of worn red ribbon.

Lou was staring at me angrily. 'Your father won't think that's funny. Especially if he's hung over.'

I nodded dumbly, my mind racing, trying to make sense of this vital clue. Of course I recognised it. It was the ribbon off my own cow's tail, not that I could remember losing it but obviously I must have. I strained to remember when I'd last taken it anywhere.

'Get away from there.'

My mother stood on the balcony, hands on her hips, staring down at us angrily. 'Come inside now. Leave it alone. The policeman's on his way. Come inside and eat your breakfast.'

Lou and I walked obediently up towards the house. We were almost at the door when suddenly I remembered. I must have given a gasp because Lou stared at me intently. 'What?' she asked sharply.

I fumbled for an excuse. 'Babe,' I finally said. 'We've forgotten Babe.'

I broke away from Lou, running down the path calling to Babe but my mind was reeling from the sudden realisation. The dead bull lay there before me, so white against the dull red of the blood-soaked gravel. I knew where I must've lost the ribbon. I knew who had killed Dante. I knew without a doubt. The ribbon had been tied as a sign for me, so that I alone would know.

Roy Schluter.

But what did he mean by the ribbon? Was it a warning? This time a bull, next time me? Or was Roy claiming the tail of the dead bull for himself? Was he trying to tell me he wanted a tail too? That he wanted to be like me. I stood there staring at Dante and began to cry. I tried to convince myself that it was impossible that Roy could have done such a thing, yet as I looked at the slaughtered bull and felt the slippery sheen of the ribbon between my two fingers, I knew with a gripping certainty that Roy had to have been responsible.

When Babe clasped my hand, I jumped. 'I found a trail of hay,' she said proudly. 'Just like Lou said. And the gate had been left open. I shut it.'

'Well done,' I muttered, wiping my tears away.

Together we walked up the house. I knew I wouldn't be able to eat. I felt sick from what I now knew.

As soon as Constable Hubble arrived, Lou dashed outside to tell him about the trail of hay. Sitting at the breakfast table, we could hear Hubble exclaiming outside, 'Is that so, Louise? Really?'

Then my father reeled into the kitchen. My mother had obviously roused him out of bed. I could see his pyjama jacket beneath his bush shirt. He went out and brought Hubble inside and sat him down at the table with a cup of tea. 'Now then,' the policeman finally said, after a sip of tea.

Lou began to speak but my father silenced her with a forbidding stare. 'Jamie, tell the constable what happened.'

Jamie explained. I sat there twisting the ribbon in the pocket of my shorts as Jamie spoke in terse sentences, prodded along by Constable Hubble's questions. When the constable could provoke no more information out of Jamie, he sighed and turned to the rest of us. 'Anyone got anything to add?'

I stared at the bowl of cereal I couldn't bring myself to eat and said nothing. I couldn't confess what I knew. To tell would inevitably mean telling a lot more than I would want to. Roy knew that. Knew I wouldn't tell because it would mean explaining things that were too forbidden. I sat and prayed for the policeman to be gone.

My father walked Constable Hubble down to his car. They stood outside by Dante for several minutes talking quietly. Lou sidled over to the window trying to overhear, but my mother noticed and ordered her to start doing the dishes.

When my father returned, he was in a real temper. My mother offered him some breakfast and he snapped at her. 'It's all because of you this has happened. You and those bloody weird things you do on the balcony. That's why they've killed my best bull, to give you a fright and make you stop. Entwining yourself into those unnatural positions. It's bizarre and people don't like to see it happening in front of their own eyes.'

We were all astonished by his outburst. Finally, my mother broke the shocked silence. 'They can't see me unless they're watching me through their binoculars.'

'Well people are always looking through binoculars checking on their sheep and so on, and they don't like being startled by coming upon you. It's provocative. I can imagine someone wanting to shoot down such a spectacle.'

Jamie excused himself to use the phone. We all knew he was trying to phone Belinda. 'I mentioned her to Hubble,' my father said in a whisper to my mother. 'Told him it'd be worth his while to talk to her.'

The phone was slapped down. My father raised an eyebrow but said nothing. Jamie slouched back into the kitchen. 'Is it okay if I go into Glenora?' he asked my father.

'Actually, I'm going to need your help for a few hours this morning. We have to dispose of the bull.'

I presumed that Dante would be given a burial. I think we all assumed his carcass would be treated with great dignity. It wasn't.

Maybe it was because my father was hungover. Or maybe he was ashamed by his behaviour of the night before and was trying to atone for his hysterics by proving he could be cold-hearted and thrifty. Whatever the reason, he asked my mother to sharpen his knives. My father intended to skin Dante and chop him up for dog tucker. What was even worse he expected us to help him do it.

Jamie obeyed sullenly. Lou went pale when my father told her to make a start on Dante's massive back leg. Babe fled in tears to her bedroom and I would have liked to have done the same. Only the dogs were enthusiastic. They had been howling all morning at the smell of blood in the air. My father shouted at them periodically but it didn't quieten them for long. 'They're going to enjoy their dinner tonight,' he chuckled to Jamie, who merely grunted in reply.

Finally, Dante was skinned, his head severed and thrown down the offal hole. It was easier to think that it wasn't Dante once the head was gone. It was just meat. We hung it by its back feet to the tractor's front forks and then lifted it up in the air over the offal hole. But the carcass was so huge that even when the forks were as high as they'd go, the front legs still rested on the gravel. Lou sat in the tractor, operating the hydraulics. She had to constantly raise the forks as the weight of the carcass kept pulling them down. I looked away when my father slit the stomach open but even the sound of the guts spilling out in a great rush was bad enough. 'Do you want Dante's tail then Billy-Boy? It's longer than the other one you've got.'

I couldn't answer. The tail went down the offal hole with the guts. My father had me wash the carcass down with the garden hose. Then he and Jamie took it in turns, standing on a ladder and sawing through the backbone with a gigantic saw. I had to hold the carcass steady. Up in the cab of the tractor, Lou was grinning at me. 'We need a chainsaw for this job,' my father joked, but neither Jamie nor I laughed or even smiled.

Grampy arrived just before the carcass had been divided into two. He stood there watching. There was a grim smile on his face. My father gave an almighty grunt as the saw severed the last of the bone. The two halves swung back and forth wildly. Grampy limped forward. Maybe his damaged forth wildly. Grampy limped forward. Maybe his damaged leg was giving a special twinge as he watched one of the 'white beasts' being cut up.

'Hubble came and saw me this morning,' he said tersely.

My father didn't even glance at him. He was busy explaining to Jamie how each side should be divided, where the cuts should be made. 'Yeah?'

'Seems you named me as the prime suspect in the murder of this here white beast.'

My father turned to face Grampy. 'I said no such thing.'

'Well you must have said something because he came and asked me what my movements were last night.'

'All I said was . . . he asked me if there was anyone I could think of who would do such a thing.'

'And you named *me*.'

'I was joking. Hubble knew that. Besides it's true. You always hated my cows. You were the first person, the only person I could imagine who'd do such a thing.'

Grampy snorted and turned away, walking stiffly up to the house. He'd be going to give my mother an earful over a cup of tea. I was sent off to find as many old sacks as possible. Half an hour later, Dante was finally laid to rest. Chopped into manageable pieces, bagged up and stowed in the dog tucker freezer.

'That was gruesome,' said Lou, as we washed our hands afterwards before going inside for morning tea.

Jamie didn't join us. He got in his car and drove off without having a shower even though he was covered in blood. He returned a few hours later, looking worried, but no one dared to ask him what had happened.

We found out the next day. Velda Pile rang with the news. Belinda Pepper hadn't turned up for work at the boutique and Julie, having heard about 'our incident' (the entire Serpentine county had heard about it within twenty-four hours) sent the constable round to check on her. There was no answer to the repeated knockings. Eventually, with the help of several curious next-door neighbours, they forced the door. Belinda was gone. But in the ashtray next to her bed, Constable Hubble found the remnants of a marijuana cigarette.

The flight of Belinda inspired a flurry of unlikely stories. Velda insisted she was a key figure in an international drug ring. Marcia Pepper claimed she'd flown off to enter the Miss New Zealand contest. Tracey Ingham put it about that her throat condition had proven to be incurable, had spread into her brain and she'd gone mad, hence her antics with the shotgun. While the bowling club ladies were certain that *this time* she must be pregnant and had left town overcome by shame and remorse.

The constable came back to the farm to question Jamie, commandeering the kitchen for the interview. The rest of us sat in the lounge, with the television volume turned right down so that we could hear. We were all shocked to learn that it had been Belinda who'd dumped Jamie.

'She'd bought a ticket to Sydney and she just told me she was going. Just like that. No warning. I said I'd come with her, just as soon as I got the money, but she said she couldn't wait. Belinda always wanted to do things straight away. As soon as she'd decided on something, she had to go and do it.'

'And did you know she smoked marijuana?'

'What's marijuana?' I asked.

'Sshhh,' said my mother and father in unison, but it was too late. Jamie's answer to that particular question was lost in their hushing of me.

'It's drugs,' whispered my father sternly. 'And you're never to touch it, do you hear?'

'What does it look like?'

'It's a plant.'

'What sort of plant?'

'I don't know.' My father was exasperated. 'We don't have it in the Serpentine thank goodness.'

But that wasn't accurate at all because they'd found it at Belinda Pepper's place, and I knew where she'd gotten it from. I slipped out of the room. No one noticed. Everyone was too preoccupied listening to Jamie describe the fight he'd had with Belinda and how he'd tried to rip her airline ticket in half.

I ran over to the woolshed, all the way without stopping. But the closer I got to the toilet, the more convinced I became that I was too late. Sure enough, when I opened the toilet door, there was nothing there. It was gone. Just when I'd discovered what it was. That was what Jamie had been doing in the middle of the night.

But had he moved it and hidden it somewhere else? Or had he destroyed it? I opened the door wide and got down on my hands and knees. That was what 'The Famous Five' would do. They would look for clues. I even peered down the long drop. It smelled as though it had been used recently and I retreated hastily. There were no clues. The plants had been removed and Jamie had swept the toilet clean.

I wandered back to the house. The policeman was about to leave. Jamie had to drive into Glenora with him to identify a shotgun that had been found carelessly hidden beneath some leaves behind the old gaol. The location of the gun confirmed without a doubt what I knew. Roy was responsible. Lou tugged at my arm, rousing me out of my thoughts. 'It's the perfect opportunity,' she said. 'We're going to search Jamie's hut for clues.'

We waited until Jamie drove off after the police car and then we bolted over to the hut. While Lou was only looking vaguely for clues, I knew exactly what to search for. I checked his toilet and all around the back of the hut. There were no plants. I walked back into the hut and checked under the sink. The bucket was back where it belonged. Then I thought to look in his ashtray. It had been wiped clean. Lou had gone through everything else she could think of. Under his mattress. In his shoes. Through all his cupboards. All his pockets. 'He's gotten rid of the evidence,' Lou announced. 'He must've guessed that the policeman would come back.'

We were just about to leave, when I thought to look in the rubbish bin and there it was. Not exactly a clue, but certainly something significant. It was the photo of Jamie and Belinda that had been stuck to the mirror. Neither Lou nor I had noticed that it was no longer there. Now it was torn into pieces. Quickly, I fished them out and stuffed them in my pocket. I didn't want Lou to see and requisition the pieces as evidence. Later, I patched it together so that I had a photo of Jamie. The bits of Belinda I burnt.

14

My father arranged for a truckload of gravel to be dumped on the driveway where Dante had lain. Several days had passed but the blood was still discernible. It clung to some of the stones. There was an unmistakeable rusty red patch. Visitors, and there were lots of visitors that week, were fascinated by that patch. Some of them even took photographs of it. Desmond Sully, the local councillor, arranged for the county grader to come and spread the gravel, free of charge. 'For what you've all suffered,' he said as he ushered the grader up the driveway.

Once that gravel was smoothed into place, my parents seemed more relaxed about what had happened. They started talking again. Prior to that things had been tense. My mother had taken to doing yoga on the balcony whenever any callers dropped by. This was to spite my father for his far-fetched accusation the morning after the incident. My father would hastily direct the visitors' attention to the blood stain, hoping it would be fascinating enough to distract any interest in my mother's contortions. When the gravel was dumped on top of it, this strategy was lost to him. He had to apologise. Babe and I eavesdropped on the apology. 'Fine,' said my mother. 'Apology accepted. Now you can apologise to your father. He is boycotting

Christmas dinner because of what you did to him.'

My father said nothing to that and he said nothing to Grampy either. Their feud continued. Grampy avoided our place and it was at Aunt Evelyn's that I saw him for the first time since that morning. He took me aside and told me very seriously that he'd changed his will and was leaving his farm at Crayburn to me. I would have liked to have said 'please don't' but it didn't seem like a very polite response.

The feud between Grampy and my father became common knowledge round the Serpentine. It fuelled the speculation about the incident, a speculation which ran even more rampant than for any of the Belinda Pepper scandals. To her shame Aunt Evelyn appeared to revel in discussing our family's misfortune. She was in the perfect position of authority. She was family by marriage, not immediate family. There was just enough distance between her and us for people to feel comfortable about ringing her to comment on the various theories that circulated. Aunt Evelyn made sure my mother heard all of those theories. 'You more than anyone else have a right to know what they're saying,' Aunt Evelyn insisted, sweeping into our kitchen three days after the shooting, a casserole dish stretched out ceremoniously before her.

My mother lifted the lid of the casserole and grimaced. I knew it had to be beef stew. 'Really Evelyn, you needn't have taken the trouble . . . '

'A death is a death,' Aunt Evelyn said. 'Everyone rallies round at times like these. It's a tradition to bring food and verbal comfort.'

'It was only a bull,' said my mother.

Aunt Evelyn's voice dropped to a penetrating whisper. 'Yes, but it was murder.'

According to Aunt Evelyn, the most popular theory behind the shooting was that my mother was responsible. 'They say you were persuaded by members of that vegetarian sect of yours to assassinate the bull, as a sort of protest against eating meat,' said Aunt Evelyn, giving a short laugh to emphasise how ridiculous she found it, though her eyes were sharp, watching my mother closely.

'Really,' said my mother in a tight voice.

Aunt Evelyn quickly hurried on to outline the other prime suspects. Grampy of course, who everyone knew had hated the Charolais ever since he was maimed by one. But my father was ascribed a motive as well. 'They say the bull was a dud. Defective in the privates,' said Aunt Evelyn. 'And that Jack shot him for the insurance money. Was he insured?'

My mother replied that she had no idea.

After Aunt Evelyn left, I was instructed to take her stew and feed it to the dogs. 'I'm sure they'd appreciate some variety,' said my mother. 'They'll be eating nothing but Dante for the next few months.'

A few days later, when Constable Hubble let it be known that he had some important questions to ask Belinda Pepper in regard to the incident, Aunt Evelyn came straight over. I think she hoped to corner Jamie and interrogate him, but he made himself scarce when he saw her coming. She discussed this latest development with my mother instead. 'But what could her motive have been? I'd believe anything of Belinda Pepper but she still had to have a motive.'

Aunt Evelyn pursed her lips, something she always did when she was perplexed. 'Do you suppose it could have been for love?' she mused. 'Love can arouse violent passions.'

She clapped her hands, clasped them together and gave a triumphant sweeping stare about the room. She had decided upon the motive. Yet she floundered to provide the circumstances to back up her theory. In the end she gave up but let it be known around the Serpentine nevertheless that

Belinda had been driven by forces of passion. People gasped and clamoured for further detail, but Aunt Evelyn would say no more. She would sigh as if it was too tragic for any further elaboration. She left it to their imagination, perhaps thinking someone might come up with a plausible scenario where she had failed to, which she could then verify as true.

All the locals were relieved that the blame had been allocated. No one wanted to contemplate the possibility that there was someone in the district with a grudge and a good aim. Everyone agreed that Belinda's sudden departure implicated her. It was the act of a guilty woman and though there were lingering doubts, Belinda's reputation was already so tarnished, it hardly seemed to matter if yet another crime was added to her list of sins.

Jamie refused to discuss Belinda with anyone. He hid from Aunt Evelyn whenever she turned up. I never learnt whether he believed Belinda was responsible. I did bring it up with him once and assured him that I knew she hadn't done it. I thought I'd win his confidence by saying what I presumed he wanted to hear. But he ignored my remark and I didn't persist. I knew he still thought about Belinda. He gave himself away on mail days, when he'd come in all anxious and fever-eyed, hoping for a letter bearing an Australian stamp to be sitting, waiting, on his bread and butter plate. Babe and I watched the mail just as closely. A letter from Belinda would have been a major clue. We had been instructed by Lou to steal it if it was ever delivered. No letter ever came.

I had hopes that with Belinda gone, things could return to the way they'd been before Jamie met her, when it had just been him and me. All the signs were promising. He showed no inclination to go anywhere. He didn't speak to his mates from the pub on the phone. But he was distant with me and my family too. He didn't initiate conversation the way he used to. He never lingered once the meal was over with. He'd go straight over to his hut. He was withdrawn, his usual enthusiasm entirely absent. I felt like a wallflower at the school dance. Every evening I waited for Jamie to ask me over to his hut but all he ever said to me was goodnight.

Finally, I became so exasperated and so curious as to what he was actually doing over there on his own, that I crept over to his hut one evening when my parents were engrossed in a program on television. I didn't dare to look through his window. I kept at a cautious distance and waited, hoping he might pass the window, notice me and invite me in. But there was no sign of him. The only indication that he was even inside was the music softly playing and the occasional wisps of smoke that wafted out the window, caught and illuminated for a moment in the light of his bedside lamp. I guessed he was lying on his bed smoking, probably having a beer. It seemed depressing behaviour for someone who had previously been so cheerful and companionable. It was then I noticed that his stack of empty beer bottles underneath the hut had more than doubled. I felt like just barging in then and there and insisting on cheering him up. Once, I would almost have felt sure enough of Jamie to do exactly that, but at that point, after all that had happened, I no longer knew if I would be welcome. I had a feeling I would be sent away.

Christmas drew closer and closer. My parents talked about it constantly to Babe and me. They wanted to distract us, help us to forget what had happened and hoped that by never mentioning *that night* we would. Nagged by my mother, my father finally rang up Grampy and invited him to Christmas dinner. He didn't apologise but Grampy didn't refuse to come for dinner either. It was a truce of sorts.

It was easy for everyone else to forget about Dante. It wasn't their chore to feed the dogs. It was me that had to take the bags of meat out of the freezer, thaw them out, chop them up into smaller pieces and then carry them, weeping blood, to the dog kennels, a flurry of persistent flies in my wake. Dante was several months supply of dog tucker. Every evening the smell of him, dead, was all over my hands. I always scrubbed them furiously afterwards with heavily perfumed soap but the smell of dead meat seemed to linger somehow. I was convinced I could still smell it when I lay in bed at night, trying to sleep. The smell led me to think of Roy.

I struggled, just as Aunt Evelyn had struggled, to ascribe a motive. At first I was bewildered, even a little indignant. Why had Roy done it to me? I had been kind to him. Or at least, I had been kinder to him than anyone else had been. I was probably the closest thing he had to a friend at school. I believed that quite fervently at first. Then, I began to remember things, flashes of memory which rather eroded my virtuous image of myself. I found myself thinking about Roy more and more. I began to regret my failure to say or do something reassuring at those significant moments. I even began to dream about Roy, betraying him over and over again in more horrible ways.

Finally I had to admit to myself that I had begrudged him the basics of a friendship. I'd not only forbidden him to talk to me at school but even out of school, when we were alone together, I hadn't encouraged conversation. Such a secretive, silent friendship couldn't possibly satisfy someone who had no other friends. He'd never said anything as such, but there had been occasions when he seemed to indicate he had yearned for more. I had steadfastly ignored all of those hints.

I was haunted by the image of Roy, a forlorn figure, lost in clouds of choking dust, churned up by the wheels of the school bus on the gravel road. That was my last sight of him. Shame stabbed me every time I recalled that day. The school prizegiving. The day before the fire.

Quite a fuss was made of me that day. Everyone was

particularly nice to me. No one called me names. Everyone wanted me to be on their team when we played soccer at lunchtime. They all realised these were my last weeks at Mawera school. They were Roy's last weeks too but no one liked to ask what he would be doing. Arch had put it about that the Schluters couldn't afford to send Roy to a boarding school.

Roy sat on a bench by himself that lunchtime as he usually did. No one had ever bothered much about including him and that day was no different. I glanced over at him a couple of times and was surprised to notice that he was actually watching the game of soccer. Usually he was staring off into space, in some strange world of his own. But he was watching, even frowning with concentration. Each time I glanced over, he was looking right back at me. I should have signalled him to come and join in. It did occur to me but I dismissed the idea. It was prizegiving day. Everyone was being so nice to me. I didn't want to spoil it. Lou set me up for a goal and I actually managed to kick it in between the posts. Everyone came up to me cheering and telling me what a great goal it was. I avoided looking over in Roy's direction for the rest of the game.

At three o'clock, the teacher made Roy and me stand up and gave a little speech about the two of us. I was flushed with pride and pleasure only to have those feelings slowly wane the more the teacher spoke. For he lumped Roy and me together as if we were equals. He spoke of us as if we were both equally brilliant, had both been the most exceptional pupils to ever pass through the school, were both assured of being placed in the top-streamed class at secondary school the next year. The brutal truth was that these praises belonged to me and me alone. That dull, blundering Roy should be classed alongside myself filled me with a cold fury at the injustice of it. Roy at least had the decency to recognise that for himself, for after a few moments, he relinquished the teacher's eye and stared down at his desk instead, growing redder and redder with every compliment.

But I blamed Roy. He had ingratiated himself with the teacher somehow. I didn't look at him when the teacher finished his speech though I could feel his humble eyes upon me. I barely glanced at the book the teacher gave me as my prize. I muttered a thank you and turned, hurrying away to be caught up in the camaraderie of my classmates, jostling and teasing me over what had been said of me. Everyone knew Roy was undeserving of sharing what should have been my glory. Everyone said as much to me. Roy was ignored, left to plod along behind our joyful little mob as we swept outside to the waiting school bus.

When the bus stopped at the drive to the Schluters' cottage, everyone fell silent. Roy always sat at the front of the bus by himself. No one wanted to sit beside him. He stood and turned to face us all. Perhaps he meant to say goodbye but then lost courage at the sight of our hostile faces. He said nothing. A violent blush stole up his pale cheeks and I felt a surge of bitter pleasure. He was ashamed and so he should be. I wondered if he would apologise and he did seem on the verge of saying something (sorry? goodbye?) but the redder his face became, the more difficulty he seemed to have in getting the words out. Finally, he gave up, snatched the hood of his parka and pulled it forward over his face as if to hide it. He plunged out the door of the bus.

No one called goodbye. Peter Hore yelled 'good riddance' once the bus had started off again down the road. Someone else commented that it was just as well he didn't blush very often because it made his pimples look even worse. I stared resolutely ahead. I wasn't going to wave but as the bus neared the corner that would carry us out of view, I turned to look back. He stood there in the middle of the road, that morose skinny figure barely distinguishable through the dust, plaintively waving. I lifted my own hand in response, though I knew it was hopeless. We were too far away, and the back window of the bus was too dust-encrusted for my farewell to possibly be glimpsed.

I never had the opportunity to say goodbye to Roy. The Schluters left the district suddenly. They packed up and were gone, just a few days after the fire. Various stories circulated as to why. Some said there had been a fight between Old Man Sampson and Mr Schluter about time off over Christmas, such a busy time of the year with hay-making. Someone else said it was over money. Old Man Sampson was so notoriously stingy. But Lou heard Aunt Evelyn telling someone on the phone that it had been the boys who had fought, that Roy had pummelled Arch almost to death. But Roy had always been so quiet and introverted that no one believed that story.

Roy became an enigma. He vanished and the opportunity to understand him vanished with him. Once he was gone, I found myself thinking about him more than I ever had before. Tormenting myself over how badly I had treated him but also remembering fondly the things we'd done to one another. I even began to remember him as being quite handsome and rather than strange, he seemed shrouded by alluring mysteries, mysteries that I wanted answers to. I had to know why the Schluters had left.

But I never got to see Arch, the one person who could tell me if he deigned to. With the Schluters gone, Old Man Sampson kept Arch out of school to work. It was unthinkable for me to phone him and bring the matter up in a roundabout way. It would have been too out of character. It had to happen casually. I'd despaired of ever learning the truth when one day in Glenora, just a few days before

Christmas, I bumped into Arch. He was in the newsagents, reading the comics. My heart gave a lurch. I sidled up to him, hoping to rekindle that mood that had prevailed on prizegiving day.

'Doing your Christmas shopping?' I asked.

Arch turned and I knew at once it was hopeless. He merely looked bored to see me. 'Nah,' he said, returning his attention to his comic.

There was a silence and I couldn't think of anything else to say. Then Arch closed the comic and put it back on the rack. 'My mother took me to the doctor,' he said quietly.

I studied him. He looked okay. Why had he been to the doctor? Was it possible that Roy really had beaten him up? I couldn't see any bruises, but then, Arch was wearing jeans for once, instead of his usual shorts. I hesitated to ask him about Roy. I was scared of somehow implicating myself by seeming interested. 'You alright?' I asked.

'Yeah, I'm okay.'

'Having to work hard, now the Schluters have gone?'

I was pleased with that question.

'Schluter was bloody useless,' said Arch hotly. 'Better off without him. I had to do all his work all over again after he'd made a mess of it. As for the Freak . . .'

Arch snorted as if that summed him up. I waited for him to continue but he didn't seem inclined to. 'What about him?' I finally asked.

'He was a bigger freak than we all thought, that's what,' Arch said and he bent back over the rack to pull off another comic.

It was then that I noticed. There was a big clump of his hair missing, right on the top of his head. He had a bald spot, glaring white, the vague outline of the bone prominent beneath. I must have gasped because Arch looked back at me. He gave a rueful sort of smile, tenderly touching where his hair should have been. 'Yeah,' he said. 'The Freak had a secret side to him.'

'Did he do that?' I gasped.

Arch shook his head. 'No, he didn't do that but he did something far worse.'

Now I wanted Arch to stop. He knew somehow. He knew what Roy had done to Dante. But it was too late to stop him. Arch began talking quickly, impulsively. 'He started that fire up behind our place. I found a box of matches in his pocket along with a packet of his mum's smokes. An' when I asked him about it, he just laughed. This real evil laugh. He started that fire alright but no one will believe me.'

I nodded my head. I believed him. I felt too sick to speak but Arch didn't need any encouragement to keep talking.

'I told my father an' he went over to Schluters swearing blue murder, accusing the Freak of ruining all our hill country. Schluter got all stroppy. I could hear them from half a mile away swearing at each other. Anyway Dad came back in an even fouler temper. Schluter quit on him. Refused to work another day. Dad was livid. The hay was cut, ready to bale. He needed him. So he took it out on me. Said it was my fault he'd lost his worker when he needed him most. Said I'd made that story up and deserved a thrashing.'

Arch lifted up his shirt. There were thick welts all over his torso. 'He set to with a dog collar. Beat me with it. Beat me till my hair came away in his hand. That's how he was holding me. By the hair.'

I shuddered.

'But the pain wasn't the worst part. The worst part was looking up and seeing the Freak, standing off a ways. Watching. You know, I wasn't sure about the fire till then. It was just a hunch. But seeing the Freak and the look on his face, so . . . gloating, I knew, just as if he'd admitted it aloud. It was written all over his face. He hated us. Hated me. Hated my family. I knew he was capable of anything.'

'Did you tell your father . . . ?'

'I don't talk to him no more. I won't talk to him till he apologises. Though I reckon he don't even remember half of what he did. Oh he knows he hit me but he was still half-blind from the night before. The big party we had at our place after they put the fire out. It was still going on when the sun came up.'

We said nothing for a few moments. 'Wish I was going away to boarding school like you next year. Wish I could go early,' said Arch wistfully.

I wanted to tell Arch what else Roy had done though I knew I mustn't. I stood there hesitating, unable to think of anything to say that could provide comfort. In the end, I said nothing, but picked up a comic myself and we stood there side by side at the counter, reading, until Mrs Sampson appeared in the doorway, calling Arch away, refusing his entreaties to buy him a comic. I put the comic back. In truth I hadn't read a word of it.

It never occurred to me at the time. It was only years later, as many as five years later, that it dawned on me, the obvious explanation for Roy's behaviour. I hadn't thought of Roy in a long time. It was what I discovered at the very bottom of the freezer that reminded me. It was the very last bag of Dante.

Ice had claimed the bag. That was why it was still there. It was frozen to the side of the freezer and no one had bothered to dislodge it. Being the dog tucker freezer, no one had bothered to defrost it either. I had to chip away at the ice with a spade to free it. I had no other choice. There was no other dog tucker left. My father had done his back in and couldn't kill a sheep for the house let alone the dogs. I knew he was secretly pleased by those circumstances. He hoped he might pressure me into making the kill for him, something I had refused to do for years.

Finally, after much careful chipping, I was able to pull the bag free. I heaved it over my shoulder and carried it to the killing shed to thaw. It all came flooding back to me. That night when Dante was slain and for some reason those words of Aunt Evelyn's, the theory she had concocted, *she did it for love*. That sentence rolled through my consciousness like a wave, building in connotation and portent until it broke upon me, the startling possibility, that perhaps Aunt Evelyn hadn't been entirely wrong, merely ascribed the motive to the wrong person.

Perhaps Roy had done it for love.

It was such a staggering thought that I lost my grip on the sack I was carrying. Had Roy loved me? It was ridiculous. I had been such a sight at that age. It was hard to imagine anyone falling in love with me, fat and bespectacled as I was then. I picked up the sack and continued on to the killing shed. But once the notion had entered my head, it was impossible to dismiss it. The more I thought about it, the more possible it began to seem. We had done intimate things to one another. We had kissed, caressed, made each other come. We had done what we knew people in love were supposed to do. We were so young. Perhaps Roy assumed that to do such things meant we were in love and that I loved him back. He was so lonely, so reviled. Perhaps he was desperate enough to fall in love with someone as unattractive as myself. Perhaps looks were unimportant to him or perhaps he managed to see me the way I saw myself, through the haze of a childhood fantasy, beautiful like Judy.

I had stopped walking, absorbed in my thoughts, the sack of meat was burning cold fire into my back. But I deserved the pain. Whether Roy had loved me or not was likely to remain unknown. What was undeniable was that I had treated him cruelly.

15

My parents were particularly insistent that we should spend a lot of time rehearsing for our Christmas Eve concert that year. My father even gave us time out from the hay-making which was unheard of. It didn't take a genius to work out why. They thought our rehearsals were a wonderful distraction from *that night*.

Our concert was something we'd been doing since we were very young. We always entertained our parents and Grampy the night before Christmas. It had developed over the years from a few Christmas carols on the veranda to plays that I devised and which tended to lack any Christmas theme whatsoever. This was a deficiency Aunt Evelyn could never tolerate.

Aunt Evelyn always tried to take over our concerts. She had guided us through our early efforts and despite our obvious reluctance with every passing year for her 'direction', showed no sign of relinquishing her role. She insisted on attending our rehearsals, changing everything around and incorporating Christmas carols somewhere in the show. 'It's topical,' she would say, though we all knew the reason they had to be included was because she liked joining in from the audience.

Even if our play was set in outer space, where time had

no meaning and Christmas was unheard of, Aunt Evelyn would insist that 'Hark the Herald Angels Sing' must be the finale of the show. It was her favourite carol, as it demanded all those glorious high notes that she loved to linger over.

With our parents being so supportive of our show, we enlisted my mother's help in getting rid of Aunt Evelyn. We outlined an ultimatum. The show would only go ahead if Aunt Evelyn bowed out.

My mother did it as gently as possible. She said we wanted the show to be a surprise for Aunt Evelyn. She then went on to suggest that Aunt Evelyn's contralto was desperately needed to strengthen the golf club ladies in their annual excursion to Glenora Hospital where they sang carols to the patients. Aunt Evelyn, always the actress, accepted this rebuff gracefully and the only clue to her state of mind was the thoroughness with which she began to tidy Lou's bedroom. 'She's searching for our script,' said Lou.

We didn't have one. Without Aunt Evelyn around to insist on things being done properly, we dispensed with such niceties. Our performance was going to be more free form and contemporary yet still retain the all important 'topicality'. It was inevitable that the recent events, arguably the most sensational ever to have occurred in Mawera, would influence us in our choice of a suitable drama. We had decided to re-enact the slaughter of Dante.

The casting of the roles caused considerable dissension. Everybody wanted to be Jamie and no one wanted to be my father. In the end, we had to dispense with my father as a character. No one could recreate the awful noise he had made that night. I eventually agreed to Lou being Jamie, but only after she'd created a wonderful wig out of baling twine and sprayed it black with aerosol sheep raddle. I would be the villain of the piece. Belinda Pepper.

We practised our play behind the henhouse and tied one

of the dogs by the corner to warn us in case Aunt Evelyn should come prowling about. Within a week we were ready to perform it. Invitations were issued and Uncle Arthur, Aunt Evelyn and Grampy came up for dinner on the night of the show. After dinner, the adults all took their chairs outside and lined them up on the lawn opposite the back veranda. This was the traditional venue for our concerts. The veranda was raised up from the lawn and we always waited for the sun to go down, then turned the veranda light on, so that it gave more of a theatrical atmosphere to the evening. We also charged an admission of fifty cents for the same reason. It just made things so much more authentic and professional.

The play was entitled *Belinda Pepper: She Did it for Love.* It was Babe's job to walk out on stage, announce the title and then launch into her opening line after the applause subsided. She was bewildered when she announced the title and the audience failed to clap. She stood there waiting and waiting, despite our urgent whispers to continue regardless. Finally, she sidled off the stage. 'Why didn't they clap?' she asked.

It wasn't a promising beginning. Lou pushed her back onto the stage and I strode on after her. I sat down on the bale of hay which was centre stage and began to twirl strands of my long black hair round my fingers. Babe kept glancing between me and the audience, wondering if she might still be greeted with the applause she'd been denied. The audience remained implacably silent. She stood there biting her lip, her line forgotten. I jumped forward to my first speech.

BELINDA: Rodney. Rodney darling. Climb up the haystack and let me ply you with kisses.

Babe stared at me angrily. She had been cheated out of one of the few lines she had to utter.

BELINDA: Climb up my hair. The knots and tugs in it will serve as your steps.

From offstage, Lou began to quack. She was the sound effects. In between quacks she hissed at Babe to climb the haystack. Babe approached the hay bale and I twirled my pigtail at her provocatively. She failed to seize it as she was supposed to. She was sulking over her lost line. I yanked her up onto the top of the hay bale and grabbed her in a fierce embrace. I would have liked to strangle her for being so useless. Lou erupted into a frenzy of quacking and I gave Babe a push (rather harder than necessary) off the hay bale. She fell to the floor and writhed about, her moans much more convincing than they'd ever been in rehearsal.

BELINDA: Sorry Rodney. I could never be your nursemaid. I want a career in fashion.

Lou entered wearing a red cross armband and the two of us transferred Babe onto the hay bale and bore her off the stage. I re-entered.

BELINDA: I'm so bored in my new job already. I wish this shop had a menswear department.

Enter Lou as Jamie, wearing some clothes of his that we'd borrowed off the clothes line. There was an exclamation of recognition from the audience.

BELINDA: Hello sir. Can I help you?

JAMIE: I hope so.

BELINDA: What do you want?

JAMIE: You.

Belinda squealed with delight and ran from the stage with Jamie in pursuit.

Babe was sulking and refused to help me with my first costume change. Into swimwear. We'd cut up one of my old singlets, painted it and a pair of my jockeys brown, and then dabbed yellow dots all over the top of that. I hadn't been too keen on wearing this bikini and revealing so much of myself in front of an audience, especially Jamie, but Lou insisted it was vital to the drama. When I did actually put the costume on for the first time, with the wig, I was amazed by the transformation. From a distance, I really did look identical to Belinda Pepper in that photograph.

No one cheered or whistled when I made my entrance, as Lou had assured me they would. The silence was unnerving. I began to pretend to drown, and Lou as Jamie rushed onstage to rescue me and give me the kiss of life. I wished she could resuscitate the show as well. This was the romantic conclusion of act one and still no one had clapped.

'They're being very unresponsive,' I complained as I struggled out of the bikini offstage. 'This was our best costume.'

Lou peered out at the audience. 'I can't understand it. It's our most ambitious production ever.'

I joined her to peek out at the audience. It was impossible to see anyone's expression. It had grown so dark out on the lawn. But their silence and the way the men had their arms folded so rigidly across their chests, suggested a grim response. Then Aunt Evelyn leaned forward to stare at Jamie, and for an instant her profile caught in the light from the veranda and I could see that her lips were pursed in disapproval. That was a very bad sign. We had expected Aunt Evelyn to commend our originality.

'I thought your mother would like it at least,' I said. 'Seeing that it's a theatrical challenge.'

'It doesn't have "Hark the Herald Angels Sing" though,

so she wouldn't like it on principle,' Lou whispered back.

The beginning of act two was the dramatic climax of the play. Babe (playing herself) and Jamie entered.

BABE: I'm so scared that the fire will creep up in the night and consume us.

JAMIE: Don't worry, Babe. I've discovered where your mother hides her buckets and I've got them filled with water at the bottom of your bed. I'll protect you if the fire comes near.

There was a grunt from my father in the audience.

Enter Belinda.

BELINDA: Oh I'm so unhappy. I asked Jamie to marry me and save me from a life of drudgery selling pantihose and he refused. Now my life is shattered and there's nothing left for me to do but escape from my troubles by smoking a marijuana cigarette. I hope no one finds out.

Out of my pocket, I pulled one of Uncle Arthur's cigarettes that Lou had snitched. 'Light that and I'll tan your hide,' my father growled from the audience.

'I wasn't going to light it,' I sniffed back at him.

I put the cigarette in my mouth and mimed lighting it. I inhaled deeply, then again and again, more and more frantically with every inhalation. I became a woman possessed. I dropped the cigarette and began to screech and howl and tear at my hair.

BELINDA: I'm in a murderous rage. I'd like to kill him for rejecting me. Or kill one of those stupid animals whose company he likes better than mine.

Belinda dashed from the stage. We had draped a cowskin rug over Babe's tricycle and I pushed that onto the stage and then began to stalk after it, levelling Lou's slug gun to my eye. I took aim and fired.

SOUND EFFECTS: Kaboom. Kaboom.

Jamie and Babe began to scream in terror. Belinda stared dumbly at Dante.

BELINDA: Ohh, what have I done, while under the influence of a marijuana cigarette. I must flee the scene of the crime. I will flee to Australia.

Belinda ran screaming from the stage. Jamie and Babe crept forward to examine the dead Dante. Babe knelt down to stroke him and Lou made a non-scheduled exit. 'What are you doing?' I asked.

'It's not working. They're not clapping or laughing much,' Lou said desperately.

'They're not laughing or clapping at all,' I retorted. 'They hate it.'

One scene remained. The finale where Belinda sang 'Leaving on a Jet Plane'.

'Maybe you should sing "Hark the Herald Angels Sing" instead. At least then Mother will like it and it'll finish on a happy note for her. Perhaps they'll forget about the bits they didn't like.'

I didn't like this idea. It ruined the narrative which I had so carefully constructed. But after sneaking another look out at our silently sullen audience, I could appreciate the sense in Lou's suggestion. We had to redeem ourselves somehow. 'Okay,' I agreed.

I stepped out onto the stage and began to sing.

Hark! The herald angels sing,
Glory to the newborn king;
Peace on earth, and mercy mild,

God and sinners recon-ciiiiiiled.

Suddenly, my voice cracked, veering completely out of tune. I didn't know what had happened. I was the best singer in the family after Aunt Evelyn. I always performed the solos in our Christmas concerts and at school. Tentatively, I tried the line again but I couldn't make that final note. My voice wouldn't work with its usual grace and ease. I froze, humiliated. I didn't know what to do, how to save the show and myself. For once, Aunt Evelyn was showing a most untimely reluctance to join in and take over.

Then, from the audience, Jamie began to laugh. At first it was merely a slow chuckle. Then he rose out of his chair and wandered towards the stage, his laughter growing louder and louder. I watched him approach. He seemed dazed. He lurched a little as he walked, and was laughing so strangely. I sank to the floor. I didn't even have the will to walk off the stage.

'Don't . . . stop,' said Jamie, but he could hardly get the words out, he was laughing so much.

Suddenly, I felt scared of Jamie. He didn't seem like the same person. This laughter seemed maniacal, malevolent and laced with malice. It was the same laughter that I heard so often when I was teased in the playground, when names were hurled at me and everybody began to laugh and mock me. I wanted to shut him out, cut out this laughter that was echoing in my ears and jarring through every nerve in my body. Then the rest of our audience began to laugh too, the way people do, out of politeness, as if someone had told a joke, even if it wasn't particularly funny. But no one had told a joke. There was just me. On the stage. Bathed in the light.

Jamie tried to say something to me but it was impossible to hear over the clamour of mirth that he had aroused. He was still struggling to contain his own laughter, trying to be serious. I felt sure he had recognised the devastation on my face and was going to apologise. He had reached the edge of the veranda. He leant on it with his elbows, as if he needed the support, as if he was drunk. He looked at me and beckoned me to him. This wasn't the Jamie I knew and worshipped. Strangled by the shadows, his face seemed twisted and brutal, with this leering, mocking grin that I had never witnessed before. Still, he beckoned me to him. After so many weeks of what seemed like estrangement, finally he wanted me again. I crawled towards him, until our faces were only inches apart.

'Don't stop,' he whispered hoarsely and his voice gave out into a sneering laugh.

Then his voice dropped lower still and he said the words so that no one else could hear. 'I never realised what a perfect little poofter you are.'

I was stung. I sprang back from him, the words searing into me like a brand on my flesh. Jamie stood there, staring at me, as if I was some strange species, like something that the Robinson family might encounter in outer space.

Which I wasn't, I wasn't.

All I'd wanted was to look beautiful. Like Belinda. I remembered how Babe and Lou had looked at me, just before we were about to begin the show, with such a grave awe in their eyes. I felt transformed. That night I would be Belinda Pepper. A fierce beauty.

I sprang to my feet, commanding attention, fighting back the tears that threatened to undo me. I sprang onto the table, which had been too heavy to move off the stage, resuming the performance once more. I stood upon high, my mane of hair dangling in my face, my eyes gleaming with a menace of my own. Now I was the crone that Aunt Evelyn so often delighted in scaring us children with. I was a witch from

Macbeth. I was Abigail from *The Crucible*. I was revealing the unknown, accusing the unwary. I pointed my finger at Jamie as if I was inviting him to a duel and began to gabble out the words as if they were a spell.

'He gave it to Belinda. He gave her the marijuana. He was growing it over in the old toilet at the woolshed. He gave it to Belinda. It was him. It was him.'

I crumpled to the floor, the spirit that had taken possession of me spent. The accusation had been thrown out and like magic it went to work.

16

The following day was Christmas. It dawned with little prospect of joy for me. I was obliged to get up at five thirty in the morning and help my father bale the hay in the lucerne paddock. I stacked the bales into pyramids on the hay sledge while he drove the tractor. I resented every bale I wedged into place. My pyramids were short-lived. Inevitably they collapsed in a heap when I dispatched them off the sledge onto the cropped grass. I cheered to myself every time that happened. I was in a destructive mood. I watched the machinery swallow up the hay and contemplated throwing myself in after it. An agonising death. I would be gouged and pummelled to shreds. Yet the bloody spectacle of such an act seemed preferable to the silent, secret suffering of first love.

Lost love.

My father had put me in the tractor cab initially and stooked the hay himself. But my driving had been so erratic he made me get out and stook. 'It takes precision driving,' he said curtly, relieving me of the task.

I was too preoccupied. I failed to notice when I veered off-course and missed great rows of hay. I didn't hear my father's frantic yelling to get back in line. He had to jump off the sledge and run ahead, waving his arms to make me stop. I almost ran him over before I noticed him. My thoughts were elsewhere.

Relegated to the sledge, I had no time for daydreaming. The bales kept coming relentlessly, demanding my attention as they pumped out of the baler, threatening to knock me off the sledge if I ignored them. I longed for the string to run out or a shear-pin to snap so that we could stop, but for once the machinery worked efficiently. Usually, there was some breakdown, which drew everything out for hours longer than necessary. But not that day. That day, everything worked exactly, coldly, grimly.

Hay dust rose in the air and fell all about me. Great billowing clouds, stirred up by the fury of the machine. The dust was ubiquitous, irritating. It insinuated its way everywhere. It clogged my nostrils, caked my tongue, coated my glasses, then found its way beneath the lenses as well to nag at my eyes directly. It stuck thickly to the sweat on my face like ruined make-up. Bits of hay adorned my hair, lodged themselves down my gumboots, beneath my clothes. I took a piss and found a nest of straw in my underwear.

Once there had been a time when the flurry of dust and straw had seemed a frivolous thing. Jamie and I had tossed our heads back and laughed into it till we choked. It was confetti and I was his bride, grubby but smug. We worked the sledge side by side, taking a bale in turn, me struggling with the top one but determined to prove to him that I was his equal. He threw his shirt off and surrendered himself to the dust. 'It gets in anyway,' he laughed.

I studied him discreetly as we worked. We were too busy for him to notice my stares. Occasionally I brushed against him. Felt the graze of my skin upon his. Not often, not so that he would notice. Just fleeting moments. Brief shivers of sensation. If we turned a corner sharply I'd touch him as if to steady myself. The seemingly accidental was ardently calculated.

Once the glaze of his sweat wiped upon my arm and I licked it, tasted the salt of him on my tongue. I didn't want to speak after that and risk losing the tang of him. I lolled it round in my mouth while Jamie tried to joke me out of what he took to be a sulky mood.

Stooking the bales *alone* on Christmas morning was a cruel reminder of my loss. Jamie was gone.

I hadn't been able to sleep after the concert. We were all sent to bed in disgrace. I lay there listening to our parents discuss the situation, though Aunt Evelyn was the only one who spoke loudly enough for me to hear. 'I wanted to get up on that stage and close the show down,' she said at one point. 'I wanted to. But I couldn't. I was mesmerised by the sheer horror of it. I couldn't move a muscle.'

Finally, Uncle Arthur quietened Aunt Evelyn down and they drove home. My parents went to bed. Everything was silent. Except in my head. Tumult reigned there. What Jamie had said pounded at me again and again like relentless hay bales out of the machine. His words provoked so many questions and anxieties, but my overriding concern was the fear that I had alienated him forever.

Suddenly, I heard the garage doors creak open. I bounded out of bed. I knew who it had to be and what it must mean. Torn between the need for silence and for speed, I ran on tiptoes to the back door. It was often left open on summer nights to cool the house. I stood there in the doorway, hidden amongst the dangling plastic frenzy of the fly-screen and watched Jamie pack his belongings into the boot of his car. When he'd finished, he disappeared into the garage. A tear began to slide down my cheek as I waited for the engine to start. Another tear fell and still there was no sound. I listened closely. I could hear a grunt and then another grunt. Slowly,

I crept forward, down the path, ready to scuttle back inside if he should suddenly appear.

As I got closer to the garage, I realised what he was doing. He didn't want to start the engine and wake my father. Risk him storming down after him and making a scene. He knew all too well the sensitivity of my father's hearing. He was trying to push the car out of the garage so he could glide it silently down the driveway. But he couldn't heave it out of the garage.

I was debating whether I dared to sneak a look round the corner, when suddenly he loomed in front of me. We both gasped in surprise. I stood there, ashamed, not daring to look at him. I began to shiver in my pyjamas, not from the cold, but from the dread of what he might say to me. 'What the hell are you doing?' he finally asked.

The lie came to me easily. 'I came to give you a push.'

Jamie just grunted. He didn't even say thanks but turned back into the garage. 'Come on then,' he called impatiently from the depths of the garage.

I walked round the other side of the car and edged my way to the end of the garage. Jamie was already braced against the car waiting for me.

'Okay, heave ho,' he said.

I crouched and began to push. Slowly, the car began to inch backward. I pushed as hard as I could. I wanted to impress him this one last time. Though another part of me desperately wanted to apply the handbrake and beg him not to go. We cleared the garage and Jamie dashed forward and leapt into the driver's seat. He began to swing the car round so that he was facing down the driveway. I stopped pushing. Watched the car glide away from me. Jamie clambered out and began to push the car forward to get some momentum going, ready to jump back in at the last minute. I didn't move to help. I willed him to mistime things and leave it too late, so that his car sailed off down the hill without him and crashed. He wouldn't be able to go anywhere then.

But he timed it perfectly. He jumped into the front seat and slammed the door. He was leaving without a goodbye. Without a wave or even a word of thanks for giving him a push. I couldn't believe it. Instinctively, I began to run after him. The car had just begun to amble away and it was easy to catch up with him. His window was wound down. He looked round in annoyed surprise at me running alongside his car. I knew I must look a fright. Panting, desperate, tearful. 'What?' he asked testily.

Confronted by that impatient, aggressive look on his face, I was forced to acknowledge any hopes of him staying were doomed. There was nothing that could be said between us now except perhaps goodbye. Unless . . .

Suddenly, I knew what I had to say. Rather, what I had to ask. The enigma that had been puzzling me for months had finally poised itself on my tongue as a question. Jamie was leaving. I could ask him and it wouldn't matter so much what he thought of me. The car was moving faster and faster. I was breathless. I began to speak, but abruptly my nerve deserted me and all that came out was a sort of strangled moan. Jamie's expression became alarmed, a flicker of abhorrence in his face. He wanted to escape me. I knew what he was thinking. That my moan was a prelude to a declaration of passion. His fingers moved to the ignition keys. I knew it was my last chance and I snatched it.

'What's a poofter?' I asked quickly, recklessly.

His hand dropped into his lap. He stared up at me incredulously. 'What?'

I wanted to cringe, to cry, to disown the question. Yet at the same time that my doubts began to surface, I noticed a change in Jamie. Surprise had melted some of the grimness out of his face, leaving a vulnerability, a confused boyishness. The ghost of his jovial old self hovered there in his face. I felt a brief fierce flare of encouragement. I began to speak, my words an incoherent jumble. 'I don't know what it is. Whether I want to be one. It's a word that isn't in the dictionary. You said I was one and . . . and . . . I just don't understand.'

I couldn't say any more. I ran out of breath. All I could do was nod encouragingly at him, my eyes entreating. We were halfway down the drive, the car was moving faster and I was beginning to lag behind. Jamie turned away, bent himself over the wheel so I couldn't see his face. It was only then as despair set in that I noticed the pain in my bare feet. I was running on the gravel and suddenly every step was etched with pain. I was about to concede that I could no longer keep up with the car, when he gave a sigh and turned to face me.

'It's a homo. You know what that is?'

I winced and nodded. Jamie turned the ignition key. The motor began to hum. We were at the bottom of the driveway. Jamie jerked the car into gear. 'See ya,' he said, then his car jolted forward kicking up dust.

It was wrong to seize upon his words and cling to them as if they were an eternal promise. But I was so stricken with grief at his going, so wild with love for him, I couldn't help myself. 'I hope so,' I called after him and my eyes and nostrils and mouth instantly filled with dust.

It choked me. I bent over, coughing and wheezing and spitting until the taste of it was almost gone. It was a sign. I knew it. I should never have given voice to my hopes. When I'd recovered and could look up, the headlights of Jamie's car were far away. I watched them until they were lost from view altogether. *See ya* he'd said but his words were nothing more than convention. I knew I would never see him again. Ever. I began to limp back up to the house.

I went to my bedroom but I didn't go back to bed. Instead I pulled the cow's tail out of the drawer. I took it outside, holding it in front of me, pinched between two fingers, as if it smelt offensively. I tossed it into the incinerator where we burnt the rubbish. It gleamed whiter than ever against the black ashes. I had brought matches but suddenly I doubted that it would burn on its own. I would have to get a blaze going.

I ran back to my room. I knew what I would use to fuel the fire. I ripped down the poster of David Cassidy with his shirt off. It wasn't the sort of thing a normal boy had hanging in his bedroom. I couldn't believe that had never occurred to me before. It was best to burn it. I was about to leave the room when I remembered something else which should be burnt for the same reasons, a photograph I had kept hidden in my drawer with the cow tail.

I was glad it was dark. It meant I couldn't have a last look at it and lose my resolve. I took it outside with the poster. I screwed the poster up and threw it in after the cow's tail. Then I lit a match, picked up the photograph and held it to the tiny flame. The flame flickered and caught, illuminating the image as it began to consume it. The photograph was of Jamie. The one that I'd rescued from the rubbish bin in his hut and stuck back together with sellotape. Not that anyone would recognise it as Jamie. There was a piece missing. A vital piece. He had no face. Like one of those ancient Greek statues, the head lost somewhere through the centuries. I had mourned the absence of the face but now I was relieved. If it had been whole I doubted that I would've been able to burn it. The heat worried my fingers and I let go of the corner I was holding instinctively. It fell into the incinerator, the flame engulfing the entire photograph as it dropped from sight. Within a few moments, the poster had burst into a dancing blaze. I watched the fire until it died away and then crept back to the house, to my bed.

It was an odd coincidence to awaken the next morning to my father calling Jamie. I had been dreaming of him. I knew it as soon as I opened my eyes. I was annoyed to have had the dream interrupted by my father's unwelcome noise and as my irritation mounted, I suddenly realised I had lost it. The dream. It had been there just a moment before, hovering in my consciousness, waiting for me to drift back into it. But when my attention had been distracted, it had stolen away. All that lingered was the sense that it had centred upon Jamie and something significant had been about to occur between the two of us. I closed my eyes and strained to recapture the image, to lull it back. It was impossible. Outside my father's tone became terser as the prospect of having to walk over to the hut and rouse Jamie out of bed grew more inevitable. Then I remembered. Jamie was gone and with that realisation came a sharp stab of sorrow. I sank back into my pillows.

Gradually that aching sense of loss gave way to another emotion: indignation, and a conviction that I had been cheated. I had burnt my prized possessions as an act of redemption. Purged my poofter trappings, expecting my inclinations to have been destroyed along with them. But they hadn't been. My desires lived on in my dreams, betraying my new intentions. My sacrifice had been for nothing. I was still a poofter. I still loved Jamie. Only now I no longer had a photograph of him.

When my father returned from the hut, he was cursing Jamie and wishing an agonising fate upon him. He burst into my bedroom and ordered me out of bed. 'That long-haired git has snuck off in the night. I can't believe I didn't hear him. You'll have to help me with the hay. The forecast's for rain. Can you believe it? There's a drought, but it's going to rain today just when my hay's ready. No time to waste. Rattle your dags.'

It was five thirty on Christmas Day, and I had to make hay.

Lou turned up round breakfast time to relieve my father of the driving so he could go and eat. As soon as he'd taken off in the ute, Lou stopped the tractor, jumped from the cab and walked grimly back towards me. She knew Jamie was gone. I could tell. Her face was quivering with emotion. She opened her mouth to speak but the words failed to come. All the accusations she planned to fling at me, that simmered in her breast, clogged in her throat. She burst into tears.

I was stunned. Lou prided herself on never crying. I couldn't remember the last time she'd cried, it had been so long ago. Her tears were turbulent but quick. Merely a prelude to the full fury of her anger. She wiped them away with the back of her hand, sniffed and then pulled me off the hay sledge, pummelling me to the ground. 'Treachery,' she shrieked in my face. 'You've ruined everything.'

She pinned me to the ground, her knees wedged against my arms 'We had plans for next year, me and Jamie. Just the two of us. He was gunna let me use his gun. We were gunna go rabbit shooting together. He was gunna let me drive his car. He said I could be his adopted kid brother.'

Treachery? I couldn't believe she accused me of what she was guilty of herself. It was she who had betrayed me. Plotted secretly behind my back. Made marvellous plans with Jamie for the things they would do together when I was away at boarding school. She must have been counting down the days for me to leave. It almost pained me as much as the loss of Jamie. That Lou had behaved with such calculated disloyalty.

I was pleased to have unwittingly ruined her plans. Perhaps she saw that in my face, for her eyes narrowed in that shrewd, knowing way of hers. For a few moments, we simply stared at one another, the sudden rush of mutual hatred wavering against the weight of the companionable intimacy we'd known together for so long. Suddenly, she sprang off me and stalked back to the tractor.

We were making hay when my father returned. He kept glancing at the gloomy sky, muttering and swearing, and occasionally invoking Jamie as the cause of all his problems. Rain was inevitable, the unbaled hay would be ruined and it was all Jamie's fault. He relieved Lou of the driving and pushed down harder on the throttle. Lou went back to the house. There was no question of her helping me. It was a race against the elements. The bales spilled out faster than ever. But we couldn't beat the rain. I heard my father curse over the tractor's engine and guessed that the first drops had splattered on his windscreen. We still had a good third of the paddock left to bale. He kept at it for another ten minutes and then stopped the tractor. 'Damn rain,' he muttered.

He got off the tractor and surveyed the paddock, his face sinking further as he realised how few of the stooks were actually standing erect as they should have been. 'What a shemozzle,' he said. 'You can't leave the hay in such a state. The rain'll get into all those single bales. You'll have to stack 'em up Billy-Boy, protect 'em from the rain.'

I said nothing. I didn't even look at him. I couldn't believe he expected me to walk around the paddock for hours, restooking the hay by myself. 'I'll send Lou back with a parka for you so you don't get so wet. Maybe she'll give you a hand.'

I knew his concerns were inspired less by the rain and more by what the neighbours would think. He had a horror of the neighbours witnessing any task shoddily done. Unfortunately, the hay paddock was right next to the road. Everyone would see this monument to my ineptitude. 'It won't take you long,' lied my father. 'And then when you've finished, I've got a special Christmas present for you.'

I knew what his special Christmas present was. My school uniform wrapped up in Christmas paper. He'd made a big fuss about my school uniform, announcing that he would take me to Hallensteins himself and have me outfitted. The two of us drove down to Dunedin after an early dinner one night. This allowed my father to spend the night with his old school friend Herb Day and reminisce about their school days over a few Scotches. Herb's son Ian had already been at school for four years and they tried to embroil him in their reminiscences, comparing their achievements with his own. But Ian was taciturn. 'Ian'll help young Billy settle in,' Herb assured my father, though the look Ian gave me behind his father's back seemed to contradict that.

Later that night, when Ian and I lay in our twin beds, the light just switched off, he informed me that seniors didn't bother talking to juniors and not to come up to him and embarrass him in front of his friends. He turned away from me and went to sleep.

The shopping expedition was as humiliating as I knew it would be. There were no shorts or jackets to accommodate my shape. The only jacket that would actually button up came to round my knees. 'Maybe he'll grow into it,' the shop assistant said. 'They do grow around his age, don't they?'

She peered at me over her glasses. 'Or has he done it already?'

My father glared at her and then at me in the jacket. It looked ridiculous but he bought it anyway. 'With some adjustments, it'll be very smart,' said the shop assistant.

My father strode away from me across the hay paddock to where the ute was parked at the gate. I didn't even want to open his present. He would insist I put the stupid uniform on, which was still unadjusted, and everyone would laugh at me. He glanced back at me and I ambled towards a muddle of bales as if I intended to fix them. He drove off in the ute and I sat down on the bales instead. I didn't have the strength or inclination for any more work. I'd had enough of working on Christmas Day and I didn't want to have to face Lou again either. The ute had disappeared out of sight. I decided I was going on strike. Though I couldn't go home, there was somewhere else I could go.

I walked across the paddock and out the gate, across the road and then slipped through the fence on the other side. I was going to Dragonland. Christmas had already been ruined for me. I decided I'd disappear for the day and miss it altogether. I enjoyed thinking of the distress my absence would cause my family. I felt a pang of disappointment about missing Christmas dinner: the turkey and new potatoes and then four different desserts for afterwards. But I told myself that sitting opposite a baleful Lou would kill any sense of pleasure I might have taken in the food.

The rain didn't let up. I was wet through but I didn't care. I hoped I would catch a cold, get sick and have an excuse to stay in bed and avoid more hay-making. Maybe contract pneumonia and make my father feel guilty. I walked through the paddock above the road and then slipped through the next fence onto the hill block. I stopped to catch my breath. The rain had settled in. I couldn't even see across to the other side of the valley. I was isolated in a cold grey alien world. I was in outer space. I was Judy. I began to toil up the hill. I knew strange life forms lurked behind the craggy rocks, watching me pass, admiring my silver spacesuit, wanting to capture me and wonder at my exotic beauty.

The sheep track I trudged up grew more and more treacherous from the rain. My gumboots gave no grip and I slipped a few times. There was no Lou to come to my aid. I had to pick myself up. The rain fell even more heavily. I could only just make out the Dragon rock looming above me on the horizon, while behind me the world had been swallowed up by the rain. I could no longer see the road or the farmhouse. I wondered if Lou had reported me missing from the hay paddock. I panted from the exertion of the climb.

By the time I reached the rock, I was shivering from the cold, exhausted and beginning to feel pangs of hunger. I had convinced myself that I was on the brink of pneumonia. There was only one place to shelter. The Dragon's mouth. Standing at its entrance, it seemed even darker and more forbidding than ever. But I was too wet and cold to have irrational qualms about it. I ducked my head and crept into the cave, sitting as close to the front as I could without getting wet.

Gradually, I began to feel more at ease. I stretched out on the rock cautiously, rolling around, trying to get more comfortable. It was impossible. I was lying on a big crack. I rolled aside, and as I did, I noticed there was actually something stuffed down the crack. Some papers. I pulled them out, and slid down to the entrance of the cave so that I could see them more easily out of the shadows. They were pages from a magazine. I unfolded them carefully but my hands were wet and the pages became sodden. Nevertheless I recognised them. It was the photo spread from the *Playboy*, the one Arch had brought to school and which had gone missing.

I managed to spread the pages out. I studied the photos: the big breasted women slapping one another, the astronaut who'd crash-landed on their planet and found himself promptly stripped of his spacesuit. It was very peculiar that Lou had stolen them. *Playboys* were for men, just as *Cleos* were for women. Had Lou stolen them for the shots of the naked man, not that you saw much of him? Or for the women? I didn't know what to think.

I was still puzzling over what I'd found when suddenly I

looked up and saw Lou striding towards me. My first impulse was to stuff the pages back down the crack in the rock. But then I thought of what she'd said to me in the hay paddock. How she had hurt me. I decided I would enjoy watching her realise that I had discovered her secret.

Unfortunately, she had the hood of my parka pulled forward tight, clasped by her hand, half shrouding her face. I could only see her mouth. It wasn't smiling. She stopped a few feet short of the cave and stood there. Eventually, she pulled the hood off her head. I expected her to be blushing, her eyes staring at the ground, not daring to look at me. Or perhaps to fix me with one of those famous contemptuous stares of hers which would slowly waver away with her mounting shame. But her expression was bland, totally unreadable. 'My mother told me to come and get you. She gave Uncle Jack an earful for leaving you out there in the rain. Said he was a heathen to be working on Christmas Day and forcing you to do the same.'

I forgave Aunt Evelyn everything. She was still my kindred spirit. 'I figured you'd be up here when you weren't in the paddock,' she continued.

I didn't say anything. I was a bit disappointed. I had wanted to see Lou rattled. She calmly undid the buttons of the parka and flung it aside. She was wearing Jamie's clothes underneath, the ones we'd stolen for our show. He had left without them. 'Put the parka on,' she said.

'I'm already wet. It doesn't matter.'

We stared at one another. 'Well? You coming?' she asked.

'I've caught pneumonia,' I said resolutely. 'This cave is my grave.'

'But I've come to save you,' said Lou, equally firmly but with a glimmer of a smile.

Did I want her to save me? Did I really want to keep playing the same roles in these childish games: me the helpless maiden, Lou the chivalric hero. I didn't know anymore. 'Go on,' said Lou. 'Put it on.'

'I want to die,' I moaned, closing my eyes.

I lay there like that for a while, feigning death, but the silence that followed prickled my curiosity. I couldn't resist peeking at Lou to see what she was doing. She wasn't even looking at me. She was fumbling in her pocket. When I peeked again she had her knife clasped in her hand. That made me open my eyes. She flicked the blade out. I lay back prone on the rock. 'Kill me,' I commanded her. 'I don't want to live anymore.'

Lou grinned at me and slowly approached. The expression on her face was of grim concentration. It was exactly the same look she had when she approached possums she'd trapped, that she was about to bash on the head with her hockey stick. I began to have second thoughts about dying. Lou raised the knife in front of her face and I knew she was going to plunge it into my diseased heart. I began to protest and then to scream, begging her to stop, not to do it, when I realised what she actually intended the knife for. I sprang forward to try to stop her but it was too late.

I was silent, in awe of what she had done. She was staring at it too and then slowly a grin stole across her face. 'It's your Christmas present,' she said and she held it out to me, with both hands.

Her long red plait.

I didn't know what to say. All I could think of was how Aunt Evelyn would carry on. 'This will ruin your mother's Christmas,' I said.

Lou shrugged. 'It's too late now. It's done.'

I stared at the plait, entranced, still shocked by the rashness of Lou's act. 'It's better than a cow's tail,' said Lou. 'Even if it is the wrong colour for Judy. It's the real thing.'

I smiled and reached out for it. 'Thanks,' I said.

'Just a moment,' she said.

Deftly, she undid the ribbon at the end of the plait and retied it at the top to keep the cut ends together. Then she tucked it up under my hat and took a few moments to arrange the plait so it draped over one shoulder. I couldn't help thinking that Aunt Evelyn would have been delighted to witness Lou fussing over her own hair for once. She stood back to admire the effect and clapped with delight. 'It looks better on you than it ever did on me.'

'And you look just like Jamie without it,' I told her.

It wasn't true. It hurt me to even say his name to her. But I knew it was what she wanted to hear more than anything else. It was Christmas after all. Lou beamed with pleasure.

I slid forward to sit on the brink of the cave. The rain had eased and there was even a glimmer of sun, hinting its intentions through the clouds. The closed-in look to the valley was dissipating. I could see the river meandering through the swampy flats, and the Field of Blood surely greener than any other paddock in the entire valley. Lou was staring at the view too, her fingers constantly at her hair, fascinated by the rough, cropped feel of it. 'Everything is going to be different when you go away,' she murmured, so softly I wondered if she meant for me to hear.

I muttered some reassurance but it wasn't convincing. I'd had a change of heart about boarding school. I had been looking forward to it because it meant escape from the farm and all the chores I hated. I'd managed to ignore the ominous stories that filtered through of what went on at boarding school. But the time was drawing closer and closer. The school uniform was bought. It was no longer so easy to ignore. Our visit to the Days' had been intended to fuel my anticipation and reassure me of what lay ahead.

But instead, both Ian and his father had made remarks which filled me with foreboding.

Ian Day had deigned to give me some advice as I dressed the next morning, while he lay in bed smoking. 'I wouldn't wear those glasses next year if I was you. They'll spell trouble right off. Mark you out as a poofter.'

While his father, over breakfast, had urged me to visit them on weekends. 'You'll need to get away, son. It's a tough place to grow up for a country lad like yourself. Boys can be cruel. But you're welcome here anytime.'

'I wish next year would never come,' I said to Lou, a tremor of intensity in my voice. 'That this summer could last forever.'

Lou turned to face me, her expression electric and for a moment it was true, she did look like Jamie. She had his same infectious smile spread right across her face and it transformed her. She winked at me and I knew she must've been practising that in the mirror.

'We can string it out,' she whooped. 'You bet we can.'

She skipped towards me and I sprang to my feet. 'Is that my spacesuit?' I asked her, pointing to the parka.

Lou giggled. 'It's your antipneumonia spacesuit,' she corrected.

'Help me put it on,' I said, and Lou held it out so that I could slip into it easily.

'Come on, Judy,' she said. 'There's nothing to eat on this planet. It's lifeless and barren. Let's go back to the spaceship.'

We started prancing down the hill together, Lou playing with my hair, unravelling it out of the plait. We'd only gone about a hundred yards when we heard Babe calling us. She was right down by the first fence, too scared of the dragon to venture any further. 'Come and open your presents,' she was calling. 'I can't wait any longer.'

The sun flashed through the clouds, dazzling and brilliant, as if to reinforce the promise of the final childhood summer that lay ahead of us. Lou and I exchanged glances and began to run, screaming to Babe, in between our laughter, that the dragon was chasing us and we were having to flee for our lives. Lou stumbled on Jamie's jeans that were too long for her but I didn't wait for her. I ran, borne up by the sensation of my hair flowing out behind me loose and lush. I could imagine how glorious it must look, glittering red in the sunlight, almost as if Judy's beautiful blonde hair had been set aflame by the furious gasp of the fire-breathing dragon.